TIME AND RESTORATION

Time Trilogy - Book Three

Colleen Reimer

COPYRIGHT PAGE

Published by Colleen Reimer at Smashwords, 2019
Copyright 2017 Colleen Reimer.

Smashwords Edition, License Notes
Thank you for purchasing this book. This book remains the copyrighted property of the author, and may not be redistributed to others for commercial or non-commercial purposes. If you enjoyed this book, please encourage your friends to purchase their own copy from their favorite authorized retailer. Thank you for your support.

All scripture quotations in this publication are from the Holy Bible, NEW INTERNATIONAL VERSION®.
Copyright © 1973, 1978, 1984, 2011 by Biblica, Inc. All rights reserved worldwide.
Used by permission. NEW INTERNATIONAL VERSION® and NIV® are registered trademarks of Biblica, Inc. Use of either trademark for the offering of goods or services requires the prior written consent of Biblica US, Inc.

ISBN: 978-0-9953219-5-3

This is a work of fiction. Names, characters, businesses, places, events and incidents are either the products of the author's imagination or used in a fictitious manner. Any resemblance to actual persons, living or dead, or actual events is purely coincidental.

Front cover art created by Kurtis Molvik and Matthew Reimer.

Dedication

I dedicate this novel to all those who are searching for restoration in their lives.
Sometimes restoration can come in unorthodox ways.
Far be it from God to stick to conventional methods although he is allowed to work in whatever way he chooses.
Out-of-the-box methods are not beyond his litany of choices.
Be prepared!
After all, he is God!

Acknowledgment

I wrote the third book of the *Time Trilogy* a few years ago. Continuing the saga of the Time Trilogy was an adventure as I sought a creative way of bringing time travel back into the series.

There are a few I would like to thank for bringing *Time and Restoration* to the printed page. My daughter, Felisha, proofread it and marked corrections for me. My friend, Jenn Kononoff, also read the manuscript and marked corrections.

I want to thank my editor, Julene Schroeder, for another stellar job in editing my manuscript. Her suggestions were mixed with positive comments that gave me the boost to keep writing. She is a great encourager and I am so thankful for her.

My husband and our four children have been a huge support as I write. Jerrie, my husband, has been my greatest advocate, allowing me to explore my creative side. My husband passed away in 2018 and I miss him so much! He was always such a blessing to me. Thank you Jerrie!

I also thank God for the gift of writing. Without him this book would not exist.

My readers also deserve a huge thank you for following my work and reading what I write.

CHAPTER 1

The box sat on the kitchen table like a millstone to Sally's soul. The contents threatened to take her carefully crafted life and drown it in a storm-tossed, turbulent sea. Not only did she feel irritation at the box's presence in the room but her most-unwelcome, old terror returned with it.

Sally glared in irritation at her mother sitting across from her and said, "You can take it back. I don't want it in my house."

Melody smiled sadly. "I'm not taking the box back. These pictures are yours. They belong with you."

"I never asked for them."

"That doesn't mean they're not yours."

"I don't want them."

Melody remained calm. "I'm not taking them back with me, Sally."

Sally glared at her mother in exasperation. "I don't need this risk in my house."

"What risk?" Melody asked.

"The danger of Isabella finding them."

Melody raised her shoulders with a sigh and lowered them again. "You've kept her in the dark until now. I don't see how these pictures will change anything."

Sally crossed her arms. "Isabella is smart. She'll put two and two together and recognize him."

Melody smiled. "She might. She is a spitting image of him."

"Exactly. So take them back to Toronto with you when you leave."

"I'm doing no such thing. I didn't fly them all the way here just to turn around and drag them home again. This box is heavy. Do you have any idea how cumbersome it was bringing it with me?"

Sally threw her arms up and let them drop in her lap. "But I didn't ask you to bring them in the first place." She felt bad for shouting, but her mother could be so infuriating at times.

"Look. I've just barely arrived. This is my first night here. Why don't you put the box in a secluded place, somewhere that Isabella wouldn't consider looking? Think it over for a few days. You might come to see the wisdom in keeping the photos. Your whole childhood is in there."

Sally shook her head. "It's the other photos I'm concerned about."

"You're still afraid of him," Melody declared.

"Only of him getting into Isabella's head."

"She's not a baby anymore, Sally."

"She's my only baby and I *will* protect her."

Melody leaned back against her chair and shook her head. "Isabella is a teenager. In just over two years she'll be an adult. You can't shield her forever."

"Watch me."

"Sally!" Melody looked exasperated.

"What?" Sally snapped, feeling the usual irritation and defensiveness when her mother looked at her this way. That Melody could still get to her after all these years angered her. "I'm her mother and I'll raise her the way I see fit."

"It could backfire on you."

"I don't see how."

"Your stubborn refusal to share the past with her could drive her away." Melody's look held warning.

"What she doesn't know can't hurt her."

"You don't know that, Sally."

Sally stood, feeling fully done with discussing the photos and the history which came with them. She'd been successfully vigilant in keeping the past in the past. There was not even an inkling of desire within her to dredge up all those unpleasant memories. This first night of her mother's visit had turned into an argument, something she'd vowed not to allow.

Why couldn't the two of them communicate on a gentler tone? Melody had mellowed over time, wasn't as critical but had become much more supportive in the last ten years or so. They actually got along fairly well most of the time and her visits were welcome.

Her daughter, Isabella adored her grandmother. It was always a huge thrill for her when Melody came.

Sally pushed her chair toward the table and said, "I'm tired, Mom. I'm going to bed."

Melody sighed loudly and said, "I'm sorry I brought this up tonight but I thought it best to give you the box right at the start. You can hide it somewhere and decide what to do with it. Leaving the box in the guestroom where I'm staying feels risky. Isabella might stumble across it and look without asking."

"Thank you for that," Sally said, relieved at her mother's forethought. "And I'm sorry for getting upset. It just brings up memories I never want to revisit."

Melody stood and nodded. "I understand." She looked tired.

Sally went to her mother and embraced her. "Thanks for coming, Mom. I love you."

"I love you too, Sally." After a tight embrace, Melody left the kitchen and headed to the guestroom.

Sally stared at the box. An involuntary shudder ran through her. She was terrified of her daughter finding it and determined to conceal it well. For now, she decided to stick it in her closet and find a more suitable hiding place later, a spot Isabella would never think to look.

CHAPTER 2

Isabella was on a mission as she crept from her upstairs bedroom and descended a few steps. Spying was becoming a habit of hers. But that was the only way she was going to find answers to all her questions. She was fascinated that there was a story of her life she didn't know and wanted to discover why her past was such a dark secret.

Her grandmother, Melody Windsor, on her mother's side — the only side she knew — had flown from Toronto two days ago and had brought a box with her. She'd heard her mom arguing with her over it that first night as she hid in the hallway eavesdropping. Sally had demanded that Grandmother take it right back home with her. She insisted she didn't want a single reminder of her past in her house.

Isabella hadn't deciphered much more of that initial conversation. It had been hard to make out most of the whispered dialogue but it had certainly piqued her interest. She'd been too nervous of being discovered so she hadn't eavesdropped for long.

It was late, past eleven. Isabella could still hear their voices in the kitchen. They were probably drinking tea or coffee, sitting at the table and visiting. She took a seat near the top of the stairs and strained to hear. Only spits and spots came through to her waiting ears. Silently, she crept down the stairs again and slipped over to the kitchen door. With her back to the wall she listened. Their words were much easier to detect. She decided to stay as long as she could and find out as much as possible.

"…and I don't think that's a good idea."
Grandmother said, "Don't you think she needs to know?"
"No."
"But she's already fifteen. She'll be sixteen come December."
"No."

"Sally, listen to yourself. She's growing up and has even been asking me questions."

"Isabella's been prying you for answers?" Sally sounded angry.

Grandmother must have nodded because she didn't answer. Eventually she said, "She deserves to know."

"Huh-uh. If I have my way, she'll never know."

"Don't you think that's unfair?"

"Why is it unfair? He lost his privileges when he did what he did."

"But what about her? She wants to know. She's curious and won't stop until she finds out."

"Do not tell her anything," Sally said with conviction.

"Then what do I say to her?" asked Grandma.

"Nothing." The clinking of a spoon stirring in a cup was the only sound for a while. "By the way, what have you told her about him when she's asked?"

"Just that she looks like him."

A grunt of disgust came from Sally's mouth. "That's already too much information for her."

"Why?" Grandma sounded as confused as Isabella usually felt.

"I don't want her knowing anything about him. He's not worth the time."

"You need to forgive him."

Sally made an exasperated sound. "I have forgiven him."

"It doesn't sound that way to me."

"Well it's true."

"You've still got your back up about him; that's easy to tell."

"Well, do you blame me?"

The next room fell silent for a while.

Isabella couldn't believe her good fortune. She couldn't remember ever hearing about her father before. Hopefully they'd delve deeper into the subject. She was desperate to know something, anything.

Grandma took a sip of her mug. Isabella could hear the customary slurping sound. When the cup chinked on the table, Grandma said, "At some point you'll need to tell her, show her his picture. Promise me you'll keep the box. Hide it for now and when the time is right, show her."

Not a sound.

Grandmother cleared her throat. "Sally?"

"I heard you."

"And you should keep the ones his mother gave me too. They include his childhood photos, his side of the family."

"What a memorial that will be," Sally declared cynically.

Isabella wondered why.

"Still, it's Isabella's heritage."

"With that kind of heritage, she doesn't need one. Don't you think it's best left buried and gone? What good will that kind of information do her? It will only damage her."

"Your secrecy is damaging her. She wants to trust you but how can she when you keep things from her."

Isabella clenched her hands in nervous anticipation. The excitement of her good fortune caused her heart to pound against her ribs. *Go, Grandma, go. Give it to her with both barrels!*

Sally said, "If she ever does find out, it will ruin her forever. That's why I keep it from her."

Isabella lifted a hand and rubbed her forehead in confusion. Why would knowing about her father ruin her? What was her mother so frightened of?

A chair squeaked as it pulled away from the table and Isabella scurried back to the foot of the stairs and waited.

Sally's voice filtered down the hall. "I'm tired, Mother. I'm going to bed."

"Please, just promise me you'll keep the box of pictures."

"I don't know. I'll think about it."

"By the way, where did you hide them?"

Sally took a while to answer. "In a place Isabella never goes and would never think to visit."

Isabella heard more movement in the kitchen and scooted up the stairs to her room.

~~~~

Isabella pulled on the loop hanging from the attic with the pole designed to reach it. As she tugged, the hatch creaked in protest, opened and the ladder slowly unfolded until the base rested on the upstairs floor. She wasn't concerned about the noise she made. She was the only one home. Her mother wasn't here to stop her.

Melody, her grandmother, had left two days ago and flew back to Toronto to be with Grandpa. He came less than she; he still had a part time job and didn't want to lose it.

Isabella didn't mind fending for herself. Either she was in school or at home alone. Her mother worked late and then usually came home so exhausted there was little quality time left. Isabella didn't mind. She was used to living life on her own terms, doing what she wanted, when she wanted to. Being raised by a single parent made the situation what it was.

It wasn't that uncommon for a fifteen-year-old to chaperone her own life. But whom was she kidding? Her mother was no slouch. Sally Windsor demanded accountability, responsibility and, above all, morality. At least that's what she preached.

Lately Isabella had been wondering and questioning a lot of things. Was her mother really the upright, dignified and entirely righteous person she tried to portray? There were too many things she avoided, too many questions she swept under the rug and far too many vague answers that left Isabella scratching her head in curiosity.

For the last year or so she'd been searching for answers and was no closer than when she first started. All she'd managed to gain was frustration and anger. Why wouldn't her mother give her some straight talk? What was she trying to hide? And why?

All Isabella wanted was to know about her past, the truth. What was her father's name? What was he like? Did he still live in Toronto? Did her mother have a picture of him? Did she have another set of grandparents? She'd heard Melody mention them on her visit. What about aunts and uncles or other cousins?

It didn't matter what she asked, her mother refused to answer. If she did say anything it was to reiterate that her father wasn't worth the time. It was better if she never knew anything about him. He was a complete loser who didn't want to be a father. They were both better off without him and Isabella needed to come to terms with those facts.

The pat explanations didn't satisfy. They only fueled her curiosity more. If she at least knew what he looked like, maybe that would be enough. To know his name would be a bonus. She'd done a search online, looked up the name "Windsor" in Toronto, Canada. It was only a few months ago that it finally hit her. Her mother's parents' last name was Windsor. Her mother went by her maiden name. She'd confronted Sally about it, asked for her father's last name, but she'd refused to divulge any information at all.

Isabella was completely upset and insulted. She was furious that her mother wouldn't open up about anything. She treated her like a baby, someone that needed protecting from goblins and ghosts, from all the scary things of the past. It was pathetic. Just because Sally was spooked by her past didn't mean Isabella had to be. She could handle the truth.

She stepped onto the ladder and made her way up through the dark hole into the attic. Before stepping inside, she reached and felt for the switch on the floor. There it was. She flicked it and a single bulb sputtered to life, showering light on the boxes stored there. Some of the insulation was covered by rough plywood and the rough floor extended for most of the attic. The outer edges were left undone, joists showing with pink insulation stuffed between. She was thankful for the floor, rough as it was. Navigating over the joists would be too precarious otherwise.

It was a handy storage room, one where she hoped her mother kept things she didn't want Isabella to see. This was one place Isabella never went to, a room only her mother frequented on rare occasions. Just maybe, the box Grandma brought was stored here somewhere. Her mother wasn't a packrat. What she no longer needed was donated or trashed. A thin layer of dust rested everywhere. A total of eight boxes lined one edge of the plywood floor. So, which one looked the most recently added?

Isabella walked over to the first box, stirring up the dust, which made her sneeze. Kneeling down, she removed the lid and looked inside. It was full of mementos of her childhood, drawings, cards and gifts that she herself had made for her mother. So this was important to Sally? She scanned through it, looking at the various crafts, pencil drawings and colored pages with her name scrawled at the bottom. Most of them said Isa. She remembered how difficult it had been at first learning to spell her name. Isa was all she could handle in kindergarten.

When she got to her second and third grade work, she often spelled her name as Bella. For years her friends called her Bella. About three years ago she decided to go by her full name and insisted everyone call her by it. Now hearing Isa or Bella sounded strange. Everyone called her Isabella. She liked it. Only her mother reverted back to calling her Isa at times.

Quickly, she scanned through the rest of her work, replaced the lid and moved to the next one. This one contained cute outfits she'd used as a baby, toddler and young child. They were all designer clothes — nothing but the best for Sally's daughter. Isabella grunted in derision.

"Why would a kid care anyway? Clothes are clothes."

She closed the box and moved to the third. Souvenirs from various ports of call, vacation spots and cruise lines filled the cardboard container. At least twice a year, Sally took her on vacation — every Christmas and either spring break or summer. A flood of memories filled this box, from tacky Tahitian wall hangings, a Mexican sombrero, wooden figurines from somewhere, brightly colored toys from Maui, a few leis, fridge magnets from everywhere, matching sundresses from the Dominican Republic, salt and pepper shakers from Dubai, a picture frame from Disneyworld and various other knick knacks from places she couldn't recall. Sally and Isabella were always center stage in the photo.

For a while she stayed there touching each one, memories flooding back. Her mother did put in a lot of effort into making her life enjoyable. On some vacations, she'd even been allowed to take a friend along. Those had been the best. Sally wasn't cheap. Isabella suspected that her extravagance was one way of making it up to her for having only one parent and for her endless hours at work.

Moving on, she found the next few boxes full of design folders, fashion show brochures, Sally's own collection of designs, all documented, organized and filed by date, year and season. This was Sally's life and her memorial to her life's work. She was a fashion designer, having created clothes since she was in junior high. She'd worked for a prestigious designer for years and now owned her own fleet of stores. Successful business woman she was, although as a mother she could be infuriating.

Frustration gnawed at Isabella as she moved to the last few boxes. Had her mother not placed the box of pictures up here? Where else could it be? In Sally's room, hidden in the closet? If this search ended in futility, she'd look there next. But this was the only place in the house where Isabella never went.

One box contained shoes, ones that her mother had bought for her. Isabella recognized them. She'd never worn them. They were her mother's style, not hers. Perhaps Sally was keeping them just in case she'd change her mind. Isabella smiled at that.

The last box was a mixture of stuff, Sally's childhood keepsakes. A doll dressed in pink material, frilled with lace, rested on top, a dominoes game, snakes and ladders game and checkers filled one side. There were a few picture books, one coloring book with every page colored in. They were quite well done. Sally had been artsy even as a kid. Isabella hadn't inherited her mother's knack for the creative.

Digging deeper produced a photo album. Was this it? She pulled the book out and flipped it open. Page after page was filled with Sally's young face, pictures from her childhood. Her brother Robert was in many of the photos with her. The two of them had apparently been inseparable back then. Now, miles apart, living in different cities, adjacent countries, they rarely saw each other. Uncle Robert had three kids, cousins for Isabella, but she didn't know them well. All three were younger than she.

Flipping through the photo book produced only pictures of Sally and her family, taken while she still lived at home with her parents. Isabella threw the book back into the box. A few other mementos filled the bottom, a small jewelry box filled with ancient pieces, a few school yearbooks, a stack of letters and cards and a poster of The Fonz. Whoever "The Fonz" was, Isabella had no idea. He looked cute enough.

Her search had produced zip. She was so sure her mother would have placed the box up here. She closed the lid and stood. Her legs felt stiff from crouching. Scanning the attic, she noticed there were some areas shrouded in shadow. She started walking along the outer edge of the tight room and went all the way around. Nothing.

With a heavy sigh, she started for the ladder. Suddenly her eye caught something. Wait. There, on the other side of the opening, where the ladder descended, was a section that hadn't been floored. The joists were open with insulation stuffed soundly between. If her mother wanted to hide something, that's where she'd put it, buried beneath the insulation. Why hadn't she thought of that before?

She walked to the edge and lowered to her haunches. It was hard to see with the limited light. She looked for any variance in the insulation thickness. There was one spot that bulged slightly. To reach it, she'd need to scoot along the joist first. Stepping gingerly on the board she found her balance, placed one foot in front of the other and walked over to the spot. She lowered herself and lifted the bulky insulation. There it was.

"Aha! Found it." Isabella reached for it and with determination lifted it from its resting place. Maneuvering it over to the finished floor was a challenge. The box was heavy.

She set it down and stared at it. This was it. The time of truth had come. Tingles of excitement raced down her spine. Her mother had gone to a lot of bother trying to conceal the box but now all Isabella's waiting, questions and wondering were about to be stilled. Impatience egged her on, prodding her to remove the lid immediately and look at everything. Finally she'd know what her father looked like. The anticipation was overwhelming.

Common sense overruled. Pulling her cell phone from her pocket, she checked the time. Disappointed, she realized her mother would be home soon. She'd take a quick peek now and return when she had more time.

Sitting down next to the box, she carefully removed the lid and set it to the side. Staring inside, she noticed the container was full of pictures, strewn loosely about. A big brown envelope was tucked to the side. She pulled that out first. There was nothing written on it. Setting it on the floor beside her, she lifted a picture out of the box and stared at it.

It was her mother, Sally, and a man sitting on a couch, smiling at whoever was behind the camera. Was that him? Was that her father?

Studying it closer, she saw her eyes on his face. She did look like him. It was astounding how similar their features were. Her heart beat frantically in her chest at the implication. She couldn't take her eyes off of him.

Something strange suddenly began to happen. She first sensed it in her peripheral vision. The room seemed to cloud over, shift, move in strange swirls and shapes. Looking up confirmed it. The attic was bucking, moving and twisting in odd patterns, the beams meshing together with the floor, the light stretching out in an elongated line and swirling into the meshed ceiling-floor conglomeration. It kept moving and changing, like a kaleidoscope on a grand scale. The square opening in the floor, where the ladder descended, began to lift and twist into a long, curvy smile, turning until it frowned down on her. Then it wriggled into numerous curls, gyrating like a snake. Soon it merged with the other colors swirling around it.

Isabella didn't know what to make of it. What was happening? Why? Fear gripped her by the throat. She looked back down at the picture. It was still as clear as before. Nothing about it had changed. Her body wasn't shifting and buckling but everything else around her was moving in crazy, surreal patterns. The floor beneath her was twisting, moving beneath her. What was holding her up?

Looking back up, the swirling motion shifted, now going in reverse, the colors slowly beginning to separate.

She didn't understand but she was too terrified to see what would happen when everything came to a standstill again, if it ever did. She tore her eyes from the mass of motion around her and looked at the picture. Flipping it over she placed it face down on the floor, at least where she knew the floor to be. It was still rolling and churning beneath her.

The room came back into focus and seemed in a hurry to do so. The swirls died away and the colors disengaged from one another. The curvaceous loops faded, the wood trusses straightened and the floor calmed and stilled into horizontal lines. The light merged and sucked back into the bulb. The opening in the floor contracted and lowered back into place. Everything returned to its original position and stilled.

But Isabella felt absolutely different, twisted from the inside out. She didn't understand any of it. Why had everything become unglued as soon as she studied the picture? All she felt was the thundering beat of her heart beneath her ribs. Terror overwhelmed her. She had to get out of here.

She stuffed everything back in the box, the picture face down. There was no way she was taking a chance. She closed the box the way it had been and hurried across the joist to return it to where she'd found it. After scooting back to the floor she turned to look at the box's buried location. The insulation hid it well and everything looked like it had before. Her mother would never know.

Without a backward glance, she hurried down the ladder and lifted it into place, the trap door snug to the ceiling. No hint of insulation showed around the door's edges. The last thing she needed was her mom questioning her day's activities.

Chapter 3

Isabella and her friends were at the Army Surplus Store downtown Chelsey. She loved this place and was occasionally successful in drawing Abby and Shana with her.

Abby and Shana were in the dressing rooms trying on new outfits while Isabella looked at shoes on the shelf. One pair of boots caught her interest. She took them down, kicked off her flip flops and tried them on. After lacing them and securing a knot, Abby came out of the change room and Isabella turned to see.

Abby grinned and asked, "What do you think?"

The outfit wasn't Abby's style and they both knew it. The army fatigues looked ludicrous on her and dwarfed her petite frame.

Isabella shook her head. "Huh-uh. Not you."

"Can we go to the mall after this?" Abby looked hopeful.

"Sure, if Shana's up for it."

Shana stuck her head out the change room door. "Yeah, let's do it."

"How's your outfit?" asked Abby.

Shana stepped out and twirled in place. The green tank top and camouflage shorts suited her. The shorts were cinched in with a taupe-colored belt, the tank top tucked in. With her height and long legs, the look worked.

"What do you think?" asked Shana.

"I really like it," said Isabella.

"You would," said Abby with a roll of her eyes. "The shorts are too long."

Shana studied herself in the mirror. "I don't know."

"I'd buy it in a heartbeat," said Isabella

"You'd do it just to spite your mother," said Abby.

Isabella shook her head. "No. I actually like the outfit." She pointed down to her feet. "What do you think about these?"

The girls looked, their faces registering their disdain.

"You'd actually wear those?" asked Abby.

"Of course. They'd look great with my baggy jeans. Or even with those shorts Shana's wearing."

"Do you want to try these on?" asked Shana, pointing down at the shorts.

"Sure. But I need a different top. That one's too tight."

"You'd look so great in this tank though," insisted Shana.

Isabella scrunched her nose and shook her head. After grabbing a brown t-shirt from a shelf, she headed to the change room directly beside Shana's.

"Pass me the shorts over the top when you have them off."

"Will do," said Shana.

A few minutes later Shana handed over the shorts and left her change room.

Abby said, "I can't believe Isabella's actually trying this stuff on."

Shana responded, "We should know her by now. She's completely unconventional. She's the one who dragged us in here in the first place."

"I can hear everything you're saying," declared Isabella. She undid the lock and stepped out. She'd discarded the belt and left the t-shirt hanging loosely over the shorts. She turned to view her reflection in the three-way mirror on the wall. The look was big, baggy and completely her. With the army boots she'd laced up earlier, she looked about ready to head to war. But that was not her intent. This was the look she was after. The ensemble would irritate her mother to no end.

"Are you serious?" asked Abby.

"Yeah." Isabella studied the look and liked it a lot. "It's perfect."

"You are crazy," said Shana, crossing her arms. "Your mother will go ballistic over this."

Isabella laughed. "I know."

"Okay, whatever. I wouldn't try that with my mom." Shana more or less abode by her mother's guidelines, which Isabella considered modest but fashionable.

Abby, by contrast, preferred the provocative look. The shorter the shorts and the tighter and lower the top, the better.

Isabella shrugged. She didn't care what her mother or her friends thought. This look was her and she loved it. She turned back to the change room. Abby's voice stopped her.

"Why do you wear clothes that totally hide your body?"

"You know. I've told you often enough." With that she closed the door and changed.

"I know but you could at least try and look a smidge sexy."

"Not the look I'm after."

Shana said, "We may as well give up on her. Isabella is who she is."

"But we're still going to the mall, right?" Abby asked.

"I already told you we would," Isabella said irritably. "Why do you keep asking?"

Abby shrugged.

Isabella paid and the three girls left the store. They walked over to the bus stop. The air was getting cooler, fall weather making an entrance. She wouldn't be able to wear her new outfit much longer. The leaves on the trees were already beginning to turn color with the cold nights they'd had the last week. They arrived at the bus stop just as the bus that would take them to Chelsey Park Mall pulled up and screeched to a halt.

~~~~

Shopping at the mall was exhausting and she'd only bought the items she'd liked at the army surplus store. Shana and Abby, on the other hand, had left the mall carrying bags of clothes and jewelry. Isabella was glad finally to be home. She would have much preferred going roller skating in the park, riding her bike, swimming at the recreation center or any other such activity. Her friends' choices tended to win out over hers. They were seldom in the mood for anything athletic.

The extent of Isabella's jewelry fit in a small box given to her by her mother when she was eight years old. She wore silver hoops most of the time. The rest of the stuff in her jewelry box stayed basically untouched, unless her mother insisted she wear something different to go to church.

Isabella's mother was always dressed in the best designer labels, many she'd created herself. They were always accessorized with designer shoes and handbags. Her jewelry collection was something of a topic: nothing but the best for Sally Windsor.

Isabella dropped her army surplus bag by the door, entered the living room, plopped onto the couch and switched on the TV. She scanned through the channels but wasn't really in the mood to watch anything. Her mind wandered to her friends and she smiled.

They were so different from each other and yet so close that it mystified her. Abby and Shana understood her yet still liked her. They'd met when she was seven, when she and her mother started attending church here in Chelsey, Minnesota. That's when she and her mother moved to this small, out-of-the-way town. At first she'd been furious. How could her mother move her just when she'd made friends in Chicago?

But there'd been an element of excitement as well. She found out she had a half-sister living in Chelsey. What a surprise that had been. And Tessa, her half-sister, was the spitting image of her mother. They had identical brunette curls, deep brown eyes and similar profiles. The only difference was in their lips. Tessa's lips were full while Sally's were thin and tight.

Isabella looked a little like Sally but not much. Her looks came predominantly from her father; at least that's what she'd been told. With a dark head of hair and large eyes "the color of the Caribbean sea," her mother always said, she had looks that brought too much attention. Isabella agreed. Thus the baggy, unflattering clothes. Drawing attention to herself was not her goal in life, especially the way men looked at her when she wore form-fitting outfits. No. Spacious, breathable tops kept male eyes from wandering over her body.

Sally had been forced by her mother to give Tessa up for adoption as a newborn because she was only fourteen at the time. It was only later in life, during a drug rehab stint that Sally met up with her long-lost daughter. It had changed everything for them. Tessa was pregnant when Sally first met her and had a baby girl shortly after, bestowing the title of "Grandmother" on Sally instantly. Sally suddenly wanted to pull up roots and move to Chelsey and Isabella was thrilled to learn that she had a sister. That was nearly nine years ago and Chelsey was home to her now. She couldn't think of living anywhere else.

Isabella pulled out her cell phone and checked the time. Sally wouldn't arrive for another few hours. Work kept her occupied most of the eighteen hours she was awake each day.

Having eaten a burger and fries at the mall food court, Isabella wasn't hungry for dinner. Some popcorn later with a movie sounded good.

A trip to the attic crossed her mind but she wasn't sure. It had been two weeks since she'd been there and still the memory made her shiver. She didn't know if she had the courage to brave it. If the phenomenon could be explained, maybe then she'd venture up there, but the experience terrified her.

She'd thought of asking Shana and Abby to look at the pictures with her but there was no guarantee of their safety and she wouldn't risk that. Perhaps if she could get herself to try again, find out exactly what was going on and how to get back, decipher the paranormal-alien happening, then maybe she'd ask them to join her sometime.

Just thinking about it made her sweat. She wiped the moisture from her hands on her jeans and released a nervous breath.

I won't ever get over this until I just do it. I'm so curious but terribly afraid at the same time. It's driving me nuts.

Her heart beat faster and her breaths came hard and unsteady. Did she really have the courage to do it? She checked her cell phone again. Yes, there was time to spare this time. There'd be no rush and yet that thought made her even more nervous. If she was in trouble there'd be no one to help her out of it.

She clicked the "Off" button on the remote, stood and headed to the stairs. At the top, she gazed up at the attic access, uncertainty playing with her mind.

A small corded loop was attached to the ceiling hatch. The long pole in the hall closet was specifically made with a hook to grab the loop and pull the hatch open. The ladder, attached to the opposite side of the hatch, lowered enough that she'd be able to grab it and unfold it, resting its base on the floor. It was a novel idea. Whoever came up with the design was a genius. It gave easy access to the attic above, providing a perfect storage spot.

She studied the hatch for a good two minutes. Building up her courage, that's what she was doing. At least that's what she told herself. Could she do it?

She walked to the hall closet, got the pole and headed back to the attic hatch. After debating for a while longer, she finally reached up, attached the hook through the loop and pulled.

CHAPTER 4

At the top of the ladder, Isabella flicked on the switch and the single bulb spread its light as far as it could reach. Anxious uncertainty spread from her middle and fanned her body until the hair on her neck stood on edge and her toes felt hot. She forced the wave of apprehension down and took the last few steps to the floor above.

She turned and stared at the bump in the insulation. Placing a hand over her heart she willed it to slow down. This was it — the moment of truth. She'd finally know what strange power the pictures held, if any.

Scooting across the wood beam, she reached the spot, lifted off the insulation and hauled the box from its spot. Carefully she retraced her steps back to the floor and set the box down. Staying away from the opening seemed wise, just in case her mother came home early and called up before ascending. That thought produced more goose bumps. Hopefully she could finish up long before her mother made an appearance.

Lifting the lid and placing it to the side, she stared at the pile of pictures stacked haphazardly within. She lifted the brown envelope and laid it beside her on the floor. The picture she'd studied two weeks ago still rested on the top, face down. Reaching for it, she turned it right side up, brought it closer and looked. Every few seconds she glanced up to see if anything was changing. The room didn't move.

"Hmph." She'd be lying to say she wasn't disappointed. The moment was anti-climactic after her apprehension and anticipation these past couple weeks.

Isabella placed the picture on the floor and reached for another one. This one showed Sally holding a bouquet of bright blooms, a big smile on her face. She appeared completely happy. The look was unusual. Isabella couldn't remember seeing her mother so relaxed and cheerful before. A pang of sorrow hit her. Why couldn't her mother be that way now? Had life been too cruel to her? Sapped her of all joy?

She didn't know when it started but when she looked up the room was already back in full convulsions, bucking and swirling, the colors of the attic merging in unreal patterns. The floor shifted beneath her in coils of color, the texture of the plywood convulsing, merging with the bright pink surging of the insulation. The box of pictures before her was indiscernible as it elongated and meshed with the colors twisting around and through it.

The single bulb spiraled its light into feverish swirls of white, slanting and crimping into odd shapes, mixing with the wood waves flowing around it. The sight would be completely spectacular if not for the terror it invoked. The kaleidoscope effect was mesmerizing but the fear beating in Isabella's heart was louder.

With sweaty palms, she willed herself to be brave and forced herself to endure the show. What would happen when it stopped she wasn't sure but she had to find out. Two weeks of curiosity pushed her to watch. With clammy hands and tingles of panic racing up her spine, she clung to the picture and observed as everything she knew to be real disintegrated around her.

Slowly the swirling and bucking stopped, shifted and reversed, spiraling in the opposite direction much more quickly than it had before. The whole attic seemed in a rush to unwind from the madness. The room slowed, the colors separated and everything calmed to a whisper.

That's when she realized she was no longer in the attic. Her mother, Sally, sat on a couch before her, a bouquet of flowers in her hands. The sitting room was small, much smaller than the one downstairs.

Isabella scanned the place. It looked like an apartment or condo. She was still sitting cross-legged on the floor so she stood to her feet. Where was she?

Her mother's voice sounded light and airy. The lilt in her speech was unfamiliar.

"Oh, Walter, they're beautiful. Thank you."

"I'm glad you like them."

Isabella spun around to look. Walter? She hadn't seen anyone else in the room. He stood behind her, a camera in his hands. She was in his way.

Stepping to the side, she said, "I'm sorry. I didn't know you were taking a picture."

He ignored her and walked toward Sally.

He can't see me? Or hear me?

Sitting down beside Sally, he set the camera on the coffee table, draped an arm around her shoulder and leaned in. He kissed her with passion, Sally responding in like fashion.

The intimate moment made Isabella feel awkward. She turned away and waited. Their moans and open desire were completely embarrassing. She'd never seen her mother kiss anyone before. She'd never witnessed Sally involved in any kind of romantic relationship. This open display was shocking. She'd never imagined her mother capable of such passion. Her only obsession was her work.

Where was she? When was she? How had this happened? She looked down at the picture still in her hand, straining to see if a date was posted. There was nothing.

The sounds of their desire on the couch brought her back. She couldn't bear to watch them so she focused on the far wall where an open door led to the kitchen. Was this her father? Walter? She hadn't gotten a good look.

His voice broke through her thoughts and she turned toward him. "I have a surprise for you."

"Besides the flowers?" asked Sally.

"I made reservations at a restaurant down by the lake."

"Ooh, how exciting." Sally clung to Walter's neck and placed a light kiss on his lips. "What should I wear?"

"How about that red little number?"

"You mean my Sue Wong strapless dress?"

"Yeah." He raised and lowered his eyebrows a few times. "I like that one."

Sally giggled and nodded. "Okay."

"And high heels."

"Can do."

With another light kiss, Walter pulled back and stood. "I'll wear a pair of dress pants and my Brunello sport jacket."

Sally looked disappointed.

"No?" he asked.

"Why don't you wear that new suit we bought you?"

"Which one?"

Isabella couldn't believe it. He had more than one? She should have known. If Sally was allowed to dictate his wardrobe, he probably dressed like a yuppie.

"The Hugo Boss one with the pin-striped shirt and paisley tie."

"It'll go great with your dress."

"Exactly." Sally's smile never faded as Walter headed down the hall. She followed him.

Those two were clearly in love. Sally's love-struck eyes and Walter's overly attentive manner were foreign. Isabella could hardly believe it. Her parents had actually loved each other? She'd never known that. Sally refused to divulge anything about him. So what had turned Sally against him so vehemently? He seemed a nice enough guy.

Isabella didn't know what to do. How long would it take until they made their reappearance? Was she willing to stay that long? And how exactly was she supposed to leave? Could she open the front door and walk into this world unrestricted? Did she want to? There were so many unknowns here.

Curiosity egged her to the door. With the picture in one hand she reached for the knob. It turned easily enough. She swung the door open and looked into the hall. Sticking her head out she noticed that the hall ended about five feet in either direction from her location, where reality and alien activity had collided in a swirl of color and twisting matter. It looked similar to the attic buckling episode except here the colors were more vivid and the meshing more spectacular, due to the bright décor of the hall.

Pulling back inside, she closed the door, backed up against the wall and waited.

A few minutes later, Sally and Walter reappeared from the hall. Isabella's breath caught at the sight of them. They looked amazing together. She'd never seen a more striking couple. To see her mother in such a seductive, tight-fitting dress was astounding. Her figure was lithe and curvaceous. Her high heels looked like Prada and went spectacularly with the dress. She looked model runway ready.

Walter was completely dashing and debonair. His designer suit fit him perfectly, hugged his frame in all the right places. His striking good looks made Isabella hold her breath. The blue of his eyes were the color of a Caribbean sea. They were large, mesmerizing and identical to hers. She gasped.

Walter was her father and at some point in time, Sally and Walter had loved each other. That was clear now as he helped her with her coat, kissed her neck seductively, turned her around and held her at arm's length and said, "I can't wait until later."

Sally giggled girlishly and said, "Neither can I."

Walter pointed back to the hall from they'd come. "We don't have to leave right away."

Sally sighed. "But my hair and makeup will get ruined and we'll miss our reservation."

Walter nodded resignedly. "You're right." He reached for the door and opened it.

Sally left first and Walter followed, closing the door behind him.

The small apartment fell silent. Isabella's eyes lingered on the closed door, wishing they'd come back. She'd just barely met him and now he was gone. Her earlier view of the hall made following them pointless. She was resigned to this room. To stay seemed silly but how was she going to get back?

What had she done that first time? She'd taken the picture, flipped it and placed it face down on the floor. But she wasn't in the attic. She wasn't even sitting. Standing in the middle of a room as real as her own skin suddenly felt terrifying.

How had she done this? How had she gotten here? Was this time travel? Had she somehow traveled back to this year? What had caused it? Maybe there was some type of electromagnetic force field in the attic that transported her here. It seemed a little farfetched but what else could it be? And if that were true, how in the world was she ever going to get back? Did the electromagnetic field travel with her? Could it send her back?

What if she flipped the picture over and placed it on the coffee table? Would that work? She stepped toward it holding the picture tightly in her hand.

I wonder what would happen if it slipped from my hand and dropped.

She released her grip and let the picture fall. It fluttered to the floor and came to rest at her feet, Sally's face smiling up at her. Isabella looked up and noticed nothing had changed. Being alone in the apartment suddenly felt claustrophobic. She had to find a way out. Bending over, she picked up the picture, flipped it over and placed it face down on the coffee table.

That's when it happened. The room contorted and corkscrewed wildly, sending the colors of the burgundy couch swirling into the light taupe of the walls. The doorway into the kitchen twisted oddly, curling and wriggling into an elongated curved line. The ceiling weaved its way to the floor and the two melded into a conglomeration, the couch twisting and knotting into curves throughout.

The coffee table joined the party, rising, spreading and disjointing to interlock with the colors swirling around the room. The hallway to the right wiggled crazily and then took off, whooshing beneath her feet then flew to the other side where it disengaged and split apart into two sections and melted into the color whirlwind around it. It was a psychedelic phenomenon.

Isabella watched, spellbound, as the room disintegrated around her into a moving, weaving web of paint. It made her dizzy so she closed her eyes for a second. When she opened them, the colors slowed, reversed and, with a rush, sped backwards.

Everything gradually came into focus, straightened and the colors became subdued. Grains of wood mixed with strands of light filled her periphery. The dim light of the attic began to appear and with it the drab wood ceiling, walls and floor. The plywood beneath her settled, straightened and stopped beneath her. The wavy lines of the beams above leveled out, the opening in the floor shifted and returned to its rightful place. The pink spirals around her settled back between the joists.

It took a second for the room to stop heaving. Although she still felt dizzy, she was back. Her heart was racing; she breathed deep and long.

The picture lay before her, face down. So that was how it was done. She'd safely navigated this strange time shift and survived.

She couldn't help but smile, feeling victorious. She'd taken on the box of pictures, endured the terror they created, and won. At least that's how it seemed. It was silly, really. How could a simple cardboard box full of old pictures challenge her to a dual? But that's how it felt. If she could scrounge up enough courage, the pictures would reveal everything she'd always wanted to know.

I wonder how many times or how many pictures I could view in one sitting? Would I experience the time travel with each one?

Isabella knew there was no way she'd attempt any more right now. To have done it once and survived made her feel giddy. Why push her luck? Maybe another day, when she could muster up enough nerve, she'd test her theory. Perhaps she'd even invite one of her friends to join her.

She wasn't sure about that. Going to visit the past, her heritage, felt sacred, special, spiritual, as though walking on hallowed ground. Bringing her friends into it would cheapen it. But having them here would also bring her some comfort and maybe lessen the fear attached to it.

Looking up at the ceiling, she said, "Maybe I should pray about it."

Prayer wasn't something she felt entirely comfortable with. She said her usual prayer at night, a memorized piece she'd said as long as she could remember. She'd never really needed a helping hand before. Tyler Radford, their Youth pastor at church, encouraged them to spend time with God. He said reading the Bible was the best way to get to know God. He told them that prayer was developing relationship with God. He'd suggested speaking to God as she would to a friend. She'd brushed it off at the time but now his words came back.

"Well, it can't hurt, I suppose." Looking up at the ceiling again, she said, "God, help me decide what's best, please?" She lowered her head and glanced at the picture still lying face down. "Oh, and help me figure out what's going on and why."

Now that was a thought. What if God was doing this? Was He? Isabella looked around the room for any sign of Him.

She chuckled sheepishly and felt foolish for searching for someone invisible. It was a good thing her friends weren't here. They'd send her to the Looney Bin for sure.

CHAPTER 5

Tessa Fields picked up some groceries, stopped at the school to get her three kids and headed home. They were unusually quiet in the back seat today. She looked through her mirror at Faith Grace, her eldest, and wondered.

"Hey, Faith, how was your day?"

Her nine-year-old daughter shrugged her shoulders. "Okay." That was her typical answer. She tended to be moody, quiet and kept her thoughts locked inside. Already she'd turned away and was watching the scenery hurry by.

"You didn't ask me about my day," declared seven-year-old Hope, sitting in the middle, between her brother and sister.

Tessa smiled. "Okay, how was your day?"

"It doesn't count now, because you didn't really want to ask me."

"But I did want to ask you. You just didn't give me a chance."

Hope's face scrunched in the mirror and she pursed her lips. "Are you sure?"

"Absolutely."

Hope's face lit up like a Christmas tree. "Okay, I'll tell you. Today, Megan brought in her puppy for Show and Tell and it yapped and yapped so loud." She clamped her hands over her ears. "It really hurt my ears."

"Wow."

She pulled her hands away and continued, "And Mrs. Bruno let three kids do Show and Tell today."

"That's a lot," said Tessa.

"Brian and Alyssa did Show and Tell today too. Brian showed his new dump truck, which was kind of boring and Alyssa brought in a picture she drew. It was kind of dumb and kind of good at the same time."

"Why's that?" Tessa couldn't help but smile as her daughter went on and on. Life was always interesting with Hope around. She talked enough for all her siblings.

"Well, the picture had a lot of bright coloring on it but the drawing was weird. She had all these animals but they didn't even look like they were supposed to. The picture was just stupid."

"That's not a very nice thing to say."

"I know, but it's the truth." Hope's eyes grew big and she nodded emphatically.

"Wouldn't it hurt your feelings if someone said bad things about a drawing you'd done?"

Hope shrugged. "Maybe. But her picture really needed some correction."

Tessa just shook her head and glanced through the mirror to the far side, where her son, Jed, was buckled into his car seat. He'd just started kindergarten and the full days tired him out. His eyes were drooping and he was drifting to sleep.

She missed him when he was in school. His companionship at home had been special with the girls both gone full days but now he was getting into the swing of school life and the house seemed too quiet. He'd be home tomorrow and she was looking forward to it.

Hope was talking as Tessa pulled the van into their driveway. Hope could talk non-stop and she was still giving a dictation of her day. She mostly tuned her daughter out.

"...and then you know what happened?"

It brought Tessa back. "No, what happened?"

"Lizzy smacked Tim across the face with her hand." Her eyes were big and round. "Can you believe that? I was shocked."

"Did he deserve it?"

"No, Mom. All he did was join in on the big skipping rope. Well, he didn't ask but that's not a crime."

Tessa got out, opened the sliding door and unbuckled Jed. Faith and Hope undid their own seatbelts and stepped out of the vehicle.

Hope grabbed her small back pack from the hatch and headed to the house but then stopped, turned back and said, "She likes telling everyone what to do all the time."

Tessa lifted Jed out and was about to carry him to the house when he woke up. He squirmed to be released and she set him down. Jed's awkward, lazy gait told her he was still tired.

Tessa grabbed some bags of groceries from the hatch and turned to Faith. "Could you help carry in the groceries once you've put your back pack inside."

Faith nodded and walked ahead, holding the door for Tessa.

"Thanks, sweetie."

In the entrance Jed sat on the floor pulling off his running shoes. They landed however they happened to fall and he got up and headed down the hall to his room, where all his toys were stored. That would keep him occupied until dinner.

A few minutes later, Hope was still at her side chatting up a storm. The groceries were all placed on the kitchen counter, Faith helping put them away.

Tessa remembered. "Oh yeah, I forgot to tell you girls."

"What?" asked Hope, growing quiet for a moment.

"Isabella's coming to stay with us a few days. Grandma is going out of town on business so Isabella will spend time with us."

"Yay," shouted Hope, jumping up and down.

Faith's eyes lit up with anticipation. "When is she coming?"

Tessa looked at the clock above the kitchen cupboards. "She'll be here soon."

Hope ran from the room to the front window to watch for her. Tessa could see Faith wanted to do the same but she was the quiet, responsible one, always staying to help.

"Go on. Go watch with your sister."

Faith smiled big and said, "Thank you."

Tessa watched her run off. She had two amazing daughters but they were so very opposite in character. They were both precious gifts from heaven and she was grateful.

Jed wandered into the kitchen and said, "I'm hungry. What can I eat?"

"Well, how about I cut up an apple for you?"

"Sure," he said, scooting up on the bar stool and crossing his arms on the counter.

Tessa grabbed an apple from the fruit bowl, opened the drawer to get a knife and proceeded to wedge it into slices, removing the core and placing it on the counter. She smiled at her son and asked, "So how was your day?"

He shrugged, yawned and covered his mouth with his hand. After placing his arm back in its former position, his arms crossed, he said, "It was good."

"Who did you play with today?"

"Everyone."

"Even the girls."

"Everyone except the girls. Ryan was sick today. He wasn't at school."

"That's too bad."

Jed shrugged and watched as Tessa placed a few ready slices before him. He grabbed them immediately and began to munch.

When Tessa finished with the apple, she turned back to begin dinner preparations. She'd planned to make chili and noodles. That would warm their innards on a crisp fall day.

Noise from the front room echoed back to her. The girls were shouting and carrying on about something. It was mostly Hope's voice she heard.

Tessa checked on the onions and green pepper simmering in the pot, stirred it one more time and left the kitchen for the front room. One look out the window told her what all the excitement was about. Granny's car was parked in the driveway. She and Isabella were heading up the walk to the house, a suitcase in Isabella's hand. The girls rushed to the door and Faith opened it wide. Hope flew in front of her and hopped in place, waving her hands to get attention.

Isabella grinned and said, "Hi, Hope."

"Hi, Isa. Hi, Granny."

Sally chuckled as she followed Isabella and said, "Hi, Hope. How are you?"

"I'm great."

Isabella stepped inside and set her suitcase down. Sally stopped at Hope's side and reached down to hug her.

"I wish you could stay, Granny."

"I know. Me too."

"Why don't you?"

Sally reached for Faith and hugged her tightly. "Hi, sweetie. How are you?"

"Good."

Tessa watched her daughter as she interacted with her grandmother and realized how grown up Faith looked. She appeared dignified with her composed, nonchalant attitude.

Faith asked, "Why don't you stay for a little while?"

Holding up two fingers a hair apart, Granny said, "Just a little while."

Hope closed the door behind everyone, crossed her arms and pouted. "You hardly ever come over anymore. Why?"

"Oh, Baby, I'm sorry."

"I'm not a baby." Hope's eyes were big and accusing.

"Of course not. That's not what I meant. You're a big girl. It's just that you're so much smaller than me. You'll always be my grandbaby. All three of you will be."

"Even Faith?"

"Yes, even Faith." Sally looked over at Faith who grinned at the exchange.

Hope grabbed Sally's hand and Isabella's hand with her other and dragged them to the kitchen. Mom will make you some tea. Come."

"Hope, just a minute," said Tessa. She turned to her mother, Sally. "How much time do you have?"

Sally looked apologetic. "My flight leaves in two hours. I have to leave real soon."

Tessa heard Faith ask Isabella if she'd like to put her suitcase in the guestroom and she agreed. The two walked off together.

Sally said, "Goodbye, Isa."

Isabella turned back and grimaced. "It's Isabella. And bye."

A heavy sigh escaped Sally's lips. "She can be so moody." Her eyes looked distraught, like she carried too much responsibility and not enough time to get it all done. "I can't say anything right some days."

Tessa said, "She's a teenager."

"Were you ever like that?"

"Moody?"

"Yeah."

Tessa shook her head. "No, I wasn't. I was fairly easy going."

"What does moody mean?" asked Hope, craning her neck up to look at the two adults beside her.

Granny placed a hand on Hope's head. "It means that your emotions are up and down, sometimes you feel happy, other times you're mad or sad. Your emotions keep changing."

Hope nodded, her eyes got big, she raised one hand and said, "Oh yeah, that's me. I'm moody."

Tessa and Sally laughed.

"Well, let's hope you're not too moody when you're a teenager."

Tessa headed to the kitchen to check on the simmering vegetables.

It wasn't long until Sally and Hope entered the kitchen and sat on bar stools by the counter.

It was clear the way Sally chatted with Hope that she was completely in love with her granddaughter. The way she kept eye contact and touched Hope's hair or placed a hand on her back showed that she'd missed her grandchildren. Tessa wished she'd make more effort to come visit. She knew her mom was busy with her businesses but family was still more important. Tessa wasn't about to put pressure on her, though. The look in Sally's eyes told her she carried a load of responsibility, plus.

During an unusual lull from Hope, Sally said, "Come on, Hope, let's go check what Jed's up to."

"Sure." She hopped down, grabbed her granny's hand and they headed out of the room.

Tessa smiled at the sight. It was a relief finally to have a break from her non-stop verbal daughter. Preparing dinner in peace was rare.

A few minutes later, Sally said her goodbyes and left. It wasn't long until Tessa heard the front door open and Cody's voice calling out, "It smells wonderful in here."

"It's chili," shouted Tessa from the kitchen. He was home early today.

"Daddy, Daddy," yelled Jed, running down the hall and into his father's arms.

He scooped up his son and walked into the kitchen with him. Walking toward Tessa he wrapped an arm around her waist and kissed her soundly. Jed covered his eyes with one hand but then dropped it just as quickly.

Tessa reached over and tickled Jed's middle. "Don't kid yourself, kid. You love kisses."

Jed laughed hysterically, bent over toward Tessa and kissed her too.

Having her two men in her arms felt wonderful.

"Come to my room and play with me," begged Jed.

Cody looked at him. "Jedidiah, can I have a few moments with your mother first?"

He grinned sheepishly. "I guess."

Cody set him down and patted his behind. "Go on. I'll be there soon."

Jed raced off for his room.

"How was work?" asked Tessa.

"Discouraging."

She looked at him. "Why's that?"

Cody worked at the Manor of Peace, a men's rehabilitation center. They helped a myriad of men in difficult situations, from substance abuse to all types of abuse, gambling, addictions and financial crisis. Their primary focus was drug and alcohol addiction. Their success rate was phenomenal and Tessa was very proud of the work he did there. It had been years since he first started, doing whatever job needed completing. Counseling came naturally for him. His easy demeanor and non-judgmental attitude somehow drew the men to bare their souls and deal with their difficult heart issues.

Lines creasing his forehead told her it was true. He looked stressed.

"Another man that we released a few months ago relapsed. Sid Lambert just checked himself back in today. He's right back where he was at the beginning, hooked on cocaine and he's been doing Crystal Meth. The signs are pretty clear."

"Oh no."

"He went back to his old friends. That's what did him in. I was wondering. He missed some of the group sessions and last month he never showed at all. I tried calling but he never answered his cell. I left messages and he didn't call back. In the back of my mind I was expecting it but when it actually happened it hit me hard."

Tessa took the meat mixture off the stove and went to him. She wrapped her arms around him and they held each other tightly.

"I'm so sorry."

"I know. I am too." He released a sigh filled with heavy regret. "I wish we could have done more."

"You did all you could for him. The choice was his." Tessa knew it was true yet she also understood his heart. She worked at a similar home for women, the Mansion of Hope. With family responsibilities filling her time, part time hours were all she could spare, but she'd been in his shoes and gone through the disappointment of women regressing, relapsing and making bad choices. After months, weeks and hours of work being poured into some women, helping them get set free, they would leave, only to become bound all over again. It was more than frustrating; it was completely disheartening. These were lives with eternal souls and they mattered.

"At least he came back, checked himself in. That shows he cares."

"That's true," answered Tessa. "But Crystal Meth?"

"I know."

"That stuff is lethal."

"It's highly addictive."

"But so is every other drug."

He nodded.

Cody pulled away and stood. "I'll go check on Jed. It'll take my mind off work."

Tessa nodded. "Have fun driving his cars around."

"Zoom, zoom," he said and left the room.

Later, after dinner was done and dishes put away, Isabella played Connect Four with Faith and Hope, switching between the two to make things fair. Jed looked exhausted after dinner. Tessa got him ready for bed and tucked him in. After prayers, she switched off his light and as she left the room knew that he'd be asleep in no time. The girls played a few more games then headed to bed too. It was a school night and they needed their sleep. When Isabella stayed over, she was always up late but basically kept to the guest bedroom and wasn't any bother.

Settling on the couch with Cody and watching a sitcom seemed like a fittingly relaxing pastime. They held hands, their fingers interlocked.

"Are you okay with Isabella being here again?"

Cody looked at her. "I like her. I think Sally leaves her on her own far too often. It's good for her to have family time like this. She doesn't get enough."

"I agree. I've been praying for Mom. That she'll make a wise choice. Her businesses are far too consuming. Suddenly Isabella will be grown, on her own and Mom will regret these busy years."

"Sally doesn't have much time for our kids either."

"I agree. The kids miss her."

Having Sally, her birth mother, in her life was a blessing. Their children had three grandmothers and one grandfather, enough to supply plenty of attention. Cody was raised by his mother. His father had abandoned them when he was quite young and there was no contact between the two.

Tessa said, "Did you notice how distracted Isabella seemed at dinner?"

His forehead creased as he contemplated that. "No, not really."

"Well, I did. I'm not sure what's going on but something is on her mind."

"You should ask her."

"I intend to."

Silence stretched between them for a few minutes until a commercial started.

Cody said, "Your mom's on my prayer list too."

Tessa looked at him. Cody was such a good man. Her heart swelled at the thought. "Thanks."

He grinned at that, leaned in and kissed her on the lips.

CHAPTER 6

Isabella was thankful that school was over. The halls were jam packed with students, crowding around their lockers, eager to grab their stuff and get out. Even dragging her overloaded backpack didn't take away from the euphoric feeling she had as she exited the large double doors. It was far too beautiful outside to be stuck inside. The clear blue sky allowed the sun to shed its warmth and chased the cool, fall chill away.

Abby and Shana flanked her as they made their way to the gas station across from the high school. The owners were picky about kids wandering around the small convenience store, afraid of shoplifters. Only five high school students were allowed inside at any one time.

Isabella walked in first to see if they'd be allowed. The familiar clerk behind the counter held up a hand, palm up and, with his East Indian lilt said, "No, you have to wait." There were more than five school kids in the place, more like eight. She turned and headed back outside.

Shana and Isabella followed her.

"He is so… picky." Shana laced her hand through her hair.

His rule did seem a tad overboard, kind of like Sally's statutes. Now that her mom was gone on a business trip and not expected back for four days, Isabella was not allowed back in the house for any reason. It made Isabella even more curious and eager to get back to the pictures. Since she'd finally discovered the picture phenomenon was safe, she longed to get to them. That's all she thought of lately. To learn more about her father was number one in her thoughts. Maybe she should have taken a few pictures along with her.

I wonder if that would work? Would I be able to transport into them at Tessa's place? Hmm. I never thought of that before.

Abby opened her backpack and pulled out a package of cigarettes.

That brought Isabella back to the present. Shocked, she asked, "When did you start smoking?"

"After my mother forbade me to."

Shana said, "My mother would kill me if I tried that."

Abby shook her head in condescension. "You're way too obedient. It's boring."

"At least I'm not dead," stated Shana.

Abby pulled one thin, white tube out and lit it with her lighter. After one deep drag, she started coughing uncontrollably.

Shana chuckled. "That's rich. Your mother won't have to kill you. You're doing a splendid job on your own."

Isabella shook her head in dismay and said, "This is the most stupid thing you've done. She'll smell it on you."

"I know," Abby finally said after her coughing subsided.

"That's what you want?"

Abby nodded, still too winded to say too much.

"You'll have to get a job to afford them," said Shana.

"Is that you talking or your mother?" Abby said and started coughing again.

Shana grew glum and said, "At least I'll have more money on hand to spend on clothes."

Isabella said, "Shana's right. Smokes are crazy expensive."

"I don't care. I won't do drugs. Smoking seems the safest option while simultaneously driving my mother up the wall."

"Everyone at Youth will know," said Shana.

Abby glared at her. "Does it look like I care?"

"So you're going through a rebellious stage?" asked Isabella, not able to control a smirk.

Abby shrugged. "You could say that."

"What's up with that?" asked Shana.

Abby sighed. "My mother. She won't stop nagging me, accusing me, finding fault with me. I've had enough. If she suspects the worst, then she'll get the worst I can give."

Two guys exited the gas station and Isabella and Shana headed for the door.

"Hey, I'm not done."

The two looked back at Abby's smoldering white stub in her hand.

"We'll miss our chance," insisted Shana.

Abby scanned the premises, leaned down, extinguished the smoldering end on the sidewalk, placed the half used cigarette back in its box and followed the girls.

Isabella shook her head in wonder. Abby never ceased to amuse or astonish. The three girls got tall slushies, paid at the till and headed back outside toward the basketball courts across the street. There they sat on the grass, the warmth of the sun caressing their skin.

A bunch of high school guys were playing a spontaneous game of basketball. With girls now watching, they put in more effort. One of them, Tray Warden, looked over and grinned big. His eyes were on Abby. The way she dressed, Isabella wasn't surprised. Abby was petite but cute and her short shorts and deep-cut top guaranteed to keep the looks coming.

Isabella knew that if she were the one wearing those clothes, every boy would be ogling her, so she stuck with oversized t-shirts and big shorts. It's not that she was full of herself; she just knew her assets and had no desire to advertise them. Perhaps when she found the one she'd love for a lifetime she'd be more comfortable with clothing that was less baggy. But she wasn't even sure about that. Her body already brought way too many lustful glances for her liking.

Didn't guys know she was a person with feelings? Their looks were disgusting, revolting, especially when married men traversed her body with their eyes. It made her feel violated.

"He is the cutest thing."

Isabella turned to look at Abby. "You think so?"

"He's looking at me."

Shana made a disgruntled sound deep in her throat. "And grinning like an over-sexed school boy."

Abby turned to look at her. "You're just jealous."

"Of that?" Shana pointed at Tray. "No, definitely not."

"Not your type?" asked Isabella.

Shana shook her head. "No. I like my men tall and handsome."

"You are so egotistical," said Abby.

Shana pointed at Tray again. "He's kind of short and he can't play basketball. Ever wonder why he didn't make the team?"

Abby wheezed derogatorily through her teeth. "I don't care about basketball. All I care about is finding someone who will love me for me."

Isabella cleared her throat. "Then maybe you should cover up your goods and see if he'll actually love you for you."

Abby stared at her as if she'd crawled out from beneath a rock. "Dress like you, you mean?"

Isabella shrugged. "It's a novel idea, I know."

Abby's frowned. "Never."

"Then you'll never really know why it is that Tray is grinning like a toad about to eat dinner." Isabella swatted at herself. "Where are all these flies coming from?"

Shana giggled.

Abby stared at Isabella with vengeance. "Dressed like that, you'll never find a guy."

Isabella moved her head to the side and stared at Abby. "Now that was really low."

"It's not the clothes that a man will fall in love with; it's the person inside." Shana nodded her head like she'd said something completely profound. "Isabella's the sweetest person I know. She has a heart of gold."

"Thanks, Shana. That was nice." Isabella thought for a moment and then said, "It's the lack of clothing that will bring a man panting, but for all the wrong reasons."

Abby was clearly bored of the conversation because she ignored the last comment, pulled out her pack of cigarettes and lit the one she'd doused earlier at the gas station. She took a small draft of it and exhaled.

Tray abandoned the game and headed over. "Hey there, girls. How are you?"

"Great," answered Isabella. "You?"

"Enjoying this good weather."

Abby looked at him with a coy smile. "We were enjoying the wonderful view."

"Oh, is that so?" Tray looked pleased.

Shana snorted.

Abby ignored her and gave Tray a nod.

He turned to look at Shana and then turned to Isabella. "Would you girls mind if I stole Abby away?"

"I'm not sure she's up to be stolen," declared Isabella.

"I'll speak for myself, thank you very much." Abby turned glaring eyes away from Isabella and smiled up at Tray. "Sure." She stood, threw her stub of a cigarette to the ground, picked up her backpack and the two walked off.

When they were a ways off, Shana said, "I don't know what she sees in him."

"He is kind of cute."

"I think she's just desperate. She wants a guy so bad she'll do anything to get one. And settle for anyone."

It made Isabella worry. Abby was a close friend. To see her make bad choices was disturbing.

"Now look at that guy." Shana pointed to the court. "He's got some height and he's built. I like a guy with muscles."

"I thought you liked Mark from Youth?"

"I kind of did. But he's not noticing me. He's been schmoozing with Blair lately."

"You'll have to use the aggressive approach."

"Abby's style, you mean?"

"Not necessarily. But you will need to let him know you're interested. Go up to him, say hi and make small talk."

She looked nervous at the thought. "I don't know if I could do that. I'm not the aggressive type."

"If you want change, you'll have to make a change. Get Mark to notice you instead of Blair."

The ends of Shana's fingers were in her mouth now. Biting her nails was only done under extreme duress.

"Or, you can do nothing and hope for the best. Maybe he'll just miraculously start noticing you."

Her fingers left her mouth and she stared at Isabella. "I like that scenario better."

"I thought you would."

"How about you? Who do you like?"

"No one."

"No one at all?"

Isabella shook her head. She had enough on her mind and a mission to fulfill. A guy would just muddy the waters right now. Focus is what she needed.

"Actually, you've been really distracted lately." Shana stared at her. "What's on your mind then if it's not a guy?"

Isabella shrugged. "Nothing."

"Are you sure?"

She nodded.

Shana stood. "I have to get going. I have my ballet class in an hour. I need to get home."

Isabella stood to her feet and grabbed her heavy load from the grass. "I'm staying at my sister's for a few days so I can walk with you." Shana didn't live far from Cody and Tessa's place.

"Your mother's out of town again?"

"Yeah."

Shana nodded. "We could take the bus."

"It's too nice out to ride the bus and I'll enjoy the peace before I'm bombarded by the kids."

Shana chuckled. "What's the ball of energy? Is it Hope?"

"Yes. She has enough for all three of them. When they all get wound up the house is a zoo. I'm not used to the noise. Hopefully I'll get some homework done tonight."

CHAPTER 7

The house was quiet. The kids were in bed and Isabella was in the guestroom. It may as well have been hers. She was here often enough. With her mom's endless business meetings, this was Isabella's second home.

Cody was at the church for a meeting and Tessa was relaxing on the couch with a book.

The kids had been fighting tonight. Isabella had wished she were back home where it was quiet. But now things had settled and a hush ruled the house.

Isabella opened her laptop. Keeping up with email and Facebook were important to her. After logging on, she noticed an email from Abby. According to the note, her walk home with Tray had been glorious and magical. He'd suggested they start dating and she was on cloud nine. He was taking her to a movie Friday night. That was Youth night at the church. Abby really must like him a lot to miss that.

Isabella doubted the walk was magical. The guy wasn't that much of a dream. But there was no accounting for Abby's tastes. All she talked of lately was clothes and dating. Her goal in life seemed to be to find a boyfriend.

Isabella's thoughts turned to her own mission. If only she could get back to it. Three more days felt like an eternity. It was as though the pictures were calling to her constantly.

Her mom had sent her an email too. Isabella clicked on it and read the note. Sally told her about her day in detail, the meetings she'd had, the managers she'd met with. She missed her and couldn't wait to get home. Isabella huffed. Didn't her mother realize that she was fifteen and had a life? Isabella shook her head. Her mother still treated her like a toddler sometimes. Yet Sally was her family. The two of them were a team. If only they could be a team of three. She'd longed for a father for so many years and still it felt so out of reach. She couldn't remember ever having one.

Isabella looked out the window at the darkening horizon. Maybe she wasn't meant to have a father. But she did have a father, somewhere. Did he really not care to know her? Or had Sally purposely cut him out of their lives?

Isabella sighed heavily. To think derogatorily of her mother left her feeling disgruntled, angry and empty. She loved Sally and couldn't hate her. But she did feel frustrated with her at times. Sally was infuriatingly stubborn and mule-headed. Having made a decision not to tell her a speck about her father, she was a woman of her word.

Turning away from the window, she forced herself to concentrate on her homework. That was the only way she'd get anything done tonight.

Two hours later, she'd completed her book report and was nearly done her math assignment. The thin outline of a picture stuck out from the pages of her math textbook and caught her attention. She'd put it there for safekeeping, something to remind her of how he looked. Opening the book to the spot, she gazed at his handsome face and smiled. It was a picture of just him in all his glory, face on and smiling into the camera. Their looks were so similar that it took her breath away every time she gazed at it. This was her father, the proof that he existed.

A shift in her gaze told her the room was beginning to buckle and move. With a flick of her wrist she slammed the picture face down and the room slowed, straightened and returned to normal.

"Whew. That was close." She tucked the picture back where she'd had it and flipped back to the assigned page. To know that picture travel could happen here too was scary. She vowed to be more careful.

A light knock on the door brought her head around.

"Yes?"

The door opened a crack and Tessa's face appeared. "Can we talk?"

Isabella shrugged. "Sure."

She walked in and sat on the bed. The look on her face said that something had startled her.

"What's wrong?" asked Isabella.

"I don't know." Tessa looked spooked. "I felt this strange energy when I entered, like an electrical current flowing through the room."

Isabella chuckled. "You have quite the imagination."

Tessa's concern gave way to a smile. "Yeah, you're probably right."

"So what's up?"

"Well, I was wondering how you're doing. You seem really distracted these days and I was curious as to what's up."

Two had noticed her distraction, Shana and now Tessa. Was her preoccupation with the pictures that obvious?

"I don't know what you mean."

"Are you having any trouble at school?"

"Too much homework."

"That's not what I meant."

"School is fine."

"How about at home? Are you having problems with Mom?"

"Sally? Naw, she's fine."

"You like calling her Sally, huh?"

Isabella nodded. "It feels more normal, natural. We're like two girlfriends living together."

"That's not really the truth. She is your mother."

Isabella shrugged.

"But everything's going good at home?"

"Yeah."

"Any boy trouble?"

Isabella released a disgruntled sound through tight lips. "No."

"I'm sorry. I'm being nosy. It's just that I do love you. You're my little sis and I have to watch out for you."

She stared at Tessa. Her sister did love her. She could feel the concern flowing from her. "Thanks for caring, but really, I'm fine."

"Ok." They chatted about safe subjects after that until Tessa began to yawn. "I think I'll head to bed and let you get back to your work. Cody will be home soon anyway and I'm tired out."

"You look tired."

"That bad, huh?"

"No. You always look good." For a mother of three she looked spectacular.

"Thanks." Tessa stood and went to the door. She turned and said, "Have a good night."

"Thanks, you too."

With that Tessa left and closed the door softly behind her.

Isabella turned lazily in the office chair, first one way, until the armrest bumped the desk, and then back in the opposite direction. Back and forth she went. Tessa's questions made her wonder. In what way was she different now than before? What did Shana and Tessa see in her that made them speculate? Was she quieter? Was her mind so occupied with knowing who her father was that it showed? Was that the distraction they saw in her? She'd have to be more careful.

Whom could she trust? As far as she knew, Tessa was trustworthy. She'd never broken her confidence and Isabella had shared many things concerning her relationship with Sally. Not once had Tessa gone to Sally with the information. At least Sally had never confronted her with it. Tessa didn't lie. Of that Isabella was sure. She certainly didn't tolerate it from her children. Any lie from the kids was dealt with immediately and severely.

Her mind drifted back to the picture of her father. The photo had caused things to buckle and shift here too. That was useful information and would be accommodating next time she was required to stay over here. There'd be no more obligatory waiting time to get back to the business of snooping while her mother was away. Her inquisitive quest could continue whether Sally was in town or not.

Her homework finally done, she slipped into her pajamas, washed up and slid beneath the blanket. It didn't take long for weariness to overtake her and for sweet sleep to come.

CHAPTER 8

Sally was back and a new outfit lay on Isabella's bed when she got home from school. Sally probably purchased it for her on her trip to Chicago. She must have placed it there when Isabella left for school in the morning. The Lulu Lemon outfit was gorgeous, as usual, but it wasn't her. The cute mini skirt and cami with Karma pullover matched like hand and glove and yet Isabella couldn't help the automatic scrunching of her nose. On the floor lay adorable flats which coordinated with the outfit to a 'T." A bright orange scuba hoodie was the one bright note in the ensemble. She'd use that and perhaps find some use for the flats in the future.

Some of the shoes her mother bought for her were suitable. Most of them were in a box up in the attic. It was clear that Sally was still hoping her daughter's tastes would come around.

The army surplus store was more Isabella's style or Value Village. There were some amazing deals to be had there and she could usually find things to mix and match in her own style. Sally would cringe if she knew where most of Isabella's wardrobe was procured. One of these days Isabella was going to tell her, just to see the look on her face.

Isabella left the outfit where it lay and headed downstairs to get a snack. It felt good to be home. Last night Sally's flight arrived at 7:00 and by 8:00 she was at Cody and Tessa's to pick her up. Isabella had been ready to leave. The kids were really getting to her and she was ready for peace and quiet. But Sally had missed them and wanted to linger. Finally, at 9:30, they'd left. Coming back into their own home felt blissful. The silence of the house had been like a balm.

Today, walking through the empty house felt heavenly. Sally was still at work and the house was all hers. She much preferred a haven of quiet and the house felt like treading on hallowed ground after the turmoil of Tessa's household. She purposely kept the TV off and no music disturbed the tranquil air waves. The hush in the atmosphere was therapeutic.

A look in the pantry told her their supplies were running low. Sally hadn't had time to buy groceries after her trip. Maybe Isabella should learn how to bake so she could make her own chocolate chip cookies. The idea was superb and she knew exactly whom she'd ask to teach her – Tessa. She made everything from scratch. But now she needed something quick. Her growling stomach couldn't wait for a baking lesson.

On the top shelf she noticed an open bag of Oreos. That would have to do. She reached for it and checked the "Best Before" date. It was good. After pouring a glass of milk, she took the bag of cookies and headed to the living room. Sitting on the large, white leather couch, she pulled up her legs, sat cross-legged, took out a cookie and started munching. The solitary sound of her teeth grinding in the silent house was comforting. She couldn't help but smile at the customary satisfaction it gave.

After finishing three cookies and looking through a magazine she'd bought at the gas station store, she set it down and glanced toward the stairs. It was time to head back up there. Anticipation had been building all day but fear vied for dominance. What would she discover in the pictures today? Would she like what she saw? Would it send her reeling? Or what if the time shift didn't happen this time? The disappointment that rushed in with that thought surprised her. She'd find out today.

The fear she saw in her mother's eyes whenever she'd brought up the subject of her father over the past year made her wonder. Was there anything significant to fear? The unknown still played havoc with her emotions. The only way to lay her questions to rest was to embrace the experience, go back into the pictures and relive the story they told.

She headed to the stairs, taking one anxious step at a time. It still wasn't feasible to tell how it happened or what made it possible to participate in the picture anomaly. Still, her curiosity to discover all she could of the mystery of her father egged her on. Perhaps if her mother hadn't been so secretive all these years, the draw of the pictures would be less intoxicating but, as things stood, the desire to learn all she could was growing stronger.

Once upstairs, she retrieved the pole from the closet, looped the hook through the eye attached to the ceiling access and pulled. The ladder unfolded almost on its own and was easy to straighten and set on the floor. Isabella grabbed the rails and headed up to the attic. After flicking on the switch, the single bulb cast its meager light to the recesses of the small space.

It didn't take long to retrieve the box, set it in the middle of the room, and begin to scrounge for pictures of interest. She knew what her mission was today — the brown envelope from her father's childhood. It would reveal information necessary to understand whatever came afterward. She'd heard her mother mention it a few times, that one's upbringing set the course for one's life. If that were true, then learning about her father's childhood would be vital in understanding the man.

The brown envelope lay in her lap and she stared at it for a few minutes. She felt scared and excited. Did she really want to know everything? A derogatory sound escaped her lips. Of course she did. That's why she was here. Good or bad, she was about to find out.

She opened the end and pulled out a stack of pictures. The top few were family photos, two adults and one child, Walter, in different stages and ages. That he was an only child came as a revelation to her. She scanned through the family pictures rather quickly and placed them to the side. For an only child there weren't many photos of him. The brown envelope seemed to contain the extent of his childhood.

Placing the pictures on the floor before her, she stacked the pictures featuring only her father. She reached for the one on top, a baby picture, Walter lying in a basinet. After studying the photo for a while, she noticed, in her peripheral vision, the room in motion, swirling and shifting out of place. Thinking quickly, she abruptly turned the picture face down and the room stilled, backed up and everything returned to its place.

When the room quieted, Isabella quickly scanned through the pictures, picked the ones that looked interesting and placed them in the order she wanted to see them. She held five photos in her hand. Whether she'd have the courage to travel from one to the other that many times she wasn't sure but at least this time she was prepared.

Allowing her eyes to study the basinet picture, she focused all her attention on it, waiting for the room to move. It didn't take long. At the edges of her vision, objects began to buckle and bend, agitate and roll. She looked up and noticed the floor whoosh upward, the ceiling replacing it and the light from the single bulb elongating and snaking itself into the wood of the gyrating attic. The square attic access formed into a bubble and looked oddly like a floating balloon in a wood grained sky. Then, just as quickly, the balloon separated into innumerable little flecks and dispersed throughout the room. The sight was psychedelic and bizarre.

The room suddenly stopped and moved backward with lightning speed, the colors separated and curved lines straightened. Objects began to take form and the basinet took shape before her. Gradually everything shifted, settled and stilled.

Isabella stood next to the camera operator. She glanced to the right and saw a tall man with a commanding presence beside her. He looked young and robust, obviously a proud father. He lowered the camera and gazed at his son lying in the basinet.

So far she hadn't been noticed. If this time travel was like the last, she wouldn't be.

"Walter's beautiful, isn't he?"

Isabella turned to the female voice. A young woman, no more than in her early twenties, stood at one end of the basinet, her hands resting on the top edge. She was pudgy around the middle, due to childbirth, no doubt. Her chubby cheeks were rosy and her smile was bright and inviting but her quiet, soft voice sounded insecure and her demeanor confirmed it. She'd have reached her husband's shoulders if she stood straight and erect but she was as short and unimpressive as he was tall and imposing.

What an odd looking couple. These are my grandparents?

"He's handsome," the man said with finality.

"Of course." The woman turned to admire her baby.

"It's good for you to have given birth to a male child."

Isabella looked at the man. Had she heard correctly?

"This is what you wanted," the woman said timidly.

He nodded.

"I would have been just as pleased with a girl." The woman kept her gaze on her infant.

"Lynne!" His voice boomed.

Isabella stared at the woman. Her grandmother's name was Lynne.

Nervously, Lynne startled and raised her eyes to meet his.

"You don't know what you're saying. A male child is so much more valuable. He will carry my name on to future generations."

Lynne lowered her eyes to focus on her child.

"Do you understand?"

"Yes, Sheffield, I understand."

"Look at me when you answer me."

Timidly she raised her eyes to him. "I understand."

After what seemed like forever, he finally turned his intense gaze from her face, her eyes not diverting from his.

"I liked what the pastor said on Sunday," said Lynne quietly.

"I'm not sure I entirely agree with him."

"Every child is a blessing from heaven."

"On that point I agree."

"I liked what he said about every child having a purpose and destiny."

Sheffield's look was condescending and the hint of a smile held distain. "There's not much destiny in store for a girl."

Lynne stared at him, disbelief playing in her eyes.

"To get married, have babies and keep a home would be a daughter's lot."

Isabella disliked him already and she'd barely met him.

After a moment of silence Sheffield said, "I've been thinking of trying a different church, one more to my liking."

"Again?"

"This pastor's too mealy-mouthed for me. I prefer preaching with fire, definitive and strong." He swung his fist through the air for emphasis.

"But we've only been in this church for two months. I quite enjoy it and I'm just getting to know the other ladies."

"You'll adjust."

"Please, Sheffield, I don't want to change churches."

He glared at her. "You'll do as you're told." He turned to the door.

When he left the room, Lynne's shoulders visibly lowered and a heavy sigh escaped her lips. Walter let out a disgruntled cry and Lynne went to him, lifted him into her arms and settled into the rocking chair in the corner. With a pacifier tucked back into his mouth, baby Walter snuggled into her ample bosom and dozed off to sleep once more.

Lynne hummed softly to him and rocked gently back and forth.

The sight was nostalgic. To think that the young woman held her father in her arms felt comforting, somehow. How was this even possible? The peaceful vision of mother and son in a nurturing embrace was disrupted by the incongruity of the thought.

Isabella stepped forward, closer to the pair, to get a better look. The little tike's name hardly suited him. Walter. What a name for a baby. A full head of hair peaked out from the blanket tucked tightly about him. From his profile, she could already tell he was a handsome thing. Her heart lurched at the close-up view of her father, a helpless infant tucked close to his mother's breast. The sight of him reminded her of her own baby pictures, ones her mother kept filed in photo albums on book shelves in the den. Isabella was hard pressed to tell the difference between those and this infant before her.

Placing a hand over her heart, she felt it beating frantically. Seeing Walter this way was simultaneously frightening and thrilling. She'd thought seeing him as an infant was a logical place to start, and that's why she'd picked the baby photo, but now, being here and seeing him, touched her deeply. This was her father — but he was accepted and loved primarily because he was male.

The door squeaked and immediately Lynne stiffened. It made Isabella jump and she spun to see Sheffield stick his head through the door and look at Lynne.

"I'm going out for a while."

"Where?"

"I need time alone, time to think."

"Are you going to the river again?"

"I don't know."

"Will you be home for dinner?"

"Prepare it for the regular time."

"But will you be home for dinner?" Lynne asked softly as though afraid of the response.

Irritation showed on Sheffield's face immediately. "I don't know," he said, his voice detonating through the room. Walter stirred and whimpered. "I'll be home when I'm home."

Lynne nodded submissively. Walter cried out in her arms and her focus turned back to him. Sheffield left and the room gradually stilled as Walter settled.

He's an awful man. How can he be my grandfather? I feel so sorry for Lynne. She looks absolutely terrified of him.

One more look at the pair nestled in the rocker and Isabella decided it was time to move on. She looked down at the pictures in her hand. She turned the top one face down and slipped it to the bottom of her stack. The next photo staring up at her was of a young Walter, sitting on a couch, a boy of about three, and what looked like a fabric book in his lap. His head was lowered with his eyes glancing up at the camera. Studying it with purpose, she noticed the room begin to shift and roll again. After some time, it stopped and reversed with abrupt speed, colors separating and spirals unraveling until plumb lines appeared and the room equalized. The shift had happened with greater speed this time. Perhaps already being in a photo lapse made the transfer occur expeditiously.

Again, there was a man to her right, Sheffield, holding a camera. Looking back, she noticed Lynne's rotund frame in the doorway, her hands clenched over her apron. Instead of losing her pregnancy weight, she'd gained substantially. She looked anxious, somewhat afraid.

"Read it again, Walter," said Sheffield.

"I can't." With furrowed brow he looked at his father.

"It says, 'I must always obey my father.' Now say it."

Three-year-old Walter's lips twisted. "I mus alays obey my fadder."

"Good. That's good, Walter." Sheffield went to his son and sat down next to him.

Walter pointed at Lynne. "Wha abou Mommy?"

"You obey her when she makes sense."

"Make sen?"

"You obey her." Sheffield smiled and turned to Lynne. "He'll learn soon enough that I rule the roost."

Lynne didn't answer.

Sheffield turned back to Walter, pointed to the homemade book and said, "Mommy made this book. She wants you to read it."

"You told me what to put in it," said Lynne.

He turned his eyes to her. "These things are important for his training. Did you go over it with him while I was at work?"

The light in her eyes showed defiance but she answered meekly. "We did go over it."

"Then why is it taking him so long to memorize it?"

"He's only three. He can't read yet."

"I said memorize it, not read it," he said with raised voice.

Lynne's shoulders tensed and she backed up a step. "I'll keep trying."

"That would be best." Sheffield's eyes didn't blink, didn't shift from her face as he glared at her. He suddenly stood, walked toward Lynne and handed her the camera. "I'll go start on my message. I'll be in my study."

Lynne turned and watched his back as he left the room.

Isabella rubbed her forehead in confusion as she watched her grandfather leave.

Message? He's working on a message? But why? Is he a pastor now?

"Why Daddy alays mad?" Walter had left the couch and stood beside his mother. He slipped his hand inside hers and looked up at her.

Lynne smiled at him and shrugged. "I don't know."

"I love ou," he said with a cherubic face and big, sky-blue eyes.

She bent down and hugged him to her. "I love you too, Walter."

He pulled away and said, "I go play now."

"Go on." Lynne stood and watched her son scamper off. A heavy sigh escaped her lips and quietly she said to herself, "I so wish we could attend a regular church again."

Isabella thought Lynne's eyes looked desperate and a lonely aura surrounded her. What had transpired between the baby picture and this one? They'd left a church and he'd started his own? That seemed odd. It was clear that the two still had a dysfunctional relationship. There was little love evident between her grandparents. Sheffield dominated and Lynne meekly submitted.

Lynne left the room and sounds from the kitchen filtered back.

Isabella looked down at the picture in her hand and wondered if she had the courage to do one more. Sheffield was a difficult man to like. He was imposing and commanding, stifling and domineering. Knowing that the man couldn't see her was comforting, but still, just being in the same room with him made her nauseous.

With a flick of her hand she turned the picture face down and slipped it to the bottom of the pile. The photo staring up at her was of Walter at about age eight, wearing a uniform of some sort and staring into the camera. Not a hint of a smile showed on his handsome, young face. Lynne stood beside him, one arm around his shoulders.

The room seemed in a hurry this time as items disengaged, colors meshed and everything flowed and streamed together in a mass of churning chaos. It slowed, stopped and backtracked swiftly until the colors disengaged from one another, the contortions leveling and objects appearing from the tangled turmoil.

Isabella felt slightly dizzy after that round. Placing a hand to her head she willed the spinning to cease. The room stilled, or maybe it was her own disorientation that assuaged, she wasn't sure.

Looking around, she noticed other boys in uniform, seven in all, with their parents in attendance. Cameras flashed and the boys grinned broadly. Dads slapped their sons on the back and congratulations were given out profusely.

Isabella turned and noted large windows spanning one side of the room. Through them she saw a parking lot. People walked by on a sidewalk on the other side of the glass. She wondered if this room was a storefront in a line of stores. She walked to the glass and looked out.

I wonder if I'd be able to walk out, look around and come back in? I suppose it wouldn't hurt to try.

She walked to the door and pushed. It opened easily enough and a warm breeze wafted in. Stepping out onto the sidewalk, she let the door close behind her. The sign by the road posted all the businesses located in this section. Stepping out farther into the parking lot, she turned and looked at the building. Yes, it was a strip of stores and whatever ceremony or celebration Walter and his parents were holding was being held in a rented store space.

She took the few steps back to the door and swung it wide. As she walked in, she noticed Sheffield was speaking and the gathered group stood a few feet from him and listened.

"..and I'm very proud of each of you boys. Going through the vigorous training and memorization has proven your worth. Seven of you are graduating today, moving from the Tassey Boy Scouts and entering the next phase of Tassey Youth of Valor. It is a true accomplishment and I commend each of you for your hard work and dedication."

The parents clapped enthusiastically.

Sheffield made eye contact with the parents. "I also applaud you for your commitment in bringing your boys to each and every meeting; and to those who donated their time to help train, I thank you."

Sheffield turned to Lynne, who reached to the table behind her for the medals. One by one she handed them to her husband and he called out a name. As the boy stepped forward, Sheffield placed the medal, hanging on a ribbon, over the lad's head. When all the medals were awarded, Sheffield turned to the group and waited for things to quiet, which they did rather quickly.

"We are creating young leaders, something I'm very proud of. Our boys' program has been very successful and we have five more interested boys waiting to begin. I have also received requests to start something for girls." He looked at Lynne and nodded. "My wife has agreed to teach a class for the young maidens in our congregation. We will call it Tassey Girls Club. Lynne will teach them how to quilt and crochet. We both believe these will be very useful tools for them to carry on into adulthood."

Seeing the look on Lynne's face, Isabella doubted the idea was hers.

"By God's grace and power we are raising up his church, preparing his children for life and service."

The small group clapped again.

Sheffield smiled with appreciation. It was clear he reveled in the accolades. He raised his arms high and said, "Let's eat."

The women went over to the tables on the far side and uncovered the food they'd brought.

So he's started his own church? Is that what he's done? His last name is Tassey and he's tacked it on to everything he's created. Wait a minute! If his last name is Tassey then that means Walter's last name is Tassey. Is that my last name too?

Isabella stared at Walter. He looked so young and innocent. It was hard to imagine this boy, presently filling his plate with food, was her father. He chattered with the boy beside him and they compared their medals.

She had to find out for sure. Wandering to the windows she headed to the small table she'd noticed earlier. Pamphlets and informational papers rested there. One that resembled a bulletin caught her attention. She picked it up, opened the front page and scanned the contents. It was simple and contained basic church activities, much less than what her church planned for a week. There, right at the top, was the church name – Tassey Sanctuary. Underneath that it said, "Pastor: Sheffield Tassey." So it was true. Their last name was Tassey.

Suddenly the air felt thick and claustrophobic. She found it hard to breathe. Revelation had come hard and fast this time and it was completely overwhelming. There was so much information to process and impossible to do here, surrounded and bombarded by the past. The desire to turn the picture in her hand face down was strong but she overheard something that made her stop and turn.

One of the mothers, a young, pretty-looking thing, stood close to Sheffield and with fluttering eyelashes said, "I love what you've done with this little congregation. You're so talented and when you speak the whole world seems to stand still. Everyone stops to hear what you have to say."

Sheffield held his fork in midair and smiled at her. "Well, thank you, Florence. I appreciate your confidence in me." His pleasure at her words was transparent.

She sidled a bit closer and whispered, "It doesn't hurt that the pastor is mighty handsome too." With a coy smile she looked up at him.

Interest shone in his eyes but, with control, he reined it in and said, "I'm sure Lynne would agree with you."

Florence looked flustered. "Well...yes. I'm sure she would." She looked at the food table and said, "I think I'll have more of Lorna's potato salad," and walked off briskly.

Sheffield's eyes followed her greedily but he had shown restraint. At least Isabella thought so. But she knew so little of him still. Part of her feared him and yet she admired him. She was amazed how he could rally people around that followed and respected him. From the conversations she'd heard, this little group was only a portion of the following he had. Did he rule them as sternly as he dominated at home? Would people put up with that? From the look of things, everyone here hung on his words.

She glanced at Lynne, a plate full of food balanced on her hand and one of the young mothers beside her talking and laughing. Lynne listened patiently, mouthfuls of food entering her mouth as she did. A nod now and then was the signal the other woman needed that Lynne was indeed paying attention. One thing Isabella had already concluded was that her grandmother was a woman of few words. On the other hand, her grandfather made up for her deficit with his strong character and eloquent speech.

She'd learned a great deal from only three photos but all this picture travel had drained her and she was ready to go back. Flipping the picture face down, the room immediately revolted and bucked violently, sending every person and thing in the room shimmying and swaying out of shape.

Gradually the frantic rushing and writhing slowed, stopped and began churning in the opposite direction. The buckling of the floor calmed and leveled out until the wood paneling of the floor showed. Light splayed up through the opening into the attic, the wavy lines of the access hole straightened and the square entrance took shape.

Isabella let out a sigh of relief as the room finally set back in order. A slight buzz in her head was the only remaining sign that anything out of the ordinary had happened.

Something in the corner of the attic caught her attention, like a shape of a man, but when she snapped her head to look, she saw nothing. Only a dark shadow filled the corner and silence echoed around her. The illusion made her nervous.

Isabella placed the pictures back into the box and returned it to its hiding spot. Feeling relieved, she descended the ladder and closed the hatch entrance. She felt shaken by the picture travel and wanted nothing more than to lie down on her bed and process what she'd learned.

CHAPTER 9

Sitting at her desk, with a to-do list as long as her arm, Sally had to admit that work was getting excessive. Even though she loved the fast pace and the constant challenge of managing numerous designer shops, a design studio and the production of state-of-the-art clothing, the load was too much. She was wearing down and knew it.

She'd stopped by the production studio early this morning to drop off the new designs she'd perfected. Two other designers were employed full time for innovative fashion ideas and designs. They both produced spectacular creations and yet nothing progressed to production stage without her approval. If these fashions went into her stores, they had to be innovative and cutting-edge. Nothing but the finest was formulated in her design studio.

If the businesses weren't so successful she'd have scaled down a long time ago. But they were all thriving phenomenally. Chicago Fashion Magazine had done a full-length article on her boutiques and applauded her business savvy. Since then, she'd received the recognition she'd always longed for and her empire flourished. Even Vogue had covered her in an article last year. She was finally well-known and highly respected. Just to bow out wasn't an option. She'd never make her way back in if she downsized now. Increasing her presence in the design field and building on what she already accomplished was more to her liking. No, there had to be a different answer to her exhausting dilemma than simply downsizing.

The constant demand on her time was rendering her unfit as a mother and grandmother. Guilt plagued her relentlessly along with the knowledge that regret would be a hard partner to grow old with. Something was bound to shift, break or bend. She didn't want that to be her relationship with Isabella. Her daughter meant everything to her. And Tessa, her oldest daughter, was a treasure and gift she wasn't willing to throw away either. Tessa's precious children were such a blessing.

Sally smiled thinking of them. Hope was such a card. Her spunky nature was a great joy to watch and her outspoken opinions made her laugh. Faith's quiet, demure character gave Sally great pride. Faith would become a wonderful young woman one day. And then there was Jedidiah, who loved nothing better than to play with his toy cars and trucks. He was a lad of few words and yet the sparkle in his eye and his adorable looks had done her in. She was madly in love with him, with each of her grandchildren. She couldn't afford to ignore them and have them grow up without her.

She had a meeting with a special franchise lawyer to discuss some options. An idea had come to her last month. It would broaden her scope, enlarge her empire and perhaps increase her work load for a time but the long range goal was to minimize her responsibilities.

After careful research, she came to realize that simply increasing her number of stores and retaining sole ownership would not produce financial feasibility. A search online had produced plenty of information concerning her line of thought. Other businesses, desiring to boost their influence and increase their number of stores created financial burden quite quickly, nearly making them go bankrupt in the attempt.

Averting that route to travel the path of franchising stores had brought things back around speedily for other businesses. She'd learned that franchising produced rapid, profitable growth. She could do that without giving up any control or ownership. And there would be no bills for real estate, equipment or building costs, with the added benefit of incurring no risk.

Those who bought the franchise took the risk and paid handsomely to have the business owner teach the methods of running the business, known as the franchise fee. Continuing royalties paid off the gross sales. The potential was huge and looked positive.

Her lawyer had already warned her last week, however, when she met with him, of the costs involved in starting a franchise business. But she knew she could afford it and had told him so. He'd also told her of the time frame they'd be looking at until everything would be in place. Today he'd be explaining all the legal requirements involved — and there were many.

Sally felt excited. To expand, stretch her reputation and yet have more time on her hands seemed like the solution she longed for. It would require a lot of work, research, money and establishing a new type of business but she felt positive and energized to get started.

She hadn't breathed a word of it to Isabella but she couldn't wait to tell her. Once things were set in motion and the wheels were whirling, she'd share the news. Goosebumps formed at the thought.

The phone jingled loudly beside her and brought her out of her reverie. Sally picked it up and said, "Yes?"

Latisha, her secretary, said, "You have a call on line three. It's a man by the name of Grayson Kendal."

Sally groaned audibly and placed a hand over her eyes.

"Do you want to take it or should I tell him you're busy?"

She wouldn't lie but neither did she want to deal with the man. He was extremely persistent. After a deep breath of air and releasing it slowly she said, "Okay, I'll take it."

Depressing line three, she waited a moment and said, "Hi, Grayson."

"Sally. It's great to hear your voice. I didn't know if you'd take the call. You're always so busy."

"That I am."

"Too busy to talk?"

"I'm always too busy to talk."

He chuckled low and deep. He did have a nice voice even though the man didn't know how to dress. Owning a vehicle repair shop didn't warrant suits and ties. But even during leisure hours Grayson dressed horribly. His idea of fashion was a pair of cheap jeans and a plaid shirt. Not to mention his scuffed hiking boots. His roughneck look made Sally cringe every time.

"How about I take you to lunch?"

"What? Today?" she asked, wondering where in the world she'd find the time.

"Yeah."

"Look, I'm absolutely swamped today."

"You're swamped every day, pretty lady. You have to take time for yourself sometime."

What a completely foreign thought. She didn't take time for anyone except her business, least of all herself. "I'm sorry, Grayson. I just can't. Not today."

"Okay." There was disappointment in his voice. "How about dinner sometime?"

Her stress was building steadily with the pressure. Her evenings, as short as they were, she devoted to Isabella. She had no desire to frivol it away with Grayson, no matter how charming he tried to be.

"I don't know when I'd fit that in."

"I know the perfect night."

"Oh? When would that be?"

"Friday night. It's Youth night at the church and Isabella is busy anyway."

Oh my, he's slick. I hadn't thought of that. How to find a way out of this one?

"Come on, Sally," his husky voice shimmied over the phone, "you have to say yes sometime.

Oh no I don't.

Mentally going over her normal excuses this time seemed catty and mean. He meant no harm. He simply found her attractive and was very persistent in his pursuit of her. That she didn't reciprocate his feelings didn't warrant her being cruel. What would it really hurt to have one meal with the man? Just maybe he'd realize how unsocial she was and how career-driven her life had become. That would be easy to reveal to him. He'd probably be bored to tears hearing her discuss the fashion industry. They were polar opposites, he a grease monkey and she obsessed with clothes and fashion. That they were both business owners also occurred to her but she brushed that away.

"So what do you say?" His soothing voice toyed with her mind, hopeful and prodding.

"I don't know."

"We can make it later; give you a chance to finish up at the office. Let's say around 7:30?"

"Youth starts at 7:00."

"We can make it earlier. I'll come by the church after you drop Isabella off and we can leave from there."

Her defenses were crumbling. Without thinking it through carefully, she sighed and said, "All right."

"All right? Is that a yes?"

"Yes." That's all she could manage. She was surprised she'd said that much.

"Perfect. I'll make reservations."

"But I don't want to be out late. I have some meetings planned on Saturday."

"Of course. I'll have you back at the church before your curfew."

That made her chuckle. She really was a prude, anti-social misfit.

"I'm looking forward to hearing more of that laugh." With his husky voice, the statement sounded sexy.

"All right, Grayson, I'll see you then. I have to get back to work."

"Of course you do. I'll see you Friday."

Sally set the phone back in its base and stared at it. Now, why had she said yes? It would just complicate her already overtaxed schedule. She dreaded the date already.

Grayson Kendal had shown interest for a good year now and so far she'd been able to avoid him. They attended the same church, Church on the Move, where Tessa and Cody also attended. They were the ones who got her connected there. Isabella had good friends at the church and enjoyed the Youth program.

At first the man's interest was reserved to a simple "Hi" now and then. Then it progressed to him corralling her to chat. He talked mostly of his business, his comfort zone. She graciously listened and nodded, not willing to divulge too much of her own life. Gradually he began to ask questions, asking about her hobbies, where she worked, her interests. She answered them guardedly, not willing for him to become too familiar. He'd concluded that Isabella was her daughter and he eventually learned that Tessa was also.

Then the connection was made. Cody, Tessa's husband, and Grayson's son Charlie, both worked at the Manor of Peace, helping men overcome addictions. That knowledge, as well as the fact that

Tessa worked part time at the Mansion of Hope, the rehabilitation home for women, gave them a lot to talk about. Grayson Kendal was very proud of the work his son did and loved to discuss it.

Sally was also proud of her daughter and son-in-law's occupation but she could discuss that topic only in small doses. That she lived and breathed fashion seemed to have evaded the man's notice. She couldn't really blame him, not the way he dressed.

But now they were going out on the town, Friday night no less. She swiveled in her chair and groaned loudly. There was no time for regrets or wasting the day dwelling on Grayson. She had a mountain of work to do.

After a sip of cold coffee, she turned back to her computer and tried to focus on the letter to a franchise consultant she'd found online.

CHAPTER 10

The experience was inexplicable and bizarre, and sprawled across her bed, Isabella's mind spun crazily. Trying to decipher all the data was daunting. She still felt dizzy and disoriented but maybe that was simply due to the overwhelming amount of information that had been downloaded. Sealed lips, hidden data, mystery beyond measure and a mother made of iron steel resolve was more the norm around here.

So, how was it that her father's name was Walter Tassey and she'd never once in her fifteen years heard his name? It rattled her. What was it about him that spurred her mother to keep all information in lockdown? Was he truly that evil? That twisted? Sheffield Tassey, her grandfather, was still a mystery but less than before. He ruled with complete control, at least in his home. He manipulated his wife with shameless audacity. Is that how he'd raised his son too? Had he had such an influence on Walter that it permanently distorted his character?

After half an hour of regurgitating all the information she'd gleaned, she still wasn't any closer to unraveling the inscrutability of her past. Her head hurt from all the thinking.

The cheery jingle of the doorbell roused her attention and she gratefully hauled herself off the bed and headed to the stairs. Anything to distract her was a welcome relief. She took the stairs down two at a time and hurried to the front door. Looking through the side window she saw Shana standing there, two slurpies in her hands.

Isabella opened the door, swung it wide and smiled. "Hi, Shana. Is that for me?"

"This one is." She handed the cherry one over and stepped inside, keeping the blue one for herself.

Taking the first deep slurp of the cold liquid immediately soothed the writhing agitation Isabella felt inside. Shana would be able to take her mind off the time travel dilemma, at least for the present.

Shana skirted the white leather couch and plopped herself down onto the soft surface. "So what's up?"

"Not much," Isabella said, taking a seat on the far end.

Slurping on the ice cold liquid was the only sound for a while.

"What's Abby up to?" asked Isabella, looking over the rim of her straw.

"You have to ask?"

"She's with that basketball wannabe again?"

Shana nodded. "It's all she talks of lately."

"It's getting totally tiresome."

Shana nodded again. "She was too busy to join me. So I thought, what the heck, I'm going without her. I'm not putting my life on hold for her."

"Me either." Isabella grinned.

"So what's kept you so busy lately? You never stay after school much anymore. You're turning into a hermit and Abby's acting like a love-struck, grade school girl."

"She is a grade school girl."

"Yeah, I suppose she is." Shana shook her head in dismay and then turned to focus on Isabella. "But what has you all tied up lately?"

Isabella held her breath. This was the moment of decision for her. Should she confide in Shana and take a huge risk? What would she think? She didn't even know what she herself thought. The strangeness of the experience still twisted her insides into knots, made her hands sweat and gave her goose bumps.

Shana's curious stare told her she was waiting too long to answer.

"Something's up, isn't it?"

Isabella shrugged noncommittally. "Nothing really."

"Come on, out with it." Shana's stare intensified and her slurpie sat forgotten in the folds of her hands.

"You wouldn't believe me anyway." Isabella stuck the straw in her mouth and sucked hard.

"Try me."

Making eye contact with her friend, she could tell Shana was serious. "It's too bizarre."

"What is?"

"Something strange is up in my attic."

A crooked expression slowly formed on Shana's face. "Ghosts?"

With a grunt deep in her throat, Isabella retorted, "No."

"Then what?"

She shrugged. Fear kept her from blurting it all out. Shana probably wouldn't believe her anyway. Risking their friendship this way seemed precarious and futile.

Impatience flitted across Shana's face. "Come on, tell me. You can't throw out something as mysterious as that and not tell me.

"I shouldn't have said anything. It's just way too out there and it's quite private."

"Isabella. You have to say now. I'm dying of curiosity."

The look in her friend's eyes would have made her laugh if the subject weren't so near her heart.

"Isabella."

She looked at Shana. Could she handle it? Would she accept it without ridiculing her? Would she insist on seeing for herself? That might not be such a bad idea. To enter the pictures with a friend seemed less terrifying.

"Please?"

After a deep breath and lengthy exhale, Isabella nodded. "Okay." She waited a moment to conjure up a bit more courage. "There are these pictures up there that my mom hid. They're in a box and she hid them beneath the insulation. They're pictures of my dad."

"I thought you didn't know anything about him. You've never seen him."

"I have now."

"Wow. That's a switch. Does your mom know you've seen them?"

Isabella shook her head.

"That's what you've been praying for, right? You've wanted to know more about your dad."

"Yeah."

Shana looked confused. "So what's the problem? You've seen pictures of him and now you know what he looks like. That's great."

"That's not the point."

"What is the point?"

This was it. The moment of truth. After releasing another pent up breath of air, Isabella said, "I go up there when my mom isn't home."

"Is that why you never want to hang out after school? You're too busy investigating?"

"Yes."

Shana nodded. "And?"

Here I go. "Well, whenever I study a picture, the whole attic starts to shift and move. Everything comes undone and colors swirl and swish together. When everything stops again, I'm actually in the picture, seeing everything as it happened."

Disbelief was stark in Shana's eyes. "Like, you mean, back in the past?"

Isabella nodded and hoped for the best.

"Does it happen every time?"

"Every time I go up there and study a picture. I've discovered that I can hold a few pictures at a time and move from one to the other rather quickly."

"How does that happen?" Fear crept into her eyes along with a touch of skepticism.

"I don't know."

"And when you're done, can you decide when to come back? Or do the pictures decide when you're done?"

"So far I've been able to control everything."

Shana shook her head. "It sounds way too strange." Fear gave way to a chuckle until she was laughing hysterically.

Isabella didn't even crack a smile.

Shana realized and quieted rather quickly. "I don't get it."

Isabella remained silent.

"What is this supposed to prove? I mean, why does it happen and what's the point?"

"I've learned some things about my dad's past. I've learned his name."

"Really?"

She nodded.

"What is it?"

"I'm not ready to divulge that yet."

"Why not?" Shana looked miffed. "You told me the rest."

Isabella shrugged.

"Can you show me?"

Isabella racked her mind for a safe picture that wouldn't reveal too much and that wouldn't increase the load on her overtaxed emotions. This was the only way she'd prove herself right. To have a best friend share the experience would bring some comfort. The picture came to her then. Hopefully there wasn't more behind the scene than what was warranted to see.

"Okay." Isabella stood nervously and headed to the stairs.

Shana was right on her heels. "So how will this work? Will we both study and enter the picture together?"

"I'm not sure. I guess we'll figure it out."

"That's not very reassuring."

It didn't take her long to get the pole, open the hatch and pull down the ladder. Setting the pole to the side, Isabella started up first and switched on the light at the top. As Shana made her way to the plywood floor, Isabella had already shimmied over the joist to the box and lifted it carefully to her arms. Cautiously, she stepped back to the floor and placed the box down. They both sat, cross-legged, before the box. Shana's eyes were large and full of curiosity.

Isabella removed the lid and set it to the side. She placed the brown envelope beside her on the floor and searched the box for the picture she had thought of. It was one of her when she was just little, lying on the floor playing with a jungle gym. Sally would have been on the other side of the camera. It seemed like a safe one to venture into.

She found it and held it for Shana to see.

"Is that you?"

"Yes."

"I was hoping to see one of your father."

"I'm not ready for you to see one of those." Hopefully he wouldn't be sitting in the background of the picture, waiting for them once they entered.

"Just a peek?"

Isabella pondered that. It couldn't hurt anything, could it? She reached back into the box and found one of the two of them, Sally and Walter. A quick look shouldn't hurtle them into the past. She held it up for Shana to see.

"That's him? Wow. He's hot."

Lowering the picture, she said, "Shana."

"He is. I'm just being honest."

Isabella threw the picture back into the box with the others.

"You look like him."

"I know."

"Now we know where your hot looks come from."

"Oh, please."

Shana only shrugged and raised her eyebrows.

But her friend was right. That he was her father was as clear as day. She held up the picture she'd chosen and said, "This is the one we'll enter."

"Don't say that."

Confused, she turned to Shana. "What?"

"It freaks me out to hear you say that."

"It's what happens."

"Just show me."

With a shaky voice, she said, "Okay." Isabella held the picture so they could both see it. After studying it for a moment, her peripheral vision told her things were already shifting and moving. "Do you see the room moving?"

"No. Everything's normal."

"What?" Isabella turned the picture over quickly and placed it face down on the floor. Colors and lines scurried back to their original place and form. When the room settled completely, she turned to Shana and stared at her. "You didn't see anything move?"

She shook her head. "Not a thing."

Isabella pondered this carefully.

"Maybe I should hold on to you. Perhaps you're the connection to all this weirdness." Shana grinned crookedly.

It made Isabella chuckle. It felt good to have a friend here with her and helped to release the tension. "Let's try it that way. Hold onto my arm and I'll study the picture."

Shana nodded and reached for her arm.

Isabella turned the picture around and held it up. Studying it again, it didn't take long for the room to pucker and scrunch into odd shapes, disentangling from reality and meshing into a swirl of color and diverse contortions.

Shana's scream from beside her told her that this time she was seeing it too. Her grip on Isabella's arm tightened exponentially and she could feel Shana shivering in fear. Her focus was important now to make sure they made the trip completely and didn't get caught in the crinkle in time. She wasn't sure if that was possible but she was in no frame of mind to find out.

The whole room crimped and bucked crazily, the kaleidoscope display and changing mirage dizzying in its effect. Gradually it slowed, stopped mid-stride and backed up. The colors hurried backwards, new ones appearing as the room swirled around them until they all slowed, came into clearer vision and the room stilled once more.

They found themselves standing beside a young woman. It was Sally, a much younger Sally, taking a picture of her young daughter. A couch stood at their back, a rocking chair on one side and a recliner on the other. A small fireplace graced the wall behind them. To their front, on the floor, beneath a jungle gym, lay a baby, Isabella.

Slowly Shana released her hold on Isabella arm. The shock on Shana's face was almost as fascinating as seeing her mother so young.

Shana said, "I can't believe it."

"And you let go of my arm and are still here."

"That's right." Shana's eyes swam with fear. "Don't you dare leave me here."

The idea brought with it a slew of questions. "I hadn't thought of that one. I wonder what would happen…"

"Don't even go there!"

"I won't leave you behind."

A look of relief filled her eyes. After looking at the scene, Shana said, "So they can't see us or hear us?"

Isabella shook her head.

"That's comforting."

Sally lowered the camera, looked at her baby on the blanket in the middle of the floor and said, "Hey there, Pumpkin. Are you a happy girl today?"

Baby Isabella cooed on the floor, delighted with the attention. She batted at the hanging toys above her and watched in fascination, her eyes shifting from toys to mother interchangeably.

"You're such a smart girl. Yes you are." Sally knelt down to watch Isabella more closely. Pride and joy filled her features.

"She really loved you."

"Past tense?"

"Well, you were a very cute baby. You can hardly blame her."

Isabella chuckled.

"So where's Daddy?"

"Probably at work."

"Was he around much when you were little?"

"Like I'd know?"

"What has your mom told you?"

"Nothing actually."

"She hasn't told you anything?"

"Nada."

"But why?"

"Who knows. For some unknown reason, she's afraid of telling me about him."

"Do you think that's what this is all about — God's answer to your prayers?"

Isabella turned to stare at her friend. "What do you mean?"

"It could be God's way of unraveling the secrets. Giving you the answers you've begged for."

"So it's God who's making this time/picture travel possible?"

Shana shrugged. "I'm just saying it could be."

The idea made the time travel mystery less terrifying. If this truly was God's doing, then he would protect her through it. At least that was her assumption.

Sally's voice brought them back to the happenings in the room. "I love you, Isabella. You are the most precious thing in the world to me, a gift from heaven."

"Aw, how sweet," said Shana.

Isabella punched her arm.

"Ow."

"You deserved that."

Shana just grinned.

Sally slowly stood and headed to the kitchen.

"Can we walk around, look at the place?"

"I've done it before. I've even stepped outside a building in one place to learn more."

"Let's do it."

"I've also tried doing the same thing at another place and been stopped. Actually, it happened right here in this apartment."

"How?"

"Come." Isabella walked to the door, opened it to the hall and glanced down the corridor. It was the same as last time. Five feet from the door the hallway disappeared into a swirl of moving colors and shapes. "That's what I mean."

"Wow. That's trippy." Shana turned her head to look down the opposite direction. The same scene greeted her scrutiny. "This is so weird."

They reentered the apartment and Isabella closed the door. Shana turned to her and asked, "How often have you done this?"

"A few times."

Shana looked shaken and a little spooked. "What if you walked into that moving swirl down the hall? Would it send you back to the attic?"

"I haven't thought of that. Maybe."

They watched as Sally reentered the room with a bottle in her hand. "I don't know if you're ready for this. You're nearly too happy to eat."

When baby Isabella spotted the bottle, she started to whimper.

"Ah, I suppose you are ready, hey, Pumpkin?"

Her little arms waved frantically, waiting to be picked up.

Sally moved the jungle gym away to the side, lifted her daughter into her arms and headed for the rocking chair. After getting comfortable, she placed the bottle nipple into the baby's mouth and Isabella sucked lustily. Sally's eyes fixed on the baby in her arms and she hummed a quiet tune.

"She looks so young," said Shana.

Sally still looked like Sally. "She still looks young."

"Yeah, but not as young as that." Shana pointed.

"She still looks good."

"I didn't say she didn't look good."

Isabella looked at her friend with some frustration. Shana could argue about anything, given a chance. Looking back at mother and daughter, she'd seen enough.

"Ready to go?" she asked Shana.

Shana looked at her and said, "This isn't that exciting of a moment."

"Let's go then. Hold onto my arm."

Shana did just that and Isabella lifted the picture and turned it face down. Within moments the room began to move, shift and buckle. With violent force, the floor heaved upwards replacing the ceiling, while lights from up above hurled down below their feet.

Shana screamed and Isabella felt her grip tighten to the point of pain.

Shana's voice shook with fear beside her, "When will it end?"

"Soon it'll stop and reverse. It won't be long after that."

"Good."

Then it happened. The movement of the room slowed, stopped and reversed rapidly. Colors scurried around frantically, suddenly in a rush to leave. Wood grain began to dominate the color scheme, curves straightened into lines and leveled out and dispersed light sucked sideways and melded into a single bulb. The access hole became visible beside them, curves giving way to a square opening, filtered light lifting through it. The room finally stood still, silent and meek after all the harried energy and fervor.

"We're back." Shana sounded relieved.

"Yes we are." Isabella placed the picture back into the box and placed the lid on top.

Shana's unusual silence felt out of place. Isabella stood, turned and looked at her friend still seated on the floor. "You okay?"

"No, I'm absolutely not okay."

"Why, what's wrong?" Isabella heaved the box up and held it tight.

"We just got sucked into a picture, saw you and your mother from years ago, got transported back here somehow and you're asking me what's wrong?"

Isabella grinned. "It is kind of far out, huh?"

"Completely far out." She stood and waited for Isabella to carry the box back to its hiding spot. When Isabella returned to the wood floor, Shana asked, "So she doesn't know about this?"

"My mom?"

"Yeah."

"No. She has no idea and that's how it needs to stay. You can't say a word."

With one shaky hand raised, Shana said, "I promise I won't say a thing."

After descending and putting everything back the way it was, the girls headed downstairs and sat on the couch. Isabella turned on the TV. Shana often came over after school to watch TV with her. It was their habit and one Isabella was thankful for at the moment. It would help take her mind off of the past for a while.

A look at Shana told her the girl was still shell-shocked. Her eyes were glazed; the game show on TV wasn't penetrating at all. Jeopardy was usually enough to get the brain juices flowing but Shana's mind was obviously someplace else at the moment.

"You sure you're okay?" asked Isabella.

Shana shook her head. "No, but I'll live."

"You're awfully quiet."

"I'm processing."

"I'd feel better if you processed louder."

"I just can't get over it." With a slight shake of her head she said, "We'll have to tell Abby. She deserves to know."

"She deserves to know? She's abandoned us for the basketball wannabe."

"She'll come slinking back with her tail between her legs when she discovers what she's missed."

"I don't know."

Shana grew quiet and Isabella focused on the show, her emotions too frazzled to speak.

CHAPTER 11

Coming home was always a relief. The peacefulness of the house was a balm after a frazzled day of work. Sally slipped out of her high heels, set them on the shoe rack in the front closet and headed to her room. Passing the living room and seeing the empty slushie cups on the end tables told her one of Isabella's friends had been here, maybe both. Guilt assailed her again. Her wristwatch declared it was nearly 8:00. They always ate dinner late. Isabella spent way too much time on her own and Sally hated it. At least having friends pop by stemmed her daughter's loneliness, not that Isabella ever complained. She seemed to understand Sally's schedule and took it in stride.

There was no sign of Isabella. That wasn't uncommon. She preferred her room, sitting with her laptop and listening to music. It seemed to be her haven and Sally was glad. Everyone needed a place of tranquility.

Walking up the stairs took effort but to change into something more comfortable would be worth it. Her designer lounge pants called to her. That reminded her. She hadn't seen Isabella wear the new Lulu lemon outfit she'd bought her. She'd have to ask her about it. It was difficult finding outfits that suited Isabella's taste, especially designer fashion. Why Isabella hated designer labels boggled her mind. To dress well made a statement; it spoke of status and self-confidence. She often wondered if her daughter struggled with inferiority.

Some of the clothes that girl wore made her cringe. The boots she'd bought a few weeks ago from the army surplus store looked horrid. And those shorts she sported with them made her look homeless and poor, the t-shirt even more so. Hopefully, as she matured, her taste in style would also.

At the top of the stairs something caught her attention. A piece of pink fluff lay on the carpet down the hall. She wandered over, bent down and picked it up. Touching it, she was sure it was insulation, the kind she'd seen in the attic. Looking up confirmed it. The hatch opening was closed tight but a piece of pink insulation stuck out from the side, just barely visible.

That's strange. I haven't been up there in weeks, not since Mom's visit. So, what in the world?

She'd have to check on things later. Sally turned to Isabella's room, knocked and waited for her muffled reply. Opening the door, she walked in and smiled at her daughter relaxing on her bed, a bag of Doritos sitting beside her and crumbs littering her bedspread.

She'd always loved Isabella's room. They'd redecorated it nearly a year ago and it still brought her delight. They reverted from the pink, frilly things and the cutsie wall paper she'd loved as a kid to something more grown up and more Isabella. The deep purple bedding, interspersed with orange and green swirls made a bold statement. They'd painted the walls a light mauve, bought paintings in the same bold colors of the bedspread and splattered the room with coordinating knick knacks. Even the lamp on her nightstand matched the décor. It was funky and modern. At least in room styles Isabella was adventurous.

Sally stepped in and said, "Hi, there. How are you?"

"Hi, Mom. I'm good."

Sally went to sit on the corner of the bed. "How was your day?"

"Good."

"I saw the empty slushie cups downstairs."

Acknowledgement lit her eyes. "Yeah. Shana dropped in for a bit."

"I'm glad. She didn't stay long?"

"Two hours or so. She had to get home for dinner."

Sally sighed loudly. "Yeah, dinner. I sure don't feel like cooking."

"We could order in," suggested Isabella.

"I think that's a great idea."

"Chinese?"

"That sounds wonderful."

"How was your day?" Isabella asked.

"Busy like usual. I had a few meetings, worked on some designs and did some conference calls."

"Sounds boring."

Sally grinned. "I guess you could say that. I personally find it invigorating." Silence stretched between them and Sally lifted the piece of insulation she'd found in the hall. "Do you know why this was in the hall? Have you been up in the attic?"

A touch of fear flitted across her daughter's eyes which made her wonder.

Isabella said, "Oh, I put some shoes up there. I didn't realize I made a mess."

"Which shoes did you put up there?"

"A bunch that I never wear anyway."

"Does that include those army boots you recently bought?"

A small smile tickled Isabella's lips. "No."

"Here's hoping."

"Sorry about making a mess."

"You rarely make a mess. It's the blessing of having only one child."

"I don't think I could handle sharing you with a sibling."

"Why's that?"

"I get too little of you as it is."

Guilt lifted its ugly head once more but Sally forced it down. She would not allow it to ruin the little time they did have together. The temptation to reveal her business plans was overwhelming but it was too premature. The time would come soon enough.

Sally reached over to touch Isabella's leg and squeezed. "I miss you more than you know."

Isabella nodded but looked sad.

That's why she was doing what she was doing. If the franchise idea worked, things would be different around here.

"I'll go change and then order some Chinese."

"You'll tell me when it arrives?"

"Why don't you come down earlier and we can sit and chat, maybe have a cup of tea together."

Isabella looked surprised. "You don't want to soak in the tub first?"

"I'll do that later."

"Okay. I'll be down in a bit."

Sally stood and headed to the door. "See you in a few."

After changing and heading back down to the kitchen, wearing warm fuzzy slippers on her feet, Sally filled the electric kettle with fresh water and switched it on. While it hummed to life, she took down two mugs, retrieved two tea bags from the canister and got out the sugar bowl. She leaned against the counter, crossed her arms and wondered about the attic episode. The startled look in Isabella's eyes had thrown up a caution sign. She had the uncanny feeling her daughter had lied but couldn't for the life of her figure out why.

Then it came to her. The box. Her mother. The pictures. It all fit. Suddenly it became hard to breathe.

She wouldn't have. Would she? She had no idea my mother brought a box of pictures. I put them up there as soon as Mom gave them to me. Isabella never saw them. I'm sure of it.

And yet the dread wouldn't leave. She determined to find out. She'd wait until Isabella was asleep, head up to the attic and take a look around. The first logical step was to see if the box had been tampered with. If it had been, she wasn't sure what she'd do, but she had to know.

A sound on the stairs told her Isabella was coming. She had to hide her misgivings. Time with her daughter was so rare that she was willing to put on a grandstand production to veil her agitation.

Later, at 3:00 in the morning, with the moon in full command of the sky, its light filtering through the blinds, Sally's alarm woke her. She rubbed her eyes, looked at the clock and switched it off. After waiting fifteen minutes, to make sure Isabella had fallen asleep again if the alarm woke her too, Sally swung her legs out of bed. She slipped her feet into her slippers and reached for her robe at the foot of her bed.

As she tied the waist straps around her, the idea of snooping suddenly felt completely unfounded. She needed sleep far more than a nighttime foray investigation of the attic. Didn't she trust Isabella? Yes, she did. And yet it wasn't Isabella that caused alarm to tighten its grip around her heart. Terror filled her when she thought of the possibility of Walter reentering into their safe and peaceful lives. She'd do anything to stop that from happening. Taking a deep, calming breath, she headed for the hall.

Once there, she retrieved the pole for the attic access, hooked it into the loop and pulled gently. It opened quietly, the ladder descending and stopping at eye level. She reached for it and pulled it all the way down. Placing the pole on the floor, she reached for the ladder and made her way up.

She switched on the light as soon as she reached the top and took the few last steps up to the wood floor. Looking around, nothing appeared out of place. And yet, how had that insulation managed to get from between the joists and down to the floor? Someone must have wandered close to the open insulation and it would mean a deliberate walk over there.

Sally stepped over to the edge, where the plywood floor and open joists met. Looking over to where she knew the box to be, the slight bump was still there, covered carefully with the bright, pink insulation. Was that enough proof? She wasn't sure. She stood carefully and maneuvered herself across the joist, one foot in front of the other. Once there, she lifted the insulation and placed it to the side. A careful look would tell her a great deal, not that she had paid much attention to the box or its contents when her mother brought it. Now she wished she had.

The lid fit tightly over the opening like it had been when she placed it here. Sally removed it and looked inside. A brown envelope lay on top. Yes, she remembered her mother telling her about that. The envelope contained pictures from Lynne Tassey, her former mother-in-law, pictures from Walter's younger years. Sally pulled it out and perused the photos lying loose and unorganized within. There was nothing out of the ordinary here.

With a sigh of relief, Sally placed the envelope back on top, replaced the lid and folded over the insulation to cover it all. There was no need to relocate it as she'd planned to do if she'd found foul play. Carefully, she stepped back to the plywood floor, took one more look around, determined everything was as it should be, and flicked the switch, sending the room into darkness. Faint light filtered up through the access hole. Meticulously, she lowered her foot to rest on the first wrung and descended slowly, cautious not to make a sound.

At the bottom, she closed the hatch as quietly as she could and returned the pole to the hall closet, making sure not to leave any telltale signs of her visit. There were no pieces of insulation left behind. Gratefully, she headed back to bed and sweet sleep overtook her.

CHAPTER 12

The night was long and sleep escaped Isabella. In the morning it proved hard to function and the restless night was the culprit; she was sure of it.

Sally left the house an hour ago but she'd come into Isabella's room at least three times to wake her. The last time she shouted for her to get up.

"I'm leaving and you have to wake up, Isabella. You can't miss school."

Isabella groaned and complained but she was finally awake. Once Sally knew she wouldn't doze off again, she finally left for work.

A strong cup of coffee might do the trick, left over from the regular pot her mother made each morning. Not that Isabella particularly liked the stuff but she found the caffeine fix did wonders for a droopy, sleepy state of mind. It might get her through morning classes without falling asleep during one of Mrs. Tingle's boring lectures. She was dreading that class already. It should be against some type of school regulation to make an English class that dull.

After a bowl of instant oatmeal and one more cup of coffee poured into a travel mug, Isabella locked the door and headed to the bus stop. It wasn't far to walk to school and she usually did on a nice day, but today she just wasn't in the mood. Besides, she was late.

She waited ten minutes before the bus pulled in to the stop and screeched to a halt. Finding a seat at the back suited her today. The free seat by the window looked ideal. She sipped the black mix in her bright orange mug slowly as the bus pulled into traffic, her mind suffused with questions.

During the night, noises from up above had broken through her sleep and shaken her awake. She'd stayed where she was, tucked beneath her warm comforter, and listened, hardly breathing. The sounds from the attic had alarmed her. She knew her mother was investigating at a time she thought Isabella would never suspect. Sally was checking the pictures.

What did Sally find up there? I sure hope I didn't leave any clues. Did she take the pictures? Hide them someplace else? If only I'd had time to check this morning and make sure they're still there.

Fear wrapped itself around her throat like a snake. She'd barely discovered her father and now the possibility of losing this priceless avenue of information was terrifyingly real. She'd been too careless. With Shana there, she hadn't done a careful survey, making sure everything looked as before. In the future she'd be more vigilant. That is, as long as the pictures were still where she'd left them.

The day crawled as slowly as a turtle on vacation. Her classes felt long, drawn out and entirely cumbersome. Mrs. Tingle took this day to belabor deep meanings found in the book, "Pride and Prejudice." Although reading was one of her favorite pastimes, this book was proving burdensome to finish. Some girls in the class were in awe over the love story, but Isabella found it dull. Adventure, a murder mystery or a good thriller were more her taste, anything with action.

At lunch she met Shana and Abby in the cafeteria. Abby's high ponytail, tight jeans and low-cut top brought plenty of looks as she passed tables and sat down across from Isabella. Shana's modest looks went unnoticed as she followed Abby to the table.

Isabella looked down at her plain outfit. Her jeans were a size too big and were held up with a wide belt. The large, striped t-shirt she wore over a blue cami hid everything well. She'd worn her army boots today. They made her feet sweat but the look was worth it.

Tray Warden was looking over and trying to catch Abby's eye. Isabella said, "Looks like someone's noticing you."

Abby looked up from her sandwich but kept her eyes averted from Tray. "I know. Tray's really interested."

"And you're not?" Isabella felt surprise. Had something changed in the last week?

"I think it's time to play hard to get. It makes males more interested."

"Or he'll give up and move on to Tia." Shana pointed to the girl a table over.

Isabella looked. Yes, Tia was quite the looker. She was already surrounded by a fan club, girls and boys.

Abby made a sound low in her throat. "Like that would happen. I've given him enough bait to lead him on. He's not going anywhere."

"What do you mean?" asked Isabella.

"I've shown interest, spent time with him. He asked me out to a movie for tonight but I declined."

"Why?" asked Shana.

"I want to be pursued. I don't want to be too easy."

Shana looked confused. "Well, don't spurn him too many times or he'll go searching elsewhere."

"Naw. He won't."

"You sound pretty confident."

"Watch and learn." Abby turned, looked at Tray and smiled.

His eyes lit up immediately, he stood and headed over.

"See. Just like that." Abby looked smug and superior.

"I didn't realize how desperate teenage boys can be." Isabella felt a sick churning in the pit of her stomach.

"Hi, Abby." Tray turned to the other two. "Hi, girls."

"Hi, Tray," said Abby and Shana simultaneously.

Isabella leaned over and took a slurp from her straw, stuck into her diet coke. She preferred to avoid conversing with the basketball wannabe.

"Hey. I know you said you couldn't hang out tonight but what about tomorrow night?"

"I'm sorry, but I have something up tomorrow too." Abby's eyes blinked steadily. Her self-control was quite impressive, knowing how much she actually liked the guy.

"Okay." Tray looked somewhat deflated. "Sunday?"

"What do you suggest?"

"Seeing a movie?"

"What time?"

"Afternoon sometime?"

Abby took a deep breath and slowly exhaled. After a long sip from her lemonade, she looked up at him and said, "All right. I suppose that'll work."

The relief on his face was hilarious. Isabella forced a chuckle down and lowered her eyes to her food.

"I'll come pick you up at two."

"Sure."

Tray nodded, turned and walked back to his table and his friends.

Abby waited until he was out of earshot. "That's how it's done, girls."

"Really?" Shana looked dubious. "And you're the expert?"

Abby's eyes exuded a haughty look. "I don't see you dating anyone."

"Maybe I don't want to."

"Not even Mark from Youth group?"

Shana shrugged and turned her attention to her sub, taking a nibble off the end.

"Do you really like Tray?" asked Isabella.

"He's okay. He's a little on the short side but he is cute." Abby finished her sandwich, scrunched up the plastic wrap and said, "How about going shopping at the mall after school?"

Shana's eyes lit up with interest. "Sure."

Isabella had no desire to go anywhere but straight home. Both girls looked at her, waiting. "Uh, no. I don't want to shop."

Abby said, "But, why not? Looks to me like you're in need of it more than we are."

The negative appraisal of her attire was uncalled for. "I like my clothes."

"That makes one of us." Abby lifted a single finger skyward.

Tilting her head, Shana said, "Her clothes aren't that bad."

With a triumphant look, Abby retorted, "That proves my point. Her clothes aren't that bad? You may as well have said she looks awful."

"No," objected Shana. "That's not what I meant." Shana faced Isabella and said, "I didn't mean it that way."

The whole conversation seemed ludicrous. Didn't her friends know by now that she didn't care what they thought of her wardrobe?

Isabella cleared her throat and said, "Look, I'm not going shopping. I need to go home right after school. There's something I need to do."

"What?" asked Abby.

"It's a personal matter." With that, she stood, grabbed her Diet Coke and took her trash to the garbage can.

Abby voiced more questions and reasons why she should join them but Isabella ignored her and headed to her next class just as the buzzer sounded. All three were in different classes for the next period, actually for the rest of the day, and she was glad. She had no desire to answer Abby's questions. The girl's curiosity knew no bounds. There were certain to be more questions and Abby wouldn't let things rest until she knew what personal matters were calling Isabella home.

When the last bell of the day finally rang, Isabella rushed to her locker and headed outside to the bus stop.

When she arrived home, she threw down her backpack just inside the door, undid the ties of her boots, left them on the entrance rug and raced up the stairs. Suspense had been haunting her all day and there was no time to waste.

Getting the pole from the hall closet, she hurried to the attic access. Pulling the ladder down fully to the floor, she thought of her friends' shocked faces at her flat out refusal to shop. It made her grin. What if Shana told Abby about the picture experience? There was no way shopping would keep Abby's attention if she knew some mysterious thing was taking place up in this attic. But Isabella needed some time alone first.

Flying up the ladder, she switched on the light and headed straight to the joists, shimmied over carefully and removed the insulation. Seeing the box lying there, the lid tucked on tightly without a hint of disturbance, caused the frantic beating of her heart to slow. It was safe and sound, just where she'd left it.

The uncertainty and fear that had plagued her today, however, gave her an idea. She couldn't leave everything to chance. She'd have to take control of the pictures. They were far too valuable to gamble with. It was clear her mother was determined to keep them concealed. But her mother didn't know how determined she was in discovering everything she could about these pictures.

If her mother could play games, well, so could she.

Isabella rushed downstairs to gather supplies. With all the shoes being purchased in this household, it wasn't difficult to find some flat, low boxes that would conceal well beneath the insulation upstairs. She also grabbed a stack of paper from the paper recycling bin and took that with her.

Back up in the attic, with the box of pictures hauled to the middle of the plywood floor, Isabella transferred the pictures carefully to the smaller boxes. With all the pictures out, she glanced inside the large box and stared in surprise. At the bottom lay another brown envelope. Funny. She hadn't noticed that before. She lifted it out, opened the flap and glanced inside. It was filled with newspaper clippings. This wasn't the time to search through it though. There was a time crunch to consider.

She stuffed that envelope in one of the small boxes with the first brown envelope. They seemed to belong together. She transferred all the pictures to shoe boxes until four were filled. After padding the big box full of useless recycled paper, she positioned a few pictures on top, ones that she wasn't interested in pursuing, to make the box appear legit. A random brown envelope she'd found in the recycling box was perfect for the top. A few more papers stuck in there would make it look full enough and would be a good replacement.

Isabella sat back and scrutinized it. There were too many newspapers close to the top and she could see the drab newsprint peak through between the pictures. It completely destroyed the illusion she was attempting to generate. She removed all the items from the picture box, found some magazines in the paper stack with bright pictures and realized that a scissor would be a useful in creating the deception.

After a quick trip downstairs, she returned carrying scissors, their blades held firmly in her grasp, just like she'd been taught.

Cutting the magazine into picture-sized pieces would help with the facade. Minutes passed as she cut picture after picture out of the stack of fashion magazines. She felt some shame at her blatant deceit and yet to safeguard these pictures from her mother's misguided need to shield her was paramount at the moment. She told herself it wasn't really a lie. She was simply camouflaging an invaluable trove of information, a heritage that had been concealed from her for too long.

After placing a good stack of drab pieces of newsprint, flyers and random printer paper at the bottom, she placed a few full sheets of brightly-colored magazine pages over top and scattered the picture-sized pieces she'd cut over them. Satisfied with the appearance, she carefully placed the few pictures she'd held back and positioned them on top of the magazine clippings. The look was perfect. Her mother would never suspect just looking in, unless she dug deeper. Placing the brown envelope on top completed the look. She returned the box to its hiding place and covered it carefully until it looked completely untouched.

Isabella released a sigh of relief and felt the weight lift from her chest. The pictures would be safe now and she'd hide them carefully on the other side of the attic, beneath the insulation there, where the light hardly reached.

Her stomach grumbled in hunger as she lifted one rectangular shoe box and carried it to the far side, in the corner, lifted the insulation and placed the box between the joists. She wouldn't have to maneuver over any more joists to get to the precious pictures. They'd now be in easy reach, directly beside the plywood floor, the corner cloaked in darkness. She got the second shoe box and hid it between the next two joists. Soon she had all four boxes tucked beneath the insulation on the far side within easy reach.

Stepping back, she surveyed her handiwork. There was no sign of anything having been moved, just pink insulation doing its quiet job. No bump in the pretty pink fluff revealed something hidden beneath. It was perfect and she felt pleased. Inhaling deeply, she released her breath slowly and then turned to the opening and descended.

Looking up, she decided to leave it open for now. She needed a snack, something to quiet the ferocious growling in her middle and then she'd be back.

In the kitchen, she went straight to the pantry and pulled out a bag of Oreo cookies. After pouring a glass of milk, she went over to the kitchen table. Sitting there by herself didn't feel awkward. Perhaps it should. When Abby or Shana came over, they always commented on how quiet her house was. It freaked them out. Isabella didn't know what they meant. A house full of rowdy kids was far more disturbing. Abby and Shana both had siblings. Abby had two brothers and Shana had a sister and a brother. Where they were comfortable with noise, she was soothed by the sound of stillness.

Lack of noise in the house suited her perfectly. The hum of her computer was okay and she occasionally cranked up the tunes on her iPad and danced in her room where no one could see her. There was never anyone home to observe her actions, especially in her bedroom, which seemed a safer place for such activity.

After finishing her third cookie and placing the bag back in the pantry, the doorbell rang out with a merry jingle.

Isabella smiled as she headed for the door. She'd calculated accurately. That was probably Abby and Shana now. She looked through the side window and saw them standing side by side, expectation plastered over their faces. They'd dropped by for a show.

Isabella unlocked the door and pulled it wide. "Hi."

"Hi, Isabella," cooed Abby in her sweetest, high-pitched voice.

Shana looked sheepish. "I told her."

"I thought you would."

"Really?" Shana looked surprised as she stepped inside. "You didn't even trust me to keep it secret?"

"And it looks like my instincts were right," Isabella said as her friends moved inside so she could close the door.

"I'm sorry. I'm not very good at keeping my mouth shut."

"I don't mind. I kind of like having a friend along for the ride."

Abby looked beside herself with impatience. "So where do you get to the attic and how does this time warp stuff happen?"

"It's best shown, not explained."

"Then show me."

"Follow me." Isabella led the way upstairs and stopped at the ladder.

"This is it?" asked Abby.

"Uh-huh."

"You don't have spiders up there, do you?" Abby looked worried.

Shana said, "They have these really huge ones up there that dangle down from the ceiling and hang in your face. And the webs are insanely big."

"Ugh. Stop it, Shana! They do not." Abby turned to Isabella. "Do you have spiders?"

Isabella chuckled. "No, not that I know of."

"Good." Abby stared at her, waved her on with her hand and said, "Well, go on then. Lead the way."

Isabella started up the ladder, flicked on the switch and stepped up to the plywood floor. When the other two girls had joined her, she turned to them and said, "I had to transfer the pictures to a safer place. My mom was up here last night snooping around. It woke me up and I heard her. It freaked me out. I think she was suspecting something. I was terrified she had taken the pictures or moved them."

"So what did you do?" asked Shana, her eyes big.

"I repacked them into smaller boxes and hid them over there." Isabella pointed out the spot.

Shana nodded. "Good thinking."

Abby looked confused. "Your mother was up here snooping? Isn't this her house? Isn't she allowed to snoop if she wants to?"

"She doesn't want me to see any pictures of my father. I think she came up here to make sure I hadn't found the box. She hid it over there." Isabella pointed to the bump in the insulation close to the light. "She probably wanted to make sure I hadn't found it."

Abby shook her head. "I don't get you two. Why is your mother so determined to keep information from you? I thought you were close."

"We are."

"And?"

"I don't know." Isabella felt stupid for not knowing. "She has this hatred for my dad. She can't stand him and doesn't want me learning anything about him."

"But you're time-traveling back into the pictures, right?" asked Abby.

Isabella nodded.

"So you are learning about him, right?"

She nodded again.

"But your mother has no idea?"

"No."

"She would kill you if she found out, right?"

Shana rolled her eyes. "Enough with the questions already, Abby."

Isabella ignored Shana and said "She wouldn't kill me. She'd be extremely upset, yes. And she'd confiscate the pictures."

"She must really hate him."

Isabella nodded.

"Ooh, this sounds like fun." Abby turned toward the corner. "So they're over there where it's dark?"

"Yes."

"You'll go get them, right?"

"Abby!" Shana looked frazzled. "Stop with all your questions."

"That's the only way I'll find out what's going on."

Isabella turned away from them and headed to the corner, retrieving one box with all the loose pictures. She wasn't ready for her friends to delve into her father's past. That was too personal and too disconcerting, even for her.

Placing the box on the floor, she sat down and her friends joined her, surrounding the box. Isabella lifted the lid, took a handful of pictures and studied them one by one. She picked a few that looked somewhat safe. Once she'd decided, she looked up and said, "We'll start with these."

"How many are we going back to?" asked Shana, looking worried.

Abby said, "I want to do a whole bunch. This is so exciting."

"I picked three. If they go real quickly, then we can come back later and choose more."

"What do mean, if they go real quickly?" asked Abby.

"Some of the pictures don't have much story behind them and there's not much to see. Others are more involved and continue on for a while. So we'll see how these pictures go and decide what we'll do when we're done."

Shana stared at her. "You don't mind us seeing your past? Your father, mother and what happened between them?"

"If I don't like what's happening, I'll just send us back."

"Wait, wait. What do you mean by 'send us back'? How do you do that?" Abby was beginning to look worried.

"You'll find out," assured Shana.

"That's not very reassuring."

Isabella said, "It's best experienced. It's kind of tough to explain."

Inhaling deeply, Abby said, "Okay, I guess I have to trust you on this one."

"You two have to hold onto me. Just touch my arm while I study the picture. As long as you don't let go, we'll all end up at the same place together."

Abby's eyes started to get round but she scooted over close to Isabella's side. Shana moved in on her other side.

With their hands resting on her arms, one on either side, Isabella looked at the picture and focused. It didn't take long for the room to shift and move.

CHAPTER 13

A kaleidoscope of color swirled around them and, with Abby groaning and whimpering in fear beside her, the room slowed, reversed and the colors speedily disengaged and separated until distinguishing objects began to appear.

When everything settled, Isabella didn't recognize the place. She'd never been there before. Sally was young, in her teens, sitting on a bed with a glass of ice and some clear liquid in her hand. A bottle of vodka sat on the nightstand. Another teen, a girl, stood beside the three visitors with a Polaroid camera. The developed picture slid out and the girl gently took it in her hand. Isabella judged that Sally was about her own age. It was appalling to see her mother drinking alcohol. It was something she adamantly forbade Isabella to do.

"Look at your mom," said Shana in surprise. "She's drinking."

"That is quite shocking," agreed Abby.

"Yeah, I suppose she wasn't much of a saint at my age," Isabella said.

All three focused on Sally as she spoke.

"Why'd you take a picture?" asked Sally.

"We have to document this momentous occasion."

"It doesn't feel very momentous to me. I'm in a heap of trouble."

"Not yet." The other girl flopped onto the bed on the other side, set the camera down and picked up her glass of spirits. After a long sip, she set it down, turned to Sally and said, "It's not every day a girl gets pregnant."

Sally fell back on the pillows with a grunt. "My mother will kill me."

"You don't have to tell her. Just go get an abortion and it'll be over quickly and no one wiser for it."

"I don't know."

"What's not to know? I've done it."

Sally turned and stared at her friend.

"What?" protested Sally's friend.

"How do you live with it?"

"With what? Not having to raise a baby?"

"Amber!"

Isabella put two and two together. This was Sally's good friend growing up, Amber Woods, the one who'd had two abortions and struggled with depression almost continually. That is, she did until she finally turned her life to God and received some counseling and appropriate medication for her melancholy state.

Isabella concluded they must have caught the two after Amber's first abortion, during Sally's pregnancy with Tessa and before Amber's second. The knowledge was heavy and the air in the room thick with possible scenarios.

"Okay," said Amber. "Yes, I feel a bit guilty sometimes but I can't raise a baby. "I'm only fifteen, for crying out loud. What would I do with a baby? My parents would refuse to raise it and I certainly don't want to be a mother yet."

"What if you get pregnant again?"

Amber scrunched up her nose.

"It's a real possibility, especially the way we party," said Sally.

"I'll be more careful next time."

Sally chuckled.

"What?"

"Not if you're drunk and stoned out of your mind."

Amber shrugged. "I'll just get another abortion."

Sally sat up and stared incredulously. "Just like that?"

"Why not?"

"It's killing a human being, that's why not!"

"It's not really a human being. It's just a little embryo, a few cells stuck together. Better to do away with it before it turns into anything."

Sally looked away and shook her head.

"What's wrong with you?" asked Amber. "It's no big deal."

"I don't think I could do it."

Isabella felt tremendous respect for her mother at this moment. So, she'd made some horrible choices and ended up with an unwanted pregnancy. The worst thing she could do, in her mind, was add to it by killing the baby. And, she'd never have a sister if Sally'd gone through with Amber's suggestion.

"I'll help you get the money. It won't be a problem. The guy who knocked you up will help pay."

Sally looked sheepish. "I don't even know who he was."

Amber laughed at that. "We were both so stoned that night; it could have been any one of the guys."

Sally didn't laugh.

Abby and Shana both made stunned, choking sounds beside her. Isabella looked over at them. Their faces were mesmerized and completely engrossed in what had just been revealed. Growing up in Christian homes hadn't prepared them for such blatant recklessness. She couldn't blame them. Sally had protected her from a lifestyle like that, instilling a standard of morality and right living in her.

To see Sally in this light, in her former lifestyle, was outrageous even to her, even though she knew much of what took place back then. She'd have to ensure her friends kept this information to themselves. Sally would be furious if she knew Isabella was sharing this information with them.

"What if I keep the baby?"

Amber stared at Sally with a wide-open mouth. She finally got her wits about her, closed her mouth and said, "You're not serious?"

Sally looked worried. "I think I am."

"Why would you? Your mother will go ballistic. She won't let you."

"But, what if she did? Wouldn't that be better than killing it? Give it a chance at life?"

Guilt paraded across Amber's face and a scowl creased her forehead. "That's stupid, Sally. No teenager keeps her baby."

A look of determination filled Sally's eyes. "I'm going to try." She turned to pick up her glass of vodka and took a sip.

"You shouldn't be drinking that stuff if you're planning to keep the baby."

Sally looked at the clear liquid longingly, set it back on the nightstand and nodded. "You're right. I shouldn't."

"You're seriously going to go through with this?"

Sally nodded, resolve filling her eyes.

"Let me know how you make out with your mother. I wish you luck."

"It'll be a tough sell."

Amber made a mocking sound deep in her throat. "If she's as religious as you've made her out to be, there's no way she'll let you raise that baby. It would ruin her reputation."

The worried expression on Sally's face deepened a few degrees. "What do you think she'll say?"

Amber shrugged. "She might just suggest an abortion." She grinned at that.

"I don't think so. She doesn't believe in murder."

An angry, sullen look passed through Amber's eyes. "I didn't murder anyone."

"I'm sorry. I didn't mean it that way but my mother would see it that way."

"Any religious nut would."

Sally let the comment slide.

It took control for Isabella not to say something. She didn't like anyone slandering her grandmother. To say she was a religious nut was completely insulting. Her grandmother was an amazing woman and admitted to praying for Isabella faithfully. She absolutely adored her grandmother. To hear her trashed like this was hurtful.

Isabella turned to Abby and Shana and said, "It's time to move on. Hold on to me and I'll switch pictures."

They both stepped toward her and grabbed her arm. Isabella slipped the top photo down beneath the others and studied the picture on top.

The room immediately came unglued, the colors and forms elongating and swirling together at a terrific speed. Pinks, purples, yellows, shades of white and the brown shag rug beneath their feet all converged into a conglomeration of color and shapes. The swirling, diffused effect was psychedelic and the motley vision produced a hallucinogenic feel.

Just as suddenly as things disintegrated, colors rapidly connected and found each other again until solid objects began to reappear. The floor stilled and the ceiling above sucked in tightly. Light that had been dispersed throughout the color montage now converged on two points, two lamps that sat on end tables at either end of a couch. Two women were seated on the couch, facing each other. Neither one looked particularly happy.

The grip on Isabella's arm was excruciating and she let out a yelp. "That hurts."

Abby turned an ashen face toward her and whimpered. "I'm sorry. I was just so terrified." She released her steel grip and rubbed Isabella's arm in conciliation.

Shana also let go and looked to see if she'd caused any damage. "I behaved myself."

All three turned as they heard a man's voice beside them. He smelled of alcohol, his eyes looked red and his face was flushed a deep crimson. He lowered the camera and went to sit down in the chair beside the couch. A small smile curled the edges of his lips.

Isabella knew immediately who the man was. This was her grandfather, Vern Windsor, in the days when booze was a god to him and when his parenting was less than ideal. At least that's what she remembered Sally telling her. Sally had forgiven him for his indiscretions and now they enjoyed an amiable relationship. All she knew of the man was that he was the only stable male relative she had and she loved him dearly. The acceptance and love she felt from him was a solace to her lonely life.

To see him this way was disturbing. Knowing a historical fact about someone you love is entirely different than seeing them right in the grips of that fact.

Isabella stared at him. He looked so much younger and yet he also looked worn out. It was a strange combination of youthfulness and destruction. Grandmother and Sally were talking but Isabella struggled to hear them, so engrossed was she in the altered Vern.

"I can see why your mother got into the party scene," said Abby beside her.

When Isabella glanced at her, it was clear Abby's focus was also on Vern. She didn't respond.

"I never knew your grandfather was an alcoholic," said Shana, looking equally as surprised.

This picture travel didn't seem the best idea at the moment but what could she do now? Turn the picture over and end it? Maybe she should. The photos had looked so innocent. How could she have known they'd reveal so much? But she was as curious as her friends. She couldn't leave now.

"But I want to keep it," Sally said.

Melody looked at Vern with an angry scowl and asked, "Did you take a picture of us?"

"Yup."

"I want it destroyed."

"Why?" he asked, a little woozily. "It's a memory of our first grandchild."

"Stop it, Vern. If you can't behave yourself and contribute to this conversation in a realistic manner, then leave."

He shook his head. "It's just getting interesting."

With contempt beyond anything Isabella had ever seen her display, Sally glared at her father. Her disdain felt tangible and Isabella couldn't help but cringe inwardly. Her heart went out to her grandfather.

Melody ignored her husband and turned back to Sally. "You can't keep it."

"I am going to keep it."

"Let her keep it," said Vern.

"Not in this house, she's not," Melody declared.

"You'll kick me out?" asked Sally.

Melody looked unsure but then she said, "You can give the baby up for adoption."

"Or get an abortion," Sally said icily. Hatred for her mother oozed from every pore.

Melody stopped and considered. Slowly she said, "No, that wouldn't be right."

"Your conscience would bother you too much but it doesn't bother you to force me to give it up?"

"It's the only option."

"It is not the only option," Sally spat out loudly, emphasizing each word. "I want to keep my baby."

"It's illegitimate. I can just hear what the church ladies will say when they find out."

Vern chuckled. "Ah, so that's what this is all about. The church. And your reputation." His crooked grin and stained teeth looked amusing. "I think she should keep the baby."

Isabella inwardly applauded him and yet she already knew the outcome.

Melody looked flustered. "Be quiet. You're not helping."

With fragile hope, Sally turned to him. "Dad, please help me keep my baby."

He stood shakily and stepped toward the door. Once there, he turned to her and said, "This is up to your mother. I don't want to get involved. And besides, I'm in no shape to make a decision."

With that Sally spat out angrily, "The only thing you want to get involved in is your liquor."

"That's no way to speak to your father," declared Melody.

Vern ignored the chatter and left the room, probably to find another drink.

"He doesn't deserve any better than that." Sally looked suddenly sullen and miserable.

After a deep sigh, Melody said, "You'll carry this baby to term. I'll take care of the adoption matter."

"No. I won't let you. I'm keeping it. The baby belongs to me."

A young teenage boy stepped into the room, stopped, stared at Sally and asked, "Is it true? Are you pregnant?"

Isabella recognized him immediately. This was Sally's younger brother, Robert. Isabella stared at the younger version of her Uncle Robert.

Sally looked at him and nodded.

"Cool."

Melody shook her head. "It is not cool. It is immoral and appalling."

Robert shrugged, turned and left the room.

"I don't know how I'm going to explain your condition to my church friends, to the pastor and the congregation. You've put me in quite the pickle. You need to understand what you've done, Sally."

"This isn't all about you. It's my body and this is my baby."

"But your actions reflect on me. Have you ever thought of that?"

"I make you look bad? Is that what you're trying to say?" Hurt emanated from Sally's eyes.

Melody remained quiet.

"What about Dad? How do you explain him to the church? He must be a real problem for you."

Melody's eyes took on a cornered look.

"Why don't you just do away with him too? It would make your life so much simpler and less embarrassing. You sure are quick in wanting to get rid of my baby. Is that your answer for everything difficult?"

"That's enough. You've said more than enough." Melody stood, signifying the conversation was over.

"I'm not nearly done!" Sally shouted.

Melody stepped over and slapped Sally hard, leaving a red mark on her cheek. "Yes, you are." Then she turned on her heel and walked out.

Sally's hand went to her cheek and her eyes filled with tears. She blinked and tears trailed down her cheeks unhindered. "I hate her." Sobs began to wrack her body. "I hate him." After a few minutes she sucked back her raw emotions, wiped her face, stood and stomped out of the room.

The anger in Sally was hard to watch. Never had Isabella imagined her mother going through so much emotional agony. She'd heard stories of her past but seeing it was difficult.

Sound beside her brought her around. Both girls were staring at her.

"What?"

"That was ballistic," said Abby. Her eyes were wet and a tear trickled down one cheek.

"It was horrible," said Shana. "I never knew your mother went through so much." She looked visibly shaken.

Isabella shrugged. Sally went through far more than that. If they could see it all they'd be a weeping, bawling mess.

"She didn't keep the baby, did she?" asked Abby, her voice shaky.

"No. The baby she's carrying is Tessa."

Both girls nodded in understanding.

"She only met her later in life, right?" asked Shana.

Isabella nodded. She looked down at the three photos in her hand. There was no way she had the emotional stamina to visit the third one. Feeling completely drained, she looked at her friends. "I want to go back to the attic."

Both Shana and Abby nodded in agreement, compassion in their eyes. They stepped forward and touched her arm. Isabella took the top picture and flipped it face down.

CHAPTER 14

It was hard for Isabella to focus at Youth Group. Her friends were here with her; they'd seen the same things just this afternoon. They were talking and laughing with others, like nothing out of the ordinary had transpired, but Isabella held back. What she had witnessed had hit her hard; it was much more personal for her.

She'd never look at her mother the same way. She'd always known it but to see what she went through had changed something. Maybe she felt more compassion for her; she wasn't sure what it was. Her grandmother had carried out her threats about forcing Sally to give up the baby. Now Isabella wondered how Sally had fared through that. How devastating had it been for her? Is that why she struggled so with relationships?

From what she'd witnessed, Sally's relationship with her father was tenuous at that age. And her mother was hardly supportive. How horrible it must have been for Sally. To a degree, Isabella could understand her grandmother's view. Sally would be beside herself if Isabella lived as wild as Sally had. She would never allow it. Or would she? Maybe her tough expectations were only a coverup for the fear of it actually happening.

Isabella poured some Diet Pepsi into a red plastic cup at the snack table. She went to the wall and leaned back to watch the group. Her mind was anywhere but there. They were getting ready to play a wide game. She wasn't in the mood.

The Youth leader was waving at her to join them. With a shake of her head, she opted out. She needed time to process but hadn't had the chance.

Sally had come home early last night, shortly after six. Shana and Abby had left just before she came. Stress was obviously getting to Sally again. She looked frazzled after a week of work and told Isabella she had agreed to some date. Sally never went out on dates. Apparently, some guy from church had called and strong-armed Sally into saying yes; at least that was Sally's version of it. No one strong-armed Sally. Isabella wondered what had pushed her into agreeing. Now she wondered how the evening was going and who it was Sally had gone out with.

It worried her. To have a man coming around, showing interest in Sally was upsetting. Isabella liked her life, the peace and quiet she and her mom enjoyed. She didn't want anyone else around. Sally was rarely available as it was, never mind getting caught up in dating. Annoyance rattled her and the photo travel only added to her emotional distress.

Abby shouted from across the room, "Come join in, Isabella."

She shook her head, pushed off from the wall and headed to the doors. Once outside, the cool evening air made her shiver. Tucking her jacket more tightly around her, she zipped it up tightly. Maybe a walk around the block would ease her anxiety.

She'd nearly reached the end of the block when footsteps behind her caught her attention. Turning, she saw Shana racing toward her.

"Hey, where are you going?"

"I really need some time to think."

"Do you mind if I join you? You shouldn't be wandering these downtown streets alone at night."

"Shana, my bodyguard. I feel so much safer already."

Shana grinned. "Two is better than one."

They walked in silence for a while, the only sound being their shoes scuffing the sidewalk.

Breaking the silence, Isabella asked, "So what did you think of this afternoon's photo travel?"

"It makes me want to cry."

She looked at Shana and noted that she was being serious.

"I never knew your mother went through that. I knew Tessa Fields was her daughter but I didn't know the circumstances. It must have been so awful for Sally."

All her friends called her mother Sally. It was Isabella's fault really. She called her Sally more than she ever referred to her as Mom.

Shana continued, "She lived a life I can't imagine, what with having a drunk for a dad."

"He's a wonderful man now. I love my grandfather dearly."

"Anyone can change, I suppose."

"And my grandmother is the sweetest thing. I love her so much too. I honestly can't imagine them the way they were. It was completely foreign to me to see them act like that. I just can't get over it."

"I guess they were facing a lot of pressure."

They walked on silently. The night air was crisp but it felt good to breathe fresh air and move her limbs. Although she enjoyed Youth group, her mind and heart weren't in it today.

"Thank you, Isabella."

She turned to Shana. "For what?"

"For letting us join you today. It must have been hard for you to open up and let us see your mother's past."

With a grunt deep in her throat, Isabella said, "I thought I'd picked safe pictures, ones that wouldn't reveal too much. I thought wrong."

"Oh." Shana tucked her hands into her jacket pocket to warm them. "Maybe you won't want us to join you anymore."

Isabella shrugged. "I don't know. Some things seem sacred."

"Especially where your dad is concerned, right?"

Isabella nodded. "I have to discover that on my own." They were quiet for a few minutes. "Sometimes I feel so frightened with what I'll learn. Maybe it's safer just sticking to the pictures of Sally. I can prolong finding out about my father that way."

Shana glanced over with a concerned look. "Sally has really spooked you about him."

"Yeah, she has." Isabella stopped at the crossing and waited for the walk signal. "I wish she hadn't told me anything about him. Now that I know she's terrified of me finding out about him, it makes me curious but it's also completely unnerving. I want to get to know him and yet I don't. It feels like a tug of war."

Shana nodded.

The walk signal blinked on and they headed across the street.

"Do you ever wonder where your father is right now?"

"All the time."

"Have you wondered why he's never tried to contact you?"

"Yes."

"Do you think he's tried but Sally refuses him access?"

"I've often suspected as much."

"Doesn't that make you resentful?"

"No, not really. I really think she's trying to protect me."

"That would scare me."

Isabella looked at her friend. "Why?"

"Just the idea that you need protection from your father is scary. What kind of man is he anyway?"

"That's what I mean to find out, whether Sally likes it or not."

"If you ever need company, you can count on me."

"Thanks. I'll let you know."

Half a block more and they'd be back at the church. It was downtown in a warehouse-type building, focused on ministering to street people, those caught in addictions. They had chosen an ideal location for drawing in the desired crowd. If Sally knew Isabella was walking around at night on that street, she'd flip. It felt safe though. The church had been extremely successful in cleaning up the area, bringing many into its fold and transforming them. Drug dealers started keeping their business to other parts of the city and hookers no longer gathered on street corners. Within a five block radius, this area was actually quite safe. The pastor often said that their prayers provided a covering for miles around the area and scared every demon and undesirable away. To Isabella it felt like a safe place to be.

CHAPTER 15

Sally felt tired and yet with Grayson Kendal sitting across from her, staring at her like she was the best thing since sliced bread, she couldn't help but enjoy the attention. She'd had so little time to date or feel the special interest of a man. Not that she intended to take this anywhere at all, but the respite from her constant, frenetic pace of work was nice. She found herself actually enjoying his company, especially having a spectacular dinner at one of the finest restaurants in the city.

It was clear that Grayson was trying to impress her. He'd dressed smartly in a nice pair of black pants (they weren't designer but they did look good on him). His shirt was a rich green, probably bought at a department store but it fit him well, and with his bright, striped tie he looked quite sharp. His recent haircut suited him and his clean-shaven face looked more attractive than Sally wanted to admit.

The whole evening made her feel special. Something long dead began to stir deep inside her. She chided herself for feeling like a school girl. After years of resisting any type of advances from the opposite sex, she deserved some indulgence. Monday's work day would come soon enough and besides, she planned to go to the office for a few hours tomorrow as well. This evening would be soon forgotten amidst the hectic schedule she kept. She may as well enjoy his attention and infatuation for tonight.

Over cups of steaming coffee and the restaurant's signature ice cream pie, the evening was turning out to be sublime. Sally hadn't felt this relaxed in a long, long time. After downing half of the huge slab of ice cream, she set her fork down and looked at Grayson. He'd pursued her for years, persistently sought her out on Sundays after church in the foyer. However, she'd always treated him with reserve. She felt guilty now as she watched him devour his dessert. He'd never been anything but gentle and kind, never pushy or demanding. As she'd continually resisted entering a relationship, he'd bided his time. If nothing else, he was as patient as a saint.

That thought made Sally smile.

Grayson looked up at that moment and stared at her. "What's so funny? Do I have ice cream smeared across my face?"

Sally chuckled. "No."

He was already wiping his face carefully with a napkin. Placing it down beside his plate, he looked at her and asked, "What is it then?"

She shook her head, feeling embarrassed to admit her thoughts. What did she have to lose? She wasn't really interested in prolonging this relationship anyway. "I was thinking of how patient you've been."

He studied her eyes, her lips and her entire face. His intense gaze unnerved her and that was saying something. It was virtually impossible for anyone to rattle her like this any more.

His words came husky and deep. "Anything of value is worth waiting for."

She stared at him. Had he just said that? He viewed her as something of value? Then he didn't really know her very well at all.

"What?" he asked.

"You know very little about me."

"I know you've raised a wonderful daughter all on your own. You have a flourishing company. You own your own home and you're a fine Christian woman. You attend church with your daughter regularly. I could also go on about your daughter, Tessa, and her husband, Cody. That's a whole list of positives in my book."

Alarmed that she was feeling even more disarmed, Sally fidgeted with her napkin on her lap. "I can't take credit for Tessa. I didn't raise her."

"But she has your genes. I can tell."

Sally wanted to brush that away but she liked the idea of taking some credit for the wonderful woman Tessa turned out to be.

"And I've watched you with your grandkids at church. You love those three ankle biters. I give you a lot of credit for holding your life together and managing so amazingly. You have a lot on your plate."

She didn't realize anyone noticed. It made her appreciate him even more. "Thank you." Then she remembered. "You raised your son on your own too, didn't you?"

He nodded. "My wife left me when Charlie was young. It was devastating for him at the time but he turned out well. I'm very proud of my boy."

It was clear that he was. He had a lot to be proud of. Charlie's work at the Manor of Peace helped many broken, addicted men find their way to freedom.

"Was she part of Charlie's life?"

He shook his head and sorrow entered his eyes. "No. She left and never looked back. She never called and didn't bother to connect with Charlie. I haven't seen her since she walked out the front door. I assume she moved to another city and started over. The divorce papers came through the mail and I didn't contest it. I signed them and mailed them back. That was that."

"I'm sorry."

"Don't be. It happened a long time ago and I've gotten over it."

Sally pondered that. She didn't believe him for a second, not with the pain oozing from his eyes. "Why didn't you ever remarry, find another wife and a mother for Charlie?"

He shrugged. "I never found the right one." After a sip from his coffee, he set it back down and looked at her. "Charlie was terribly angry after she left. All my energy was focused on him during those years. I have to admit that I didn't do a very good job at first. I was too angry myself. The two of us just fumbled along trying to survive."

Her heart went out to him. She could relate to his pain. Her past was like a soap opera. If he knew all she'd been through, he might not be quite so eager to get to know her.

"When Charlie was raised, on his own and finally married, it seemed somewhat pointless to remarry. I was used to my single life and liked it. My house was my haven. I guess I didn't want to disrupt my peaceful existence."

Sally couldn't stop the automatic smile. She was amused that she shared his opinions and feelings concerning her own life. She found it comforting that someone understood her. "I totally understand. So what made you change your mind?"

"Did I say I've changed my mind?"

"No."

He smiled at her but remained quiet.

Perhaps she'd assumed too much by this one date. But then, he'd been pursuing her for years. How did that information play into his life? She could feel her forehead scrunching in confusion and her eyes questioning him.

It made him laugh. "Okay. Meeting you changed my mind."

"You have very bad taste."

"I don't think so."

She just stared at him.

Leaning his elbows on the table and crossing his arms, he said, "You're beautiful, intense and completely interesting."

His confidence forced Sally to break eye contact. This was far too intimate and made her uncomfortable.

"Did I say too much?"

She tentatively glanced back up at him. "Maybe."

"How come you're such a tough business woman but avoid relationship at all costs? Why does it frighten you so?"

Defensiveness paraded in and anger right behind it. How dare he question her on her life and decisions? She wasn't afraid of anything. Just letting her guard down long enough to go on one date was exhibiting a great deal of courage. That made her stop and think.

Is that really how I see myself? That I need courage to face a date?

She stared at him while examining her heart.

"I think I've offended you but, truthfully, living in fear is no way to live, Sally."

"I'm not afraid," she stated. But why did she feel so terrified, then?

He reached across the table and offered his open hand. Sally just stared at it.

"Why don't we try to get to know each other? See each other on a regular basis and find out if we're compatible."

She trembled inside, feeling breathless. Why couldn't she hate him? Why had he dressed so nicely and treated her so well tonight?

It frustrated her. She was feeling that long forgotten stirring deep in her middle and it disturbed her tremendously. She had no desire to traverse these waters again. She'd failed every time before. It was terrifying thinking of attempting again.

"Sally?" He was gazing at her in concern.

"I don't know," she said with a squeaky voice. After clearing her throat, she gave him a weak smile.

"I promise not to be too scary."

That made her chuckle nervously.

"We can go real slow if you'd like."

"I don't have any spare time." Even as she said it, she knew it sounded like an excuse.

"You made time tonight. One night a week isn't a huge commitment."

One night a week. Could she manage that? Did she want to? She felt confused and her head was starting to spin.

"Next Friday night we'll go see a movie, eat popcorn and act like teenagers. We'll wear jeans, t-shirts and baggy hoodies."

She looked at him in wonder. Didn't he realize she didn't even own a hoodie? "I just have my designer coats."

"That'll do just fine."

Had she just agreed to his date suggestion? She should feel appalled. But his relaxed and open demeanor completely disarmed her. That she felt comfortable in his presence was becoming clear. He wasn't pushy and yet his easy bantering drew things out of her that no one else had managed to do in years.

"Or," he was going on, "you could borrow one from Isabella. I'm sure she has one to spare."

"Probably."

"Then it's set. I'll pick you up Friday night after Isabella goes to Youth."

"I drive her there."

"Well, why don't I pick the both of you up and we can drop her off together?"

What a sweet suggestion. That's when Sally noticed Grayson's hand still resting on the table waiting for hers. Shyly, she lifted her hand from her lap and placed it over his. "All right, Grayson. You talked me into it."

"I knew you'd say yes."

"Oh, you did, did you?"
He just nodded and grinned.

CHAPTER 16

Sally was at work. The house was Isabella's and, with an agenda, she was up early — if 9:00 could be considered early. After a breakfast of a toasted blueberry bagel and a large glass of milk, she cleaned up the kitchen and headed upstairs.

Standing under the attic hatch, memories of yesterday's travels sent chills up and down her spine. She'd grown to understand her mother better, which was surprising. Just the pain of giving up a baby would have sent many young girls into a pattern of bitterness and anger. But Sally had been through so much more than just that. Isabella didn't know everything but she did know there had been two divorces along the way and a number of bad relationships.

Maybe that's why having a boyfriend seemed so repugnant. Sally warned her of the pain of rejection, advising her to wait until she was mature enough to recognize the good from the objectionable. Clearly, Sally's fear had rubbed off on her. Waiting for the right man, if there ever was one, seemed prudent. Watching Abby rushing to date a guy at the tender age of fifteen struck her as reckless and dangerous.

After getting the pole from the closet she pulled the hatch down, straightened out the ladder and ascended to the attic. Switching on the single bulb, the light's limited rays barely reached the edge of the far corner. Isabella walked into the dark place and pulled out first one box, then another. Soon she had all four sitting side by side on the plywood floor. She hadn't quite decided where to venture today. She pulled the boxes over the plywood to where the light was brighter and sat on the floor. Here she'd be able to hear if her mother happened to come home early. Although, Sally devoting only half a day to work was highly unlikely.

Isabella opened the box of random pictures and lifted out the ones she'd already visited. Taking a handful of photos, she flipped through them quickly to see if any interested her. There were many of a younger Sally and her brother, Robert. She placed those aside. They wouldn't reveal much except sibling rivalry. Digging deeper she drew out more from the bottom.

One instantly caught her eye. Sally was standing beside a young man in a close embrace, smiling for the camera. The backdrop was kitchen cupboards, odd for a picture. Isabella was interested enough to place it to the side for viewing. Most of the other photos seemed pointless to visit until another caught her eye. It was a wedding picture but she didn't recognize the man. The woman was definitely Sally. The worried look on her face made Isabella wonder. She placed that photo with the other. It would be worth taking a peek.

She skimmed through the rest quickly. There were quite a few pictures of fashion design shows with the company Sally used to work for in Toronto. Many of the pictures depicted Sally standing before models who were wearing designs she'd created. The company name, "Taylor Fashion Design," stood in bold print behind the models. There were too many pictures to count and they didn't interest Isabella at all.

Isabella thought she saw movement in the corner of the attic among the shadows. She glanced over quickly and stared. It was too dark to tell. So how had she imagined something moving there? With a shake of her head she pushed the disturbing thought aside and chalked it up to nerves. After yesterday's experience, she was just edgy.

One photo jumped out at her and she stared at it. Sally and Walter sat side by side and it appeared that they were in a restaurant. Their cheeks were touching as though they were thoroughly in love. Their bright smiles and happy eyes pulled hard at her insides. Oh, how she'd longed for this, a mother and father who were in love.

As soon as the thought came, she pushed it down with a vengeance. It was a childish, hopeless wish! It was time to get over it and get on with life. To know a little about her father was all she could really anticipate. In fact, even to think this whole picture travel would end well was being too optimistic. But she was going to learn the truth even if it killed her. And she was pretty certain her desperate illusions of a good dad would evaporate like thinning clouds.

Three photos. That was enough for one morning. She was sure that was all she'd be able to stomach anyway.

Gathering up the three in the order she believed they belonged in, she held them tightly in her perspiring hands and studied the top one. The room slowly unhinged and buckled violently as it did each time.

The living kaleidoscope then slowed, stilled and inverted, rushing backwards until solid shapes began to appear. When the picture gradually developed before Isabella's eyes, she found herself standing in a small kitchen where she saw Sally embracing a young man. Something in his eyes seemed off.

Isabella looked to her left and noticed her grandmother beside her, a much younger version of herself. Melody Windsor snapped the picture and stepped toward Sally, holding out the camera.

"Here you go. I hope you're happy."

Sally took her arm from around the man, reached forward and took the camera. "Thanks."

Melody swiveled to the small table behind her and grabbed her coat, hanging over a chair. "I should go."

Sally nodded. Isabella thought Sally agreed with Melody too quickly and wondered again about their relationship back then. The man turned away and headed to the next room.

Melody shouted after him, "Good bye, Felix."

"Yeah," came the muffled reply. "See you around."

Melody's face looked tight and stiff as she faced Sally. She kept her voice low. "I don't like that young man. There's something not right about him. You should send him packing."

With a sneer of derision, Sally said, "Why should I be surprised? You've never liked anything about my life."

"Keeping him around isn't helping you. You know better than this. I've taught you better."

"Well, maybe I should marry him," Sally said, a goading look in her eyes.

"Please, Sally, don't ever do that. Not that I agree with how you're living now. Living common law is wrong. But, for heaven's sake, don't marry the loser."

Felix sauntered back into the room. He grinned crookedly. "Are you still here? You just can't get enough of my company, can you?"

Melody grimaced but didn't answer.

He opened the refrigerator, grabbed a beer and left in the direction he came.

After he was out of earshot, Melody hissed, "I don't like him."

Sally rolled her pretty eyes and sighed in frustration. She really was quite a looker in her early twenties, the age Isabella guessed she was at the moment.

Melody said, "All right, I'll go, but I'll be praying for you."

"Sure, whatever." Sally reached over, opened the door and waited for her mother to step out. "Bye, Mom."

Melody's pained eyes turned back to look at her.

"What now?" Sally said angrily.

"Nothing. Goodbye, Sally."

"Bye." Sally slammed the door shut and leaned back against it in relief.

The display shocked Isabella. She knew Melody and Sally weren't chums back in the day but the open hostility was unexpected. Is this what the forced adoption had reduced their relationship to? How long did the resentment last? Did Sally ever forgive her mother? She must have. They could visit for hours now and not exchange a harsh word. But when did the anger give way to civility? When Sally met Tessa? Was that when Sally finally forgave her mother?

Thinking it over gave her pause. Sally was thirty-nine when she met Tessa. She often spoke of it as the moment her life began, the year of healing. It was astounding to imagine living with such anger and bitterness for such a long time. Isabella could feel her heart going out to her again, softening at the torture displayed on Sally's face. She was utterly miserable but didn't know it.

Isabella watched as Sally pulled something out of a kitchen drawer, pulled up her shirt sleeve, tightened a rubber wrap around her upper arm and prepared a syringe and needle. Isabella was shocked to see her mother this way. She'd heard stories, vague and unclear but her mother had mentioned she'd struggled with drug addictions. Seeing it played out before her eyes was a lot to take in. With the needle and syringe in her one hand, she inserted it into her arm and dispensed the substance into her body. Was it cocaine? She wasn't sure. Isabella knew virtually nothing about drugs.

Once the drug had made its way into her system, Sally relaxed almost immediately; her shoulders lowered and her facial features eased. She took the band off her arm and placed everything back in the drawer.

Felix entered the room again, went to the fridge for another beer, opened it and took a long swig. He stood and stared at her for a while. "You want to go to a party?"

After rubbing her neck lazily, Sally looked at him and said, "Sure."

"Go change and we'll take off."

"You need to change too. You can't wear that dirty t-shirt."

"I can wear whatever I want, sweetheart. Now go change before I hit you."

Sally sobered for a moment as she glared menacingly at him. But there was also fear in her eyes.

"Go on. Don't keep me waiting." Felix fixed her with a threatening gaze.

She dragged her eyes from him and left the room.

Being in the same room as Felix made Isabella's skin crawl. The reality that he was ignorant of her presence didn't help. She didn't like the guy. Her grandmother's repugnance of the man was completely understandable. He was vile, crass, cruel and had no manners at all. What had Sally ever seen in him? Isabella had no desire to stay in the general vicinity of the man so she followed Sally to her room.

Through the living room and down a short hallway, she found the bedroom. Sally was slipping into a short mini-dress. It was cute on her and showed off her long, shapely legs. But it was something Isabella would never dare wear.

The drugs Sally had just taken did nothing to hide the despair in her eyes.

"I don't know why I put up with the jerk," she said softly. "He's worthless." She zipped up the dress and sat on the bed to pull on long, black boots. "He keeps my bed warm. That's his only redeeming feature." She stood before her dresser mirror and put some bright lipstick on her lips. "Well, at least I'm not lonely."

By the look on Sally's face, it was hard to believe her last statement. Isabella stared at her mother, totally mesmerized by the difference. She was startled at how her loving, responsible mother could ever have been in this state.

As Sally studied her image in the mirror, she said quietly, "Who am I kidding? I'd be happier without him."

"You're right. You would be," Isabella said. Too bad her mother couldn't hear her.

Sally left the room and headed for the kitchen. Isabella followed. Felix whistled when he saw her.

"That's my girl."

Sally ignored him and walked to the door. "Let's get out of here."

"I'm not finished my beer," Felix yelled.

With a frustrated sigh and one hand on the doorknob, Sally waited.

He gulped down the rest, threw the can into the sink and walked toward the door. Sally opened it and just like that, the two were gone.

Isabella waited a moment and then slipped the top picture to the bottom, revealing a wedding shot. She stared at it and the room came unglued.

CHAPTER 17

It didn't take long for the unhinged, swirling to slow and solid objects gradually to emerge. Before her stood a bride and groom. Sally smiled in pleasure at the man to her right. The photographer snapped a picture then instructed them to change positions. He snapped again. This went on for some time.

Isabella stood beside the photographer for a while then got bored. She assumed the groom was Milton Blake, Sally's first husband. Sally didn't mind mentioning Milton's name but she'd never once let her second husband's name pass her lips. From what Sally had shared, Milton ended up being a really bad idea. He was unfaithful and left her for another woman. Maybe she shouldn't have visited this picture. After a heavy sigh, Isabella turned away from the photo shoot and wandered farther into the room.

She recognized her uncle Robert and his wife, Emily. Sally's friend, Amber Woods, was here too. Isabella had only met her twice but she knew enough to recognize her. Emily and Amber were dressed in matching dresses, the bridesmaids. Robert wore a black tuxedo and there was another man dressed identically to him but he didn't look familiar.

A third man, wearing a long, black trench coat and top hat, stood on the far side, close to the door. It didn't appear that he was a participant in the wedding party. Perhaps he was the minister who'd officiate the wedding. Isabella wasn't sure but she didn't like the way he kept looking over at her. At least, that's how it appeared. He shouldn't be able to see her. No one else could. She turned away and ignored him.

Her grandparents, Melody and Vern Windsor, stood over in the corner. Melody was talking with Robert and their worried faces drew Isabella toward them.

When she was within earshot, she stopped and studied them.

Robert was saying, "…it's best to leave it alone. She's made her decision and there's no way to stop her. She loves him."

Melody shook her head. "If only she'd listen to some reason. Milton's nearly as old as your father. And anyone can see his eyes are prone to wander. Can't she see what will happen?"

"All she sees is a man who rescued her."

Melody made a contemptuous sound. "He took advantage of her at a low point in her life. Came in like a knight in shining armor when Felix was shot and killed. She went from a drug dealer to a carouser. Milton's nothing but an opportunist."

Robert didn't look happy with the assessment. "Don't let her hear you say that, Mom. She'd be hurt and angry. And I believe we've given her ample warning already."

"She's always angry with me. It doesn't matter what I say."

Robert looked away without answering.

Melody said, "If only we could keep her from walking down that aisle before it's too late."

"You warned her this morning. She won't listen."

"Did you talk to her, Robert?" Melody asked.

"I tried but she's adamant. She claims she loves him and is convinced Milton will stay true to her. I'm not pushing the point any further."

"Well, someone needs to."

"Mom, forget it. It won't do any good. Let it go and let her make her own decision."

"She needs God."

"Oh, please. Don't start that again."

Melody stared at her son. "He's the only hope for any of us. He's the reason I'm still sane."

Robert turned away and tried to hide a sneer.

Melody didn't notice her son's slight. Her eyes were riveted on Sally's happy face.

The photographer called for the two bridesmaids and groomsmen to assemble. Milton and Sally stepped to the side and waited until they were needed again.

Melody glanced down at her watch. "In an hour the ceremony begins. It's not a lot of time."

Robert glanced at her. "What are you intending to do?"

"I have to try one more time."

Isabella watched as Melody headed for Sally. Robert's heavy sigh filled her ears. Robert walked toward the photo backdrop and got into position with the other attendants.

Isabella walked over to join her grandmother.

"I need a word with you," Melody said.

Suspicion and caution clouded Sally's eyes. "What now?"

"Just a short word," pleaded Melody.

Sally reluctantly allowed her mother to lead her to the back of the room, where Robert had been a short while ago. Melody turned and quietly said, "Please reconsider this decision."

"No. You said plenty enough this morning at the house. I don't want to hear any more."

"Shh," she whispered. "Keep your voice down."

"Why should I when you're trying to subvert my special day?"

"I'm not trying to subvert anything. I just want you to be happy."

With a venomous tone, Sally spouted, "Then leave me alone."

Milton stepped up behind Sally, touched her arm and said, "Is everything all right here?"

Sally turned to him and gave him a shaky smile. "Yes, everything's perfect."

He gave Melody a winsome smile and said, "It'll be a pleasure to call you Mother."

With an awkward glance toward her soon to be son-in-law, Melody said, "I never imagined having a son-in-law my own age."

"I'm sure I'm a few years younger." He raised his eyebrows and smiled.

She stared daggers at him. "Not by much."

Sally gave her mother a warning look. Isabella knew the look. She'd been the recipient of that glare many a time.

"If you don't mind, we have *wedding* photos to take. Excuse us." Sally turned abruptly and walked off, Milton's arm embracing her waist.

Isabella stayed beside her grandmother and said, "I'm so sorry about Sally. She's always been stubborn and hard to talk to. When she makes up her mind about something she doesn't budge." She looked over at Melody, who stared straight ahead. "But I suppose you know all that. You're her mother."

Melody couldn't hear her but it felt good to get that off her chest. Seeing Sally so bent on marrying a man nearly twice her age was confusing. Why would she do it? Was she so desperate for a man? Sally was beautiful and could have any man she wanted, so why Milton Blake? His eyes did wander — all over Emily and Amber. Already it was obvious he wasn't committed to Sally. Why couldn't she see it? It was frustrating to watch.

Something Melody said earlier came back to her, something about Felix. She'd just met him in the last photo and now he was dead? He'd been shot and killed? The way history sped forward in this picture time travel made her head spin. Melody mentioned something about drugs. That made sense after what she'd seen in Sally's apartment. Sally was on the rebound, forced out of an entirely unsavory relationship and jumping into a hot frying pan of unfaithfulness.

Isabella shook her head at the horrible choices her mother was making. Someone needed to talk some sense into her. But then again, Melody had tried. Her words of wisdom had been soundly rejected. Sally was still too angry and bitter toward Melody to give her any heed.

The whole wedding party stood in front of the professional drop cloth and took their positions as the photographer instructed. Funny, but she'd never seen this pose before. The only picture from this wedding was the one in her hand. Had Sally destroyed most of them? Had this one photo in her hand once belonged to her grandmother? Is that how it ended up in the box of pictures?

She glanced over at her grandmother beside her. Melody looked younger but worn and her worried eyes were fixated on Sally. Isabella wished she could put her arm around Melody and let her know that everything would eventually turn out okay. She also knew there were still many years of uncertainty and concern for her grandmother left to carry concerning Sally. Never before had she realized how wearing Sally's life had been on Melody.

Every picture she visited carried a load of emotional upheaval. It wasn't so much physically draining as emotionally exhausting. It felt like her heart was being stretched, enlarged to feel others' pain. The process wasn't pleasant.

Vern walked over and put his arm around Melody. His eyes looked bloodshot, like he'd been drinking for breakfast. The smell that accompanied him attested to it. Melody accepted his embrace and reached up to grip his hand. They stood like that and watched the wedding party.

"Our little girl's getting married," Vern said with some pride.

"It's not a happy day."

Vern only shrugged, oblivious to the obvious.

It was hard to see her grandfather this way. She never knew him as a drunk. He was the most wonderful grandfather anyone could have. His love for her was boundless and he missed her terribly. She treasured each of his visits.

Movement at the door drew her attention. She expected to see the man in the top hat but he was gone. Maybe he just left and it was the door closing that she'd noticed. She decided that it didn't really matter.

It was time to move on. The conflicting emotions in this room were hard to stomach. She looked down at the picture in her hand and slipped it to the bottom of the stack. One undiscovered picture remained, staring up at her. Walter Tassey sat on a couch looking at a young Isabella on a blanket on the floor. For some reason the picture made her nervous but she had no idea why.

Studying it diligently, the room began to shift, jar and shudder. The wedding party was hard to make out as each person elongated and meshed with the walls, ceilings and floor. The photographer disappeared into a long, undulating line, his camera a round ball that rolled along his frame until it broke into numerous shapes and blended with the crazy colors dispersing everywhere. The twisted shapes, gyrating crazily throughout the room, slowly stopped and reversed.

With great speed, the curls of color traveled backwards until solid objects began to take shape. The floor calmed and straightened beneath her feet. The whole room shuddered slightly and then fell silent.

CHAPTER 18

There he was, the real breathing entity, the man who gave her life. How uncanny to see him in all his handsome beauty gazing at the infant Isabella, sitting so fragilely on the baby blanket spread on the floor. She could sense Sally beside her with the camera but her focus stayed on Walter.

He looks so distant. So emotionally detached. I wonder how he was as a father. Did he take good care of me? Did he love me? But if he loved me, why did he leave?

Sally's voice broke through the questions. "Why don't you hold her? It would make a better picture."

He turned discomfited eyes toward her and shrugged uncertainly. "I'm not good with babies."

With a hand on one hip, Sally made a sound and said, "Isabella's hardly a baby anymore. She's six months old."

He shook his head. "I don't want to."

An exasperated breath squeezed between Sally's teeth. "She won't bite you, for crying out loud." Setting the camera on the coffee table, Sally scooted to baby Isabella, picked her up and plopped her on Walter's lap.

"Don't. Take her off." He grabbed baby Isabella under her arms and held her out to Sally.

Sally skipped around the coffee table to get away, grabbed the camera and took a picture. Walter's arms were still extended, Isabella smiling and cooing in pleasure, her face turned toward Sally.

After lowering the camera and looking at father and daughter, Sally shrugged and declared, "I guess that's better than nothing."

"Here, come take her."

"No." Sally purposely took a seat across from him, the coffee table separating them.

Isabella watched in stupefied wonder. Walter appeared totally overwhelmed with her in his arms. Something seemed very abnormal. Why did he look so uncomfortable holding his own daughter? Isabella's heart constricted at the awkward sight. It wasn't what she'd envisioned when she dreamed of her father. Surely he must have spent some time with her when she was a baby. But the view before her sure didn't indicate that.

Walter stood and walked to the blanket on the floor. He knelt down, set Isabella gingerly back on the center of the blanket and waited until she settled into a sitting position. She was wobbly but she did balance out. Looking up at him, her face contorted and she broke into a pitiful cry. Frustration playing at his mouth, Walter stood and left the room.

"I told you I'm not good with babies," he said without turning to look at Sally.

Sally went over to fussing Isabella, picked her up and followed him.

Isabella took up the rear. It felt odd to be in the same room as her younger counterpart. She'd obviously been a cute baby. At least that wasn't the reason he avoided her. Was it truly because he felt inept with babies? Old feelings of rejection pierced her heart, threatening to overwhelm her. Deciding not to jump to conclusions, she stepped into the kitchen to see what her parents would discuss.

"I don't know why you won't hold her."

"I've told you before."

"It's not a good enough reason. You wanted a child too. We made this decision together. So why are you purposely ignoring her?"

"Maybe I'm not good at parenting," he shouted, his back against the cabinets, his arms bent behind him, his hands resting on the counter.

Frustration seeped from Sally's every pore. The tension in the room was thick enough to cut with a knife. Isabella didn't know if viewing this photo would help her at all. Confusion, thick as smog, swirled around her and made it hard to breathe. She didn't understand what was going on but she understood the feeling of agitation growing in her chest.

"You don't even try," screamed Sally. Baby Isabella cried harder.

"I'm doing the best I know how." Walter looked defeated and tired.

It brought Sally's voice down a notch as she said, "It's not good enough. I need you; Isabella needs you. You're hardly ever home. I miss you. Isabella doesn't even recognize her own father. It's not right."

Walter ran a shaky hand through his hair and studied the floor. "I don't know how to change it."

"You better change it or else we're in trouble. I don't know how much more of this I can take, with you being gone all the time and never here for us."

Walter looked up, a hard edge to his eyes now. "Are you threatening me?"

"If that's the only thing you'll listen to, then yes." Sally's stubborn side was coming out in full force.

Isabella had seen that part of her often, especially when it came to work or laying down the law at home. She found the exchange fascinating. To see her parents conversing was revolutionary. To see them being civil would be more pleasant but if this is all she could get, she'd take it. She'd have time later to dissect what it all meant.

"Don't you ever threaten me," Walter yelled. "I'm the head of this home and our marriage is for life."

"You sure don't act like that's true," Sally yelled right back. Baby Isabella wasn't too impressed with the conversation or else she wanted to be part of the ruckus too. Her wails increased but Sally and Walter just ignored the incessant volume and proceeded to add to the racket.

"I'm here every night."

A derogatory sound escaped Sally's lips. "You come home at midnight and leave the apartment early every morning. You're never here for Isabella. She rarely sees you and doesn't know you."

"She'll know me eventually."

"When? When she's old enough to stay up until midnight? What good does that do her now?"

"I am committed to you and Isabella. I've told you that before. I don't know what else you want from me."

"I want your time." Tears formed in Sally's eyes as she bounced Isabella in her arms and lowered her voice a few degrees. She finally must have realized she had a crying baby in her arms.

Walter turned away from her and ran his fingers through his hair again. It looked like his hands got stuck there but then it became clear he was clutching his hair in frustration.

"We can't talk about anything anymore without getting hysterical," said Sally. "Why can't we talk things through reasonably?"

With anger filling his eyes, he turned to her and said, "It's because your demands are unreasonable."

"Spending time with your wife and child isn't a reasonable request?" Sally asked indignantly.

Isabella stared at him too, wondering what he'd say.

"I don't know how to be a father." He looked deflated again. "I can't be the father you expect."

"Then let me help you. I can teach you how to have a healthy relationship with Isabella."

He was shaking his head, rejecting her suggestion.

"Why not?" Anger laced Sally's voice again.

"I can't do it."

"You mean you won't do it."

"That's not what I said."

"I don't know you anymore." Sally's eyes threatened to dump their load.

"What's that supposed to mean?" Walter said with venom.

"You've changed too much for my liking."

"Well, like it or not, we're married and we're going to stay married." He pushed off from the counter and headed to the other room.

Sally shouted, "Where are you going?"

"Out."

"So you're walking out on our conversation again?" She turned and followed him to the door. "Every time things get heated you run. Is that your answer for everything?"

Baby Isabella was still crying but it had grown softer now.

"This isn't a conversation. You're ranting and I'm done listening." He pulled on his shoes, reached for his coat and slipped into it.

"Don't go, Walter. We need to work this out."

"There's no reasoning with you." He reached for the keys on the hook beside the door.

"No reasoning with me?" Sally's voice rose a notch again.

His look of loathing was inescapable. Isabella took a step back at the sight. Then he turned, opened the door and was gone. The door slammed shut and Sally's breathing came out loud between her clenched teeth.

Isabella turned to study her mother. Sally stood staring at the door until her breathing calmed and baby Isabella squirmed in her arms. Finally she turned back into the room and allowed her body to fall back onto the couch, Isabella resting on her lap.

Sally stroked her baby's back, then her hair and a heavy sigh escaped her lips. "I love you, Isabella." A single tear spilled from her eye, wetting her cheek. "I'm so sorry, baby. Daddy doesn't know what he's doing. He should love you. You're completely wonderful and adorable. For some reason, he just doesn't get it. Something's blinded him. He's acting like a stranger lately. I can't fathom the reasons."

Baby Isabella cooed and reached a chubby arm up towards Sally's face.

Sally took her hand in hers and kissed it softly.

Isabella pulled her hand away and waved both arms in excitement. With her eyes glued to her mother, she slowed her frantic waving and made a grunt.

"He does love you. You have to know that, Isy." Sally bent over and placed a kiss on baby Isabella's cheek. "And I love you more than life." Holding the baby tenderly in her arms, Sally stood and headed down the hall.

Watching the exchange brought on a bevy of emotions. Maybe her dad didn't love her, maybe he never had. But she also knew that her mother had loved her from the beginning and that it never abated.

As riveting and interesting as the visit had been, Isabella was too mentally spent and emotionally drained to stay longer. Flipping the picture face down brought the desired result and she went hurtling back to the present.

CHAPTER 19

Sally came home around 3:00 p.m. She usually worked a shorter day on Saturdays. From her room, Isabella heard the door open and close softly. Sally called out for her. "I'm in my room doing homework," she answered.

After a few minutes, her door swung open, Sally stuck her head into the room and said, "Hi."

"Hi, Mom."

She walked in, leaned against the door frame and crossed her arms. "How was your day?" She was still decked out in her designer suit. Her heels had been discarded, probably left at the front door.

Isabella shrugged. "Okay." She couldn't tell her mother how it really went. Considering the emotional roller coaster of a ride she'd been on, she dare not let it show.

"Anything exciting happen while I was gone?"

"No, not really." Isabella could divulge the mundane parts of her day. "I cleaned the bathrooms and vacuumed the house."

"Wonderful. Thanks." Sally looked relieved.

Sally never had time to do all the housework with all the hours she put in at the office. Isabella knew that and had enough spare hours at home to help out. To see the relief on her mother's face was rewarding.

"So, what should we do tonight?"

"I'm babysitting, remember?"

"No, I didn't remember." Sally looked disappointed. "I was hoping to spend tonight with you, order in Chinese and maybe watch a movie later."

That made Isabella smile. "Sounds like fun. Instead I'll be fending off Tessa's horde of horror."

"That's not very nice." Sally shook her head. "They are the sweetest kids I know."

"Sweeter than I was when I was little?"

Sally's face scrunched as she pondered that. "Equal." With a smile, she gazed at Isabella. "So what time are you going?"

"Tessa said she'd pick me up at 5:00."

"That early?"

"Yeah, they're going out for dinner and a movie."

"Well, they deserve a night out."

"We could suggest she bring the kids here."

Sally thought it over. "I'd say yes if I weren't so tired."

"It's okay. Tessa would probably decline the suggestion anyway. If I go there, the kids can go to sleep in their own beds. It's a lot less complicated for them this way."

"You know what? We should have the kids over here next time and let them sleep over. That'd give Cody and Tessa a real break from the kids."

"She'd like that."

"I'm sure Cody would too."

Isabella nodded.

"Are you nearly done your homework?"

"Yeah, just finishing off the last question."

Sally nodded. "I'll go change and start with dinner."

"I'm not very hungry. I just ate an hour ago."

Sally stared at her. "You don't want to eat before you babysit?"

With a shake of her head, Isabella said, "Tessa usually has dinner made for the kids when I get there. And there's always lots of baked stuff in containers on the counter. She usually has cookies of some sort available."

A small smile tweaked Sally's lips. "That girl has a way in the kitchen. I envy her."

"She has more time to cook and bake than you do." Isabella hated it when Sally berated herself for her weaknesses. So Sally wasn't great in the kitchen and hated baking. She was a wonderful mother.

"That is true." After a moment of thought, Sally said, "Tessa should teach you how to cook and bake."

"I've helped her make chocolate chip cookies before. It's not that hard."

"And you've never offered to make me some?"

Isabella chuckled. "Would you like me to?"

"That would be amazing."

"I'll do that sometime."

With a nod, Sally turned and left the room, humming a tune as she went down the hall.

~~~~~

Tessa came at 5:00, stepped inside to stay hi to Sally and then drove Isabella to her house. She'd left the kids at home with Cody so when Isabella walked into their home, all three surrounded her with squeals of excitement, talking at the same time.

It was what she'd expected and Isabella knew she was in for a busy evening. Faith had already arranged three games and they sat waiting on the table. Faith rattled off the list as soon as she stepped inside. Hope was talking non-stop, telling her everything, from her day with her siblings, the week's events at school, her gymnastics class and all she had worn today. Apparently she'd gone through quite the wardrobe. A look at Tessa confirmed it. She looked a little frazzled.

"It took Hope and me a good hour to clean up all the clothes scattered over her bedroom floor."

Hope said, "Oh, but it was worth it. I was doing a fashion show and Faith and Jed watched me. Even Mommy and Daddy watched for a while. It was so epic and fun."

"So epic and fun, huh?" asked Isabella.

"Uh-huh. And, you know what else?"

She would have answered but Jedidiah's stance of frustration and his pouting mouth insisted she give him her attention. With a finger held up to stop Hope's flow of conversation, Isabella turned to Jed and asked, "How are you, buddy?"

Hope made a disgruntled sound beside her but Isabella kept her attention on Jed.

"Good." He still scowled but he uncrossed his arms and looked at her tentatively.

"What did you do today?"

"I watched Hope do her stupid dress up stuff."

"Hey," yelled Hope. "It wasn't stupid at all."

Isabella turned to Hope and said, "Can you give me a minute with Jed? He needs to talk to me right now."

"But you just got here and I haven't told you everything yet."

"You've told her plenty," insisted Faith, standing beside her sister. "No one else can get a word in edgewise, like usual."

Good for her. She's starting to stick up for herself and becoming more assertive. Go, Faith.

Isabella said, "Okay, girls. Hold up a minute and let Jed talk."

They quieted, which seemed like a miracle, especially for Hope.

Isabella turned back to Jed and waited.

"I set up a tent in my room. I played I was in the forest, hunting animals."

"That's really cool. How was your hunt? Did you shoot any animals?"

He nodded, a bright smile appearing now. "A whole bunch. I skinned them all and then I headed through the woods to the fort."

"The fort?"

"Yeah. It's in the back yard. That's where I trade my animal skins for things I need."

"The play structure," added Hope. "That was his fort."

"I'm telling it," shouted Jed with an angry stare. He turned back to Isabella.

"That's amazing. Did you learn about this in school?"

He shook his head. "No. I saw a show about it on TV."

Tessa had left to prepare for the evening but now she returned and, finding them still in the entrance, she said, "Okay kids, you have all evening with Isabella. Let her come into the house."

The crew finally backed away. Faith slipped her hand into Isabella's to lead her to the kitchen.

Cody appeared then and said, "Hi, Isabella. Nice to see you again."

"Thanks, Cody. It's good to be here."

He looked at the three hanging around her. "You're sure about that?"

That made her chuckle. "Yes, I'm not with them very often."

"I suppose that's true."

Tessa stepped beside Cody and he put his arm around her waist and squeezed.

"Are we ready," asked Tessa.

"I think so."

Tessa turned to Isabella. "There's a Creamy Penne Chicken and Broccoli casserole in the oven. It should be hot by now and I bought some fresh buns to go with it. You can eat as soon as we go."

"Perfect." Overseeing dinner would take up some of the time.

"Jed can go to bed around seven-thirty. The girls should get to bed by eight-thirty."

Cody said, "You kids listen to Isabella. I don't want any acting up. If you don't obey her, there'll be consequences."

"We'll listen, Daddy. We always listen," insisted Hope.

Faith lifted a finger and pointed it down at her sister's head. "I'll see to it that she listens."

Hope turned around and grabbed Faith's finger. "No you won't. I'll make sure you listen."

Tessa sighed and said, "Okay girls. Isabella will see to it that *both* of you listen."

"Let's go." Cody led the way and Tessa followed him.

The kids shouted, "Bye," but didn't bother seeing their parents out the door. They were still too excited about having Isabella around. After hearing the key turn in the door, Cody locking it from the outside, Isabella followed the kids into the kitchen and served the meal. It smelled fabulous and tasted even better.

The evening flew by in a whirl. The three kept her entirely occupied with myriad rounds of games. It was a pleasant break from the over-thinking she'd been doing all afternoon. She prayed with Jed and tucked him in. He was asleep in no time. After reading from the girls' devotional book and listening to their prayers, she kissed them both and turned out their light.

As she walked down the hall to the living room, she reminisced when her mother had devotions with her when she was younger. Sally only started it when Isabella was around seven years old. It was exciting to have her mother spend precious time with her just before bed. That's when Sally began to pray for her out loud before she went to sleep. It always made Isabella feel so safe and protected. But more than that, it made her feel special and loved.

As she grew older, Sally encouraged her to have devotions on her own. She bought her a teenage devotional book at the local Christian book store. Having bedtime devotions and prayer time was now a habit. Although her prayers were quite rehearsed and predictable, at least she still did it. Seeing her two nieces and nephew trained up the same way felt comforting. Cody and Tessa were wonderful parents.

Sitting on the couch by herself, the house suddenly quiet, her mind flew immediately to the picture travel. The three photos she'd visited today had affected her deeply. She couldn't stop thinking about them.

There was so much she didn't know about the past. Her mother's former life shocked and confused her. Being raised by a godly mother certainly hadn't rubbed off on Sally. The pregnancy and giving up a child for adoption damaged her a great deal, to the point of rejecting everything sound and wise. It was hard to fathom. All her bad choices had only added to the baggage she carried.

Then there was Walter. That was the greatest conundrum. Isabella's predominant confusion rested with him. He was becoming her mission, the purpose in pursuing this further. The bits and pieces she knew so far didn't add up. That he wasn't a fit father had become quite clear this morning. He showed no interest at all in parenting her, which made her heart twist in painful ways. He'd obviously rejected her and not wanted her.

Isabella stopped that line of thinking and pondered. No. He had wanted a child. They'd decided together to have her. So what was it then? What changed? Was there something from his past that prevented him from being all that he could be? Was he also damaged from his past? Sally had certainly carried a lot of damage — for thirty-nine years to be exact.

Isabella's heart cried out to God.

Please help me. I don't know what to do or how to go about this. I have so many questions and so few answers. Please show me what to do.

An idea formed slowly but made complete sense. She'd have to go back before she could go forward. The former past would help explain the more recent past. She needed to know more about Walter's upbringing. With that thought came a stab of fear. To study Sheffield Tassey and his ways didn't sound appealing but that's the only way she was going to find answers.

CHAPTER 20

The small sanctuary was packed out again. Pastor Chad and the mission heartbeat of the church drew people like bears to honey. Although Chad's messages were good, Isabella often became distracted sitting with her friends at the back.

Today he spoke of God's mysterious ways and how they are, at times, so different than what we'd imagine. Chad expounded on the fact that by God's wisdom He orchestrates our lives in such a way that everything works together for good. Isabella caught most of it because it spoke to her.

It made her wonder about the picture travel. Was it God's way of answering her often-spoken prayers about her father? Was this his way of revealing the past to her? Was it his doing or was it simply a random anomaly? The picture travel being produced by a wild shift of the cosmos or an electromagnetic field in her attic seemed a bit farfetched. Was it God or was it an irregular, arbitrary transformation of reality? Was it supernatural or electrical? Were God's higher ways involved? Maybe that part of the attic sat over the kitchen. Perhaps the microwave was malfunctioning and the radioactive waves were causing a shaft of unstable matter, shooting up through the layers of floors and hurtling her back in time.

She'd never previously articulated what her heart questioned. Now that the thoughts came she allowed them free rein. Which was it? If what Chad was saying was true, then God seemed to be the grand conductor overseeing the picture travel. If it was merely a random occurrence, then what did it really matter? It would amount to a bit of amusing entertainment and that's all. But no, there was much more to it than that. Her mind was being opened to never-before-known-information. These were answers to her long-sought prayers.

Abby and Shana were growing restless and broke through Isabella's train of thought. Abby, sitting next to her, was whispering about her night out with Tray. Her lovestruck eyes were enough to make Isabella stare. Shana, on her other side, was writing notes. Her mother would be furious if she noticed Shana goofing around during the service. Talking during church was strictly forbidden in the Lintel home. Shana kept passing slips of paper over to Abby who took them and answered in a whisper.

When the topic of Tray grew old, Shana handed Isabella a slip of paper. Isabella read it. It was a question about the picture travel.

"Has anything exciting happened lately?"

Isabella looked at her friend and shook her head. She was in no mood to go into it. Besides, the last few pictures had been hard to visit. They'd revealed more than she'd really wanted to know and she was still trying to process what it all meant. Her heart still felt tender and bruised.

After the service, Isabella and her friends gathered in the foyer with some of the other Youth. Shana's eyes were glued to Mark, who stood beside Blair. It was becoming obvious that those two liked each other. Shana's jealously was no secret either. It made Isabella smile. Shana shook her head and looked at Isabella.

"Are you okay?" asked Isabella.

"What do you think?"

Isabella shrugged. "No.

Shana moved in closer and said, "What is it about me? I can't seem to get a guy no matter what I do. I've shown him I'm interested but no, he goes for a shorty."

It was true. Blair was quite short. If she stood five foot three it was a generous guess. Mark was nearly six feet in height. Shana and Mark would make a great-looking couple. Isabella had admitted as much to Shana.

"Give him time. He'll come around eventually."

Abby overhead that and said, "No he won't. Not unless you give him some motivation."

Shana stared at her. "Like what? Wearing skimpy tops and short skirts?"

"It works for me."

"It's not my style and besides, my mom would kill me if I tried that."

Isabella couldn't believe this conversation. "It's important for a guy to like you for who you are, not for what you wear."

With crossed arms, Abby said, "And this coming from someone who has no clue about style."

The accusation rubbed Isabella the wrong way. "Just because my style is different from yours doesn't mean it's not a style."

"If you're going for sloppy, then yes, it's a style." Abby turned away toward Liana and the two started chatting.

"Just ignore her," said Shana. "She's so full of herself, it's ridiculous."

It was hard to ignore Abby, though. Her constant criticism of Isabella's wardrobe was tiring. A sight from across the room made thoughts of Abby take flight. Her mother was in close proximity to Mr. Kendal. Was that whom she'd gone for dinner with the other night? At the time she hadn't paid attention. Now, seeing him so close to her mom, them smiling and talking, she suddenly cared. She'd never bothered to know before. Sally had been on a few dates before but that's where they'd always ended. One date and it was over.

"What's going on?" asked Shana beside her.

Isabella glanced over to see her watching the two as well. "Not sure."

"What do you think?"

"They're talking."

"They look pretty smiley."

Isabella grimaced. "Smiling isn't a crime."

With a grunt, Shana said, "They're standing pretty close together, wouldn't you say?"

That made her angry but she didn't know why. She waved her arms as she spoke, for emphasis. "They're having a conversation. It's kind of hard doing that when you're at opposite ends of the room."

"Chill already. Why are you so uptight?"

Her hot air deflated quickly. "I don't know."

"It's not like they're dating, right?"

"No." But she wasn't sure. Now she wished she'd listened to what her mother told her. With whom had she gone out the other night?

"They're kind of cute together."

Isabella glared at Shana.

"Just saying." Shana giggled.

Isabella ignored her and took one more look. She saw Mr. Kendal reach over and touch Sally's arm. That was too much. Why was he doing that and why in the world would Sally be okay with it? Heat traveled up Isabella's spine and she felt a tremor course through her body.

She turned away and kept her eyes glued to the group of young people around her but her mind wasn't on their conversation. How could her mother do this? One date and she was smitten? It was completely pathetic. Work was her greatest love. Nothing could ever take its place, at least that's what Isabella had concluded until now. Of course her mother loved her as well, but she spent way more time at work than she ever did with her. To watch Sally in close company with a man made her uncomfortable. If there'd be a man in Sally's life, it wouldn't be Mr. Kendal. She'd make sure of that.

Maybe she was being childish and petty, but her mother was all she had. To see a potential threat, attempting to take her mother from her, divide what little attention she received, was infuriating.

The next time Isabella glanced over, Sally was standing at the doors talking to Pastor Chad. Sally threw her a few looks, indicating she was ready to go. Isabella bid her friends goodbye and headed to the doors.

The ride home was quiet. Isabella felt stupid for being so selfish. Sally didn't have much of a life, just work and her, that was all. Why did it feel so threatening to have someone show interest in her?

After analyzing for a few miles, she began to understand. She was afraid. That's what it was. She'd lost one parent. She didn't want to lose the other. Sally was all she had. Isabella looked at her mother. Sally was still beautiful and attractive. What man wouldn't be drawn to her? That train of thought didn't help. Fear only grew stronger. Her hands began to sweat and she wiped them of on her pants.

Sally looked over. "What should we do for lunch?"

Isabella shrugged. "I don't know."

"How about we go see a movie and eat popcorn."

It sounded wonderful. "Sure."

Purposely missing their residential turnoff, Sally headed for the mall and the largest theater in the city.

The fear slowly dissipated and Isabella began to relax. The normal turn of events brought a welcome calm. This is how things should be, she and Sally together. Isabella decided then that if in the future there ever was another addition, it was going to be Walter.

CHAPTER 21

The week flew by without a single opportunity to visit the pictures. Either a boatload of homework was assigned or a basketball game was scheduled after school, which Abby insisted they all stay and watch. On Thursday, both Abby and Shana stopped by and they hung out until Sally came home.

There was no way Isabella was visiting her father's past with them. It was too personal and revealing too much could be embarrassing. They asked about joining her but she declined and said she wasn't in the mood for picture travel. So they amused themselves in other ways.

Sally was coming home earlier from work lately anyway. That threw any plans of time travel out the window.

On Friday, Isabella went right home after school, hoping for some time in the attic. She visited the kitchen first to stop the growling of her stomach. After finding nothing interesting to still her hunger, she decided to bake a batch of chocolate chip cookies. Sally would be surprised and thrilled with such a feat.

It didn't take long to find the recipe she'd stuck in the recipe book drawer. The instructions didn't look too complicated. Tessa, of course, would accomplish the deed much more quickly, but the challenge would be invigorating.

First, she turned on the two ovens, one built into the cabinet over the other, to the correct temperature. They'd heat up while she did the rest. Arranging all the ingredients together and placing them on the counter, she got a bowl and the electric, handheld mixer. Now she was ready.

She carefully measured, mixed and added, and the dough was finally ready. The mix in the bowl was dotted with a liberal amount of chocolate chips. She used a whole bag where the recipe only required a cup. The more chocolate, the better the cookies, right? Isabella knew that Sally would agree with that.

The cookies baked in eight minutes per sheet. With the two convection ovens going, it wasn't long until the whole room smelled like heaven. After the first batch of baking, only one pan remained to go into the oven. She placed the pans on cooling racks and slipped the last baking sheet into the oven. This was going faster than what she'd anticipated and she realized how big the recipe was with all the cookies sitting on the counter. They easily had a two week stash of sweets.

As she allowed the pans to cool, she poured herself a large glass of milk. Touching the cooling cookies, she decided it was time to remove them and place them on cooling racks. The timer beeped and she removed the last sheet of baking. This was how Tessa had done it. The huge pile of cookies looked ridiculous.

She ate three cookies in a row, with sips of milk to wash them down. If she let herself go, she could eat a bunch more. Sally had trained her well in self-control, so she decided she'd only have one more.

Noise from the other room made her stop. She was sure she'd heard the front door. Was that possible? Sally never came home this early.

In a minute, the kitchen door swung open and Sally stepped inside, her eyes wide and pleasure written across her face. "You baked cookies!"

"You're home?" asked Isabella, too shocked to sound very bright.

"Yes," she said, walking into the room, "I finished up early today."

Isabella glanced at the clock. "It's only 5:00."

"I know. It must be a first for me." Sally grabbed a cookie and lowered herself into a chair, crossing her legs. "Mmm. This is good."

"I put in tons of chocolate chips."

"I love it."

Isabella scooped the last of the cookies off the pan and placed them on the racks to cool. She went to sit down next to her mother and stared at her. Sally was thoroughly enjoying her second cookie.

"You'll have to bake more often," Sally said after swallowing the last bite.

"Maybe I will." It felt good to do something nice for her mother. To see her enjoy the baking brought great satisfaction.

Sally wiped the corners of her mouth, focused her eyes on Isabella and said, "I'm going out tonight."

"Where?"

"I'm going to see a movie with a friend." Sally raised her index finger and pointed it at Isabella. "And you have Youth."

"You'll drop me off before the movie?"

"Of course. Actually my friend offered to pick us up and drop you off."

Isabella smiled in amusement. "Okay, who's this friend you keep talking about?"

A nervous look took residence on her face. "Someone from church."

Isabella rolled her eyes. She couldn't help it. Her mother was being infuriating. "Who is it?"

"Grayson Kendal."

Never had a name made her heart race so fast. Well, maybe it did when she first learned her father's name. But this was different. Her fear must have shown. Her mother's face held an appeasing look.

"We're just friends. We went out last Friday night and I really enjoyed his company. He suggested a movie this week and I thought, why not. I haven't done much of this sort of thing in a long time."

"When did the two of you become friends?"

"We talk at church sometimes."

Isabella grunted in derision. "Yeah, he pursues you and you avoid him. That's been the extent of your friendship."

Surprise filled Sally's eyes. "You noticed?"

"Of course I've noticed. I notice every man who gets too close."

Sally's forehead scrunched and her eyes narrowed. "You have a problem with men getting too close to me?"

Isabella stood then. She'd said too much already. She filled the sink with water and added detergent. Washing the dirty dishes seemed a safe thing to do at the moment.

"Isabella?"

"It's not a problem. It's just that I take notice, that's all."

"So you don't mind that I'm going out tonight?"

Of course she minded. But she couldn't say that, could she? It would appear selfish and vengeful. She turned to look at her mother, who had a curious wondering in her eyes. "Why would I mind? I'll be busy anyway."

"That's not what I meant. You don't mind if I start spending time with Grayson?"

"You said you were just friends and that you're just going out for a movie. Is this something that's going to become a regular habit of yours?"

With a mischievous wink, Sally said, "Am I allowed?"

Isabella breathed contemptuously through her teeth, turned around and soaked her hands in the soapy water. Scrubbing a cookie sheet seemed preferable to answering.

"I'm being serious. Is it okay if I start to date?"

"Grayson Kendal?"

"He's a very nice man."

"He's old."

"He's a few years older than I am, yes."

"What? Ten years older?" Isabella couldn't make herself turn around and look at her. Sally was being impossibly maddening.

"He's five years older."

He seemed ancient and the whole thing felt wrong. "I don't like it."

"Isabella. Are you serious?" Sally stood and came to her. She laid a hand on Isabella's shoulder which made her pull away. "What's wrong?"

Feeling like a heel, she said, "I don't know." She was too embarrassed to say how afraid she was.

"You're scared."

Was it that obvious? She never could hide her feelings well. With a shrug she furiously scrubbed the next pan.

"What frightens you so?"

With a sigh, she decided she may as well spit it out. Sally wouldn't leave her alone until she got her answer. Refusing to make eye contact, Isabella whispered, "I don't want to lose you."

Sally reached over, took hold of Isabella's chin and moved her head to face her. "You will never lose me, Isabella. Not ever.

You're stuck with me, like it or not. The two of us are a team. Grayson Kendal will never change that."

"Do you promise?" She had to have some confirmation, some assurance.

"Absolutely." Sally placed a hand to her heart. "I give you my solemn oath that I will always be here for you." She pulled her into a hug.

Isabella lowered her eyes. She still didn't feel reassured. There were too many possibilities.

"What is it, Isabella?"

She shrugged. "It's just that you're always so busy now. What will happen if you get all wrapped up in Grayson? You won't have any time left for me at all."

Sally nodded. "I won't let that happen."

"But what if it does?"

After a deep sigh, Sally said, "I didn't want to tell you this yet but I think it's time."

Isabella stared at her. What was it? Had she decided to marry him already? Fear pounded on her ribs and restricted her ability to breathe.

"I've decided to let go of running the stores. I'll only keep the clothing design company to supply the stores with stock."

A shock wave went through her body. "You're willing to give it all up?"

"Oh no, I'm not giving anything up. I'm planning to franchise the business, make the stores a national name, spreading them from state to state."

"So really, you'll be busier than ever."

"No. It should lessen my load. Right now, I'm very busy planning it all and getting the legal stuff done. Once everything's in place, my schedule should lighten significantly."

"When?"

"In a few months things should shift dramatically."

"Is that why you're pursuing Grayson?"

Sally chuckled. "I'm not pursuing him. He's the one pursuing me."

"But is that why you're finally saying yes to him? Because of this new business idea?"

Sally became thoughtful. "It could be."

Isabella suddenly wished Sally would leave the business as it was. Yes, with the change Sally would have more time, but she'd be devoting all her time to a new interest.

"I won't give all my extra time to Grayson, if that's what you're wondering."

Isabella stared at her and asked, "Am I that obvious?"

Sally grinned and nodded. "You never could hide things from me."

Now she was even more nervous. The photo travel was one thing she absolutely had to hide from her mother. Changing the subject seemed like a wise thing.

"I'll ask Shana's parents to take me home after Youth. That way you don't have to rush back for me."

"Are you sure?" Sally looked concerned.

Isabella nodded. "Yeah, just go and have fun."

"You are sounding more grown up all the time." Her face scrunched as she studied Isabella's face. "It's funny. Suddenly I feel like I'm the teenager and you're the parent."

It did sound that way. Isabella decided to ham it up. "I give you permission to go on a date with Grayson but your curfew is 11:00. Make sure you're home by then or else I'll be forced to ground you!"

"Yes, Momma." Sally saluted and grinned.

Isabella laughed.

CHAPTER 22

Up in the attic, the boxes situated around her, Isabella knew what she had to do. She finally decided that looking through pictures of Walter's childhood was her next order of business. The big brown envelope was all that remained of his younger years. There wasn't much in it. Sheffield and Lynne Tassey obviously weren't big into pictures.

Pulling out the small stack, she placed it on the floor and moved the photos around with her hand to see if any caught her interest. Most were of him as an infant, toddler or young boy. When he got around to ages eleven or twelve, pictures of him became extremely scarce. She picked out a couple of him around that age. There were only four that piqued her curiosity.

Her mother was at work, but not knowing exactly when she'd be home, she'd gotten up early, had breakfast and here she was, 8:00 in the morning on a Saturday. It was ridiculous how this picture travel had changed her weekends. No more sleeping in on Saturdays. This was her only uninterrupted morning to time travel.

She missed sleeping in until noon, leisurely getting up, doing some light housecleaning and hanging out with her friends. Shana and Abby might drop by later. She should have plenty of time to get everything done before then. Getting up early ensured a full day of activity.

After a long yawn, she gazed down at the first picture in her hand. Three others were tucked beneath it. Walter was sitting by a table, a birthday cake sitting before him covered in numerous candles. They were lit, making it hard to count them. The glow from the flames illuminated his face, causing funny shadows to distort it.

It was then that she noticed the room in full motion. She'd been so busy looking at the picture, trying to count the candles, that she hadn't seen the change begin. The ceiling buckled inward wildly, lowering to stare her in the face. The floor beneath her rose to greet the rafters up above and slivers of light from the bulb sliced through the wood grain. The boxes heaved upwards, hovered in mid-air, elongated and meshed with the room dynamo. With a swirling motion, the whole room danced and swayed in bizarre shapes.

It wasn't long until the snaking colors slowed and the convoluted swells took shape. A table gradually appeared. Light drained from the air and converged over Walter's cake, the glow casting a soft hue on the other items coming into focus. Walter's face appeared, smiling and bright.

Isabella looked to her left and saw Lynne Tassey standing behind a chair, smiling in pleasure at her son. To the right, she saw Sheffield, a camera in his hand and snapping a picture. He lowered it and set it on the table.

The whole scene felt normal and right. From this distance Isabella counted the candles. Walter was twelve. He looked even more handsome than ever. There should have been a gaggle of girls standing on the sidelines. With his looks, there was no way he could avoid the admirers. Isabella reached up and touched her face. She had his looks. She was as beautiful as he was handsome. Dressing sloppy kept the guys at bay. That thought made her smirk.

Lynne reached over and touched Walter on his shoulder. "Go ahead. Make a wish and blow out the candles."

Walter took a moment for thought, smiled and blew hard, moving his head to catch them all.

"Well done," said Sheffield.

"I'll get the ice cream." Lynne turned and went to the refrigerator. Opening the top door, she retrieved the bucket from the freezer.

Sheffield sat down opposite Walter and waited to be served. Lynne set the ice cream on the table and went back to the cupboards for the plates and silverware. Returning to the table, she removed the candles, sliced the cake and served it. She then went back to the counter to get two mugs of coffee and served Sheffield and herself.

As they ate, the silence at the table was uncanny. Isabella knew silence, living with only her mother, but this silence was odd.

TIME AND RESTORATION

Walter finished his cake first, took a napkin and wiped his mouth. He gazed at his father expectantly.

Sheffield finished next, sat back and crossed one leg over the other. After blowing on his hot cup of coffee to cool it, he took a long, leisurely sip.

Walter looked beside himself with impatience. It was obvious he was anticipating something.

Lynne grinned as she watched his restless wiggling. She turned and stared at Sheffield. After clearing her throat, she said, "Sheffield, are you forgetting something?"

He looked at her. "No, not at all."

"Did you get him what he asked for?"

"A bat and ball?" piped up Walter, keen anticipation in his eyes. "I want to play baseball and get signed up on a team."

Sheffield stared at him. He took a deep breath and exhaled slowly. "You're twelve now. You're a man in my eyes."

Walter still looked eager.

"This is the age where we leave play time behind and move on to the higher things of life."

Walter's countenance fell.

"I have something entirely different in mind for you."

"So I can't play baseball?"

Sheffield leaned forward, keeping keen eye contact with his son. "You'll learn to play ball God's way."

Confusion filled Walter's eyes. "I don't understand."

"You're coming with me today. It's time I start training you one-on-one. I'll take you to the church office and begin showing you what I do each day. This will be my gift to you."

Walter looked over at his mother, disappointment covering his face.

Sheffield's anger came quickly and loudly. Pounding his fist on the table made every eye turn to him. "Don't look at your mother, boy. Are you a child or are you a man?"

With a nervous, cowering tick, Walter said, "I'm a man."

"That's right. And don't you forget it." Sheffield turned to Lynne. "The time for babying him is over. You start treating him like a man. And I forbid you to go and buy him a birthday gift. His childhood is done. Birthday parties are for children. Now his training begins."

Lynne nodded meekly, gathered up the dirty plates and hurried to the sink where she busied herself.

Sheffield stood and waved for Walter to follow him.

Although going with them felt oppressive, Isabella had a feeling she needed to follow.

Sheffield grabbed his coat from the closet and Walter slipped into his jacket. Sheffield held the door for his son and the two were gone. Isabella inhaled deeply and released a nervous breath. She grabbed the door handle and opened the door. Stepping outside, she was surprised that there was nothing to stop her. The landscape was clear sailing, with no swirling mass to indicate she needed to go back.

Sheffield and Walter were already getting into a car. Isabella hurried to them, opened the back door and slipped inside. They hadn't noticed the door open or her presence here with them, making her shake her head in wonder. Walter sat in the passenger seat beside his father, the look of disappointment still covering his face.

Isabella's heart went out to him. What a horrible turn of events. No longer could he look forward to his birthday. It would only serve as an annual reminder that his childhood was officially over.

Sheffield spoke of things, church things that Walter numbly agreed to, nodding his head in submission. Isabella watched the scenery speed by, still feeling shocked that she was allowed to travel this far in a picture. She glanced down at her hand, where the picture stared up at her. It was tempting to switch to the next photo but there must be some reason she was allowed to travel further this time. Maybe there was something she needed to know, to learn.

In a matter of minutes the car pulled into a small yard, the gravel parking lot crunching beneath them. They stopped near a building. Sheffield cut the engine and got out, Walter following his lead. Isabella took up the rear.

The building was very new and construction not quite finished. The siding was partially complete and some painting was still required. It wasn't large by any means but it was tastefully done. A sign at the road was being installed. As yet, no words adorned it.

I wonder if this is Sheffield's church? It's quite impressive.

Isabella followed the two into the building. The spacious foyer held coat racks along the outer walls. The floors were bare; no carpet had yet been laid. Perhaps they were waiting until more money became available. Directly in front of them were large double doors and beyond that, Isabella could see pews in neat rows. Yes, this was a church.

Sheffield led Walter to the right through a side door. Isabella hurried to keep up. They walked down a short hall and through a door to the right. It was an office, a large oak desk taking up most of the space. Bookcases lined one wall, books filling every shelf. None of the titles caught her eye. A small window faced the yard to the rear of the church.

Sheffield sat down behind his desk and Walter took a chair opposite him, facing his father. Isabella chose to stand by the door. It felt safer from there. Standing close to Sheffield was too threatening.

Sheffield crossed his arms and stared at his son. "Now that we're here I want you to know that I have full confidence in you becoming a great man of God. One day you'll take over for me and run all of this." A small smile tweaked his lips. "I want to remind you again that your childhood is done. You are a man and from now on I'll treat you that way. If you step out of line or resist, I'll still punish you. Your training will be more intensive than ever. No more boys clubs for you. I will personally see to your training. Is that clear?"

Walter didn't look happy but he nodded.

"First of all, you need to know that your mother has finished her duty. She's raised you, coddled you and babied you long enough. Let her go. She's none of your concern now."

Walter looked confused. "I don't understand."

With great control, Sheffield reined in his rising frustration and said, "You will stay away from her. You will not join her in the kitchen and you will not speak to her unless she initiates it first. Do you understand?"

"Why can't I talk to her?"

With fist raised high, Sheffield let it fall in a thunderous pound on his desk.

It made Isabella jump. Walter jumped even higher.

"Don't ever question me again." His voice thundered just as loud as his fist had. Visibly, he controlled his anger and said, "Women are weak. Their weakness will lead you astray. It's best not to listen to them. Their simpleton ways are best avoided. They have their use and their place. I need your mother. She's vital to our home and was pivotal in your upbringing. But now that you've turned twelve, it's time to leave childish ways behind."

Walter didn't look twelve. All the former excitement and joy she'd seen when he sat behind his cake with the candles, had evaporated. His shoulders slumped and his face contorted in distress; he appeared more like a frightened six-year-old. Her heart went out to him. How could any father treat his son like this? It was horrible.

Her thoughts turned to something her mother once said. It had been her ninth birthday party and Grandma and Grandpa had visited from Toronto. After lighting her candles and them all singing happy birthday to her, Sally had turned to Grandma and said, "It's like old times. Isabella's birthday and her father not making an appearance."

Grandma had said, "It'd be completely impossible for him to show up now."

"Good thing too," Sally had responded. She then looked at Isabella, noticed her rapt attention, turned back to Grandma and said, "Let's drop it."

Not another word was spoken and in all the years that followed, Sally never mentioned it again. But now, looking at Walter and his devastation, Isabella felt the loss right along with him. This was not how she wanted to meet her father. She sure had not envisioned getting to know him this way. Revulsion and compassion flowed from her soul toward him.

What had this done to him? How had his father's training shaped him? The answers to these questions terrified her. Did she really want to know?

Sheffield's voice drew her attention back. "Now that we have set the ground rules in place we can get on with your training." He took a book from the expansive bookcase and turned to his son. "This man's teaching has been revolutionary for me. It will direct you in the right path."

The author's name was unfamiliar and the title obscure. Isabella couldn't decipher its contents by the title, which read, "Diadems of Religious Functions." It sounded hopelessly dull and boring.

Sheffield handed the book to Walter. "This book will explain my theology and vision for my church. It lays the foundation of all I believe to be true." He waved a hand mid-air. "Of course, I tweak it to suit my individual tastes and style. A church must be run with the utmost control. People are finicky and without a strong hand they tend to go wherever the strongest teaching blows. By being the strongest voice and exerting the most powerful views, a pastor is able to guide his sheep effectively. Keeping them in the fold is vital. I've heard far too many mealy-mouthed preachers in my day. People are perishing because there are no strong leaders to guide them. I, for one, will not be accused of allowing the sheep in my fold to go astray. Strong leadership is hard to find and I have dedicated my life to lead by strength."

He waved his hand again to dismiss what he'd just said. "But I'm jumping too far ahead. I must remember you're twelve. Although you're a man, we're barely beginning your training." He pointed to the book. "Start with that. Next week I'll drill you with questions and I'll see if you paid attention."

Walter did not look pleased. He leafed through the thick volume and slowly lifted his eyes to his father. "You want me to read this whole book?"

"I expect you to read chapters one through fourteen. That's one third of the book. That should be attainable for you."

By the look on Walter's face, it was clear he wanted to disagree but held his tongue.

Sheffield handed Walter a sheet of paper. Isabella stepped forward and looked over Walter's shoulder. The title read, "Membership Commitments."

"I drew up this list after the church plant. There was a need for clear guidelines to keep the people in line. Everyone who becomes a member of this church takes a vow to keep these rules and signs this document." Sheffield held it up, pointing to the signature line at the bottom.

"I signed one a few years ago," Walter said.

"Yes you did. But now I want you to understand fully what you signed." Sheffield began with the first item, expounding on its necessity, its functionality and its behavior-modifying benefit.

Isabella quickly lost interest. It was hard to stomach that Walter was forced to sit here, enduring this monotony. The boy didn't move a muscle. His eyes stayed glued to his father's face. Isabella wasn't sure whether he was feigning interest or not. After what felt like half an hour, Sheffield moved on to the next requirement on the membership list. One thing she knew for certain, she was done here. Isabella had no desire to stay for the entire, dull lecture.

She looked down at the picture staring up at her from her hand, took it with her other and slipped it to the bottom of the small stack she held. The photo which now sat on top was of Walter at a similar age. He stood in front of a simply decorated Christmas tree, red marks visible across one cheek.

CHAPTER 23

When Isabella looked up, everything in Sheffield's office had shifted and contorted into wild shapes and corkscrews. Not one thing was distinguishable. Walter and his father were impossible to make out. Colors flowed together violently in a rippling mass of modern art. The frantic churning suddenly ceased and reversed with frenetic speed, snaking and surging until items began to emerge.

A tree took shape and the lights on it became visible as they dispersed in tiny spots. Walter's face came into focus and his body appeared shortly after. The background took a little longer but it too settled and everything finally stilled.

Looking to her right, she expected to see Sheffield with the camera. It was Lynne this time. After snapping the picture, she lowered the camera. She'd been crying. Her red eyes and quivering chin gave it away.

Walter nodded and turned to walk away.

"Wait," said Lynne, reaching out to him and touching his arm.

Walter yanked his arm away, anger in his eyes.

"He shouldn't have done this to you."

"*You* shouldn't have goaded me to talk to you."

Devastation poured from her eyes. "I'm your mother."

His anger softened slightly and with a hard stare, he said, "Dad's put down rules. It's best if we all abide by them. It'll be better for you if I stay away from you."

"You mean it'll be best for *you* if you stay away from me. He hit you because you came to the kitchen to get something to eat after school."

Walter didn't respond.

"I'll come find you. I'll ask you if you want a snack and I'll bring it out to you. That will be the rule between us. Okay?"

He gave a slight nod.

She held up the camera. "This picture could be used against him, you know? We could go to the authorities."

Walter's eyes darkened. "And do what? Report him? What are you thinking, woman?" The disdain on his face was hard to watch. "Dad was right. Women are weak. I should never listen to anything you say."

Lynne looked like she'd been slapped hard. Pain and shock exuded from her eyes.

With a sneer of derision, Walter turned and left the room.

Lynne walked over to the couch and lowered herself onto it. Tears flowed down her cheeks unchecked. Sobs finally erupted and her chest heaved as she vented her sorrow. She tried to keep the sounds quiet but her whole body convulsed with the effort.

Isabella estimated that a few months had passed since Walter's training began, maybe six at the most. It was obvious that there'd been a dramatic change in his character She was astounded. If the power of persuasion was a great asset to attain in life, Sheffield's ability to manipulate and control were sure proof of that.

Lynne's strained sobs echoed around her. To watch her grandmother in such emotional pain was hard. Isabella couldn't endure any more so she glanced down and moved the picture to the bottom.

She hated the change in Walter. It was a testament to her aversion to such heavy-handed methods. Sheffield was an absolute villain in her eyes. What she feared most was that Walter would become like him if things proceeded.

But she couldn't stay here. She couldn't end her time travel on this note. Staring at the next picture, Walter looking a bit older; in her peripheral vision she noticed the room coming undone.

Lynne's cries faded away as a metamorphosis took place and the picture gradually took on reality. Curvaceous lines straightened and solid objects formed as shimmering shapes stilled.

Walter stood with his father, both in formal suits and ties. They stood side by side in the entrance of their home, Lynne with the camera. After she'd taken the picture, she set the camera on the small entrance table and walked toward the kitchen. Quietly she said, "At least I'll have a picture of him at fourteen." Not a hint of a smile graced her lips. She looked worn and tired. It appeared that the joy of family had escaped her and taken flight.

Sheffield and Walter ignored her and busied themselves removing their dress shoes, placing them in the closet by the front door. Walter headed for the stairs and descended to the basement two steps at a time. Sheffield walked to a room off to the side and closed the door. It looked like an office.

With the area empty and suddenly quiet, Isabella wasn't sure where to go. Should she follow Walter downstairs? Or should she head to the kitchen, find out how Lynne was doing? Checking on Sheffield didn't tempt her in the least. She decided to wait and see what would happen next.

A few minutes later, Lynne appeared through the kitchen door and called, "Lunch is ready."

Walter bounded up the steps and headed to the kitchen. He was taller than in the last picture. Lynne had revealed his age already; he was fourteen.

Isabella followed him through the door and stood against the wall to watch and listen. Lynne avoided Walter, staying by the kitchen counter to wipe up some spills. He was just sitting down at the table when Sheffield walked in. Scanning the room to see if it was to his satisfaction, he sat down at the head of the table. Lynne saw both of them seated and came to join them.

The smell of roast beef filled the room. Isabella's stomach grumbled in longing. Mashed potatoes, gravy, peas, a tossed salad and fresh bread completed the table's contents. Lynne was obviously a good cook. The three bowed their heads and Sheffield prayed.

They ate in silence. When they were done, Lynne went to the refrigerator and retrieved the dessert. A blueberry cheesecake sat on a pretty platter. Isabella's mouth watered at the sight.

Lynne served the dessert and coffee before sitting down and enjoying her piece.

Walter spoke up. "I enjoyed your sermon, Dad."

Sheffield nodded. "Yes. I was pleased with the delivery of it."

"I heard a lot of people talk about it in the foyer after."

"Oh?" Sheffield's interest was piqued. "What was said?"

Walter looked content to brag on his father. "One person said it was just what they needed. They said your talk on leadership styles would help them deal with issues at work. It would assist them in being a better manager. Someone else mentioned they liked what you said about the passive leader, leading by example. That fit their natural bent the best."

Sheffield nodded. "What about you? Which style of leadership do you possess?"

Isabella glanced at Lynne. She didn't even bother to make eye contact. Her eyes were busy studying her empty plate and the liquid in her coffee cup as she sipped at it.

"I'm not sure," Walter mused.

"Well, at fourteen you should have some idea."

"What would you say about me?"

"You have my strengths and my style." A small smile tweaked Sheffield's lips. "You make me proud."

Walter's face lit up with the praise.

Lynne didn't look impressed.

"You've come a long way in two years."

Lynne's quiet voice filled the space. "I wish we could have celebrated his birthday properly."

"We did," Sheffield said, staring at her. "I took him to the church. All the leadership was present, hands were laid on him and he was commissioned to teach the Youth clubs."

Walter's grin of pleasure was sign of his agreement with the direction of his birthday celebration. "It was amazing."

"But I wasn't there. I didn't get a chance to celebrate with my son." Her eyes were accusing as she said, "You didn't even allow me to bake a cake."

"I had a cake. Dad bought it and we ate it with the leadership team at the church."

Lynne appeared deeply wounded. Her eyes cried without shedding a drop.

Sheffield gazed at her. "You think me callous and uncaring."

She looked down, staring at her hands in her lap.

"Lynne?"

Slowly she lifted her eyes to him.

"I don't mean to hurt you by this. You must understand that I feel this is the best way to train him, wean him from his mother's apron strings."

Walter released a sound of derision.

Lynne turned to stare at him.

"I've been free of her apron strings for quite some time," Walter said without making eye contact with her.

"And this has been my goal." Sheffield locked eyes with Lynne. "I can see this is a struggle for you. It would be best if you learned to cope."

In a small voice, Lynne said, "It's difficult to cope with you turning him against me."

"I am not turning him against you," Sheffield shouted. "I'm turning him to God and God's work."

"Yes, you weak-willed woman," added Walter, looking at her with contempt.

Sheffield turned to Walter. "Now, son, it's not necessary to verbalize such disdain. In the long run it will not benefit you, especially having leadership over a congregation. People need to know you value them, respect them. They won't follow you if they feel you despise them. Women make up half our membership. To give them the honor they desire will be beneficial for everyone."

Walter hung on every word his father uttered. "I understand. So I should show Mom some respect?"

"It would be better and would please me."

Walter nodded but looked confused.

His father was sending mixed messages, obvious even to Isabella. It would be difficult for a child at that age to decipher what was allowed and what was forbidden. How exactly was he supposed to act around his mother? Was he to ignore her or honor her? There was a fine line being drawn for him and the rules were becoming gray and unclear. She was repulsed by Walter's change in character but also felt his bewilderment.

Sheffield stood and walked to the door. "I have work to complete in my office."

Walter got up and left right after him and the room fell silent. Lynne stayed at the table and stared at nothing in particular. She looked defeated.

Isabella's heart went out to her. If only she could say something, encourage her somehow.

Slowly Lynne stood and cleared the table, her large frame showing that the only joy left in her life was food.

Isabella turned and left the kitchen. In the hall, close to the stairs leading to the basement, she stopped and listened. The house was quiet except for the clattering of dishes from the room she'd left. Isabella didn't really want to follow Walter downstairs. His attitude was hard to stomach and being around him was becoming nearly as oppressive as being with Sheffield. She found it confounding to think that Walter was nearly her age. They were so different from each other, raised in such opposite ways that the distinction was glaring.

She looked down at the photo in her hand. There was one more picture she hadn't visited. Did she have the fortitude to continue? The next one couldn't be much worse than what she'd already witnessed. She slipped the top one to the bottom and gazed at the face staring back at her.

CHAPTER 24

The swirling slowed, the surroundings stilled and Walter's handsome figure appeared. He was absolutely breathtaking to look at, decked out in a tailored suit and tie. Isabella stood spellbound at the sight of him. She guessed he was around seventeen or eighteen. It was even more evident now that she looked like him. It was like looking at a male version of herself.

To his right, stood a young woman, his arm possessively placed around her shoulder. She was quite pretty with auburn hair pinned up in a fancy up-do and wearing a floor length, rose-colored gown. They smiled sweetly as Sheffield snapped the picture.

Isabella glanced around the room and noticed many young couples dressed in their finest. A band stood on a stage and music filled the big space of the room. Round tables fitted with crisp white tablecloths and floral arrangements filled the area. Long tables on the sides were being cleared of platters of food. A table at the end held an abundance of desserts and another table beside it had a large coffee urn, hot water urn for tea and a massive punch bowl. To her it looked like a high school graduation banquet. Tame by present-day grads, but a grad it was.

Isabella turned back to Sheffield. She noticed Lynne standing beside him and she was actually smiling. It was such an unusual sight that Isabella stared at her. The short woman was still as plump as ever but her eyes held a tinge of life now.

Isabella turned back to Sheffield as he spoke.

"It's a very special day."

Walter nodded. "I'd like to dance with my date."

"Go on. Don't let us stop you," Sheffield said.

Walter led the girl to the dance floor, held her close and they moved to the waltz, blending and flowing with the crowd there. Isabella watched in amazement. He'd dated other girls besides

Sally? The idea was revolutionary. She'd only ever considered him in connection with her mother.

The two looked good, like they belonged together. Their comfortable proximity, with his lips close to her ear, disclosed a measure of intimacy. When he whispered something, she responded with a smile of pleasure. The way she looked up at him, her eyes awash with love, spoke volumes. What could have driven them apart? It was clear they knew each other well and cared deeply.

"It can't last," said Sheffield to her right.

Isabella turned to stare at him.

"Why not?" asked Lynne.

"She'll distract him from his calling."

"That's the stupidest thing I ever heard," declared Isabella, not caring that they couldn't hear her.

Lynne said, "But he'll eventually need a wife."

"It's too soon."

"But they could date for a few years, wait until he's in his twenties and then they could marry."

"No."

"No?" asked Isabella. "Why is it always no, you dimwit?" Maybe she'd visited too many pictures where Sheffield was present. She was growing extremely disgusted with his manipulation and control.

Lynne said, "Walter really likes her. I can see it in his eyes."

"I agree. He is taken with her but that doesn't mean she's right for him."

"Why not?"

"She wouldn't make a very good wife."

Lynne stared at him dumbfounded.

Sheffield stared back. "Just consider what her mother's like."

"Lenore?"

"Yes. She's far too opinionated for my taste and verbalizes her complaints too openly. If the girl…"

"Tara."

"Yes. If Tara is anything like her mother, the match will be doomed to failure."

Lynne turned away and stared at Walter and Tara flowing with the rest of the dancers.

The two looked so happy and in love. Walter couldn't take his eyes off of her. His smile looked permanently attached to his face and they chatted freely and openly. Was this the same young man who'd been so twisted and formed by a control freak? Walter looked debonair, handsome and the finest catch in the room. Isabella noticed a number of girls casting glances his way. She couldn't blame them. He was a beautiful specimen of the male gender.

"It's a shame, I know," said Sheffield. "She is a very pretty girl."

"When will you tell him?" Lynne's voice held defeat.

That Lynne gave up so quickly galled Isabella. Why didn't she fight for her son's rights?

"I decided to wait until after the grad. I didn't want to spoil things for him."

"So you'll tell him tonight?"

"When he comes home, yes."

"He'll be devastated. He's liked her for a long, long time."

Sheffield released an impatient breath. "Yes, I know."

"What if he rebels?"

A sound of disdain squeezed between his teeth. "He wouldn't dare."

Lynne turned and looked up at him. "If he does, what would you do?"

"I'd take away all his accolades, his titles of leadership in the church. I'd strip away everything that he values, everything he's worked for."

Lynne looked away, fear filling her eyes. Nervously, she clenched her hands and rubbed them back and forth. Lines on her forehead stood out in anxious worry.

Sheffield stood tall and proud, strong resolve in his eyes as he studied Walter and Tara.

The two fell silent. The air around them was claustrophobic and stifling. Isabella left them and headed to the refreshment table. She waited there for the dance to end. As she suspected, Walter and Tara headed right for her.

Walter poured two glasses of punch and handed one to Tara. He smiled sweetly at her as their fingers brushed. He leaned in close and whispered something. She nodded and they headed for the gym doors.

Isabella followed them out into the hall. They walked to the end, around the corner and stopped by a row of lockers. Tara leaned back against them and Walter stood before her, one hand above her on the locker, supporting his weight.

"You're gorgeous tonight."

With an impish grin, she looked up into his eyes and said, "I always look gorgeous."

He chuckled and said, "Yes you do." He leaned down and placed a light kiss on her lips.

"So what happens after this?" asked Tara.

"You'll be in college."

"Yes, that's true. But I'll be staying. College in Toronto isn't that far away. I'll be commuting every day."

"And I'll be working with my father. He actually suggested I get a regular job."

"That'll be a change."

"Apparently the church can't afford two pastors, at least not yet."

"So what will you do?"

He shrugged. "I'd like to try selling real estate."

"Oh. You'd be good at that. You've got the gift of the gab. People would love you."

He smiled at her, satisfaction written on his face. "I'd have to take some training."

"You'd be good at that too. Your father trained you for the ministry and look how far you've gotten."

Tara was clearly in love with him. Her positive attitude fed his ego and she was glad to do it. Infatuation shone from her hazel eyes.

"I think I'd like the challenge."

She nodded.

A few moments of silence stretched between them, each looking into each other's eyes with longing. He reached down to kiss her again, this time with passion. Her arms snaked up around his neck and she held him close.

When they pulled away, both of them were breathless and flushed.

Walter said, "What about us?"

She smiled at him. "Yes. What about us?"

"Would you marry me?"

"Walter."

"I'm serious. We've been dating for over a year. We've known each other for years, been in the same church, serve the same God and joined the same programs and groups. We've been inseparable for as long as I remember. You're the only one for me. I want to marry you."

"It's so soon and we're so young."

"You have two years of college and I have some training to do. I need to get established as a real estate agent to be able to support you. I'm thinking in two years we'll be ready for marriage."

"Are you sure?" Tara stared at him with longing.

"I'm very sure."

"What about your father? You told me he wasn't too happy about you dating me."

"He'll grow to love you just like I have."

"You really think so?"

Walter nodded.

Uncertainty played in her eyes. "When he looks at me, I feel so naked and exposed."

"Who? My father?"

She nodded.

"That's crazy."

"I can tell he doesn't like me."

"I told you, he'll grow to love you."

"You're sure about that?"

"Yes. I'm sure." But he didn't look sure. The hesitation in his eyes gave him away.

So he already knows his father will be a hard sell. Interesting.

Isabella felt sorry for him. So many things were against him. Sheffield was determined to run his son's life, regardless of how much damage he'd cause. But if Sheffield didn't stop this relationship, Walter never would meet Sally and she'd never be born. The whole scenario was confusing and difficult to process mentally. Her heart went out to Walter and yet she was silently rooting for Sheffield, her blood-sucking vampire of a grandfather. He drained the life out of everyone around him.

"I think we should head back before my father comes looking for us." Walter held out his hand and Tara placed hers in his.

The two walked off hand in hand, Walter's shoulders not as straight and strong as they'd looked earlier. He already looked defeated.

What father went in search of his eighteen-year-old son at a grad? The idea was bizarre and completely intrusive. It was amazing that Walter hadn't rebelled yet. The iron rod with which Sheffield ruled had done its job. Over the years, Walter had been cowed into submission.

Isabella had never heard of Walter being married to anyone but Sally. Although, with the amount of information Sally revealed, there'd be no way of knowing for sure.

She made her way back to the gym. She felt a dread deep in the pit of her stomach with what she knew was coming. The cheery décor of the gym did nothing to quell the feeling.

Looking around for her family, she noticed Sheffield and Lynne seated at a table on the far side. Another set of parents sat with them and they were conversing with each other. Walter and Tara were gathered in a huddle of friends, talking and laughing.

At least he looked happy now. She'd rarely seen him that way in most of the photos. But she knew it wouldn't last. His father would see to that tonight. Oppression settled over her, a heaviness on her chest that made it hard to breathe. She had to leave.

With a flick of her wrist, the picture was turned upside down and the room unwound, disengaged and twisted into swirls of color and light.

CHAPTER 25

It took Isabella a short fifteen-minute walk to reach the Mansion of Hope. The expansive property, well-manicured yard and gorgeous, stately home, surrounded by a thick stone fence and impressive gate, always thrilled her. This is where Tessa worked, now a rehabilitation home for women caught in substance abuse. The mansion was stunning, both inside and out. Tessa gave her a tour once and Isabella was astounded at its size and beauty.

Today, Isabella had stepped inside when she arrived and spoken to the receptionist, who paged Tessa for her. She told the receptionist that she'd wait for Tessa outside, beneath the large oak tree.

It was a gorgeous fall day and Isabella loved being outdoors when the weather cooperated. A layer of colored leaves surrounded the single bench that sat beneath the extensive limbs of the century-old tree. There was still a good amount of leaves hanging on to the branches up above and she could hear birds chirping cheerfully, a peaceful spot to wait after a busy day of classes.

Tessa noticed a man in a trench coat and top hot stop on the sidewalk at the gate opening and stare at the house. He turned to look at her and nodded his head before walking on. Something about him caused a shiver to pass through her, as though she'd seen him somewhere before. She remembered a similar man in one of the pictures she'd time-traveled in and wondered what it meant.

Before long, Tessa exited the large front doors and walked towards her.

"Hi, Isabella."

"Hi."

"Should we walk today or should I get my car and drive us there?"

"Let's walk."

"Sure, the weather is perfect."

Isabella stood and they started toward downtown Chelsey. It was only a few blocks to Rena's ice cream parlor.

Once there, they stepped to the counter to order. The six booths along the window and the long order bar adjacent to the booths gave plenty of room to sit and enjoy. The checkerboard floor tile gave it a nostalgic 1960s feel and the chrome trim on the bright red tables and sit-up bar added to the bright, cheery effect. Red-and-yellow-flowered upholstered seats gave an extra zip of color to the room. Large, blown up, simple snapshots of ice cream delicacies hung on the walls to whet people's appetites. It was always fun stopping in here.

After ordering, they took a seat in one of the booths. Isabella glanced at Tessa sitting across from her. Their milkshakes in large fluted glasses sat on the table before them. The vanilla liquid was thick, rich and went down smoothly. Rena's ice cream parlor was known for its fabulous milkshakes, which made the shop very popular in town.

Tessa leaned forward, crossed her arms on the table and smiled. "We don't do this often enough."

"I know," said Isabella, still feeling unsure why Tessa insisted on this visit. Not that she minded. They spent virtually no time together except when she went over to her house to baby-sit. And then Tessa only spoke of the evening's expectation and instructions.

"I've wanted to do this for ages. Life is just so busy lately."

"It's called 'kids.'" Isabella grinned.

"You can say that again," Tessa said with a nod. "And work."

"How are they?"

"Good. They all insisted they wanted to tag along. I stood my ground and told them we were getting together after I was done work and I wasn't about to get them from school and let them join us. Cody left work early so that he could pick them up and get supper started."

"Good for you. You need a break from the rat race."

Tessa chuckled. "The crazy never ends at my house."

"I love your kids."

"It shows. They sure do adore you."

Isabella chuckled. She liked Tessa. Her way with the kids was amazing and her positive attitude infectious. She hoped she'd make as good a mother. Isabella leaned forward and asked, "So, what are we here to discuss?"

Tessa shrugged. "I just wanted to chat. I was wondering how you were. We haven't really talked in a very long time."

Isabella said, "I'm doing well."

Tessa nodded but didn't look convinced. "Any boyfriend yet?"

Isabella chortled. "No, not on your life."

"A gorgeous girl like you and not one possibility? I don't believe it."

That Tessa thought she was beautiful was bolstering. "I don't give them much to like."

"What do you mean?"

"I'm not interested and they can probably tell." She waved a hand across her clothes. "I like to hide my goods and I refuse to act like some teenage simpleton that's desperate for male attention."

Tessa smiled. "I see. But you do realize, don't you, that anyone can tell you're a knock-out beauty even with your baggy clothes?"

Isabella stared at her sister. She wasn't serious, was she? She thought she'd done an amazing job keeping everyone fooled. Tessa was saying it hadn't worked?

"Cat's got your tongue?"

"No," Isabella finally said. "It's just that I don't care about stuff like that."

"Even with many of the Youth already dating?"

Isabella shook her head.

"You're not jealous?"

She shook her head again.

Deep interest showed in Tessa's eyes. "So what do you care about?"

Isabella thought for a moment. It wasn't hard to come up with an answer, but how to verbalize it was the greater issue. After practicing the sentence a few times in her mind, she finally said, "What I really care about is finding out about my father."

Understanding lit Tessa's face. "It's really important to you, isn't it?"

"I never had the privilege of having a father, ever. Well, I guess I did when I was really little, but that doesn't count. I don't even remember it."

Tessa nodded. "My adoptive father is all I ever needed. He's a wonderful man. I love him dearly."

Isabella had to know. "So, you never tried to find out who your flesh and blood father was? You never cared about that?"

A thoughtful glow lit Tessa's face. "I've asked Sally. She has no clue who my father might be."

"Did she give you a list of names?"

"She suggested that."

"But...?"

"I declined her offer. It seemed too complicated and not important enough."

"Why isn't it important to you?"

Tessa shrugged. "I'm not sure." She pondered that question for a while. "Having a father that really loves me and has been all I ever dreamed of in a dad is probably the reason."

Isabella fell silent for a moment, processing. "I wish I had that." The compassion and concern flowing from Tessa's eyes was enough to make her cry but Isabella refused to give in to that.

"I hear Sally is dating now."

"It doesn't make sense. It's too late. I'm too old and I don't even want her to date. Not now."

"It's never too late."

"If she marries Grayson, it would change too many things. I'm used to and like our life the way it is. I don't want things shifting around."

Tessa nodded. "How about finding your father? Would you be opposed to that too?"

The question made her stare at her sister.

Does she know? Does she suspect that I've already met him? No. That's crazy. There's no way she'd know. And it's not like I've actually met him. The picture travel doesn't really count. But I have seen him, been close enough to touch him.

"How could I ever meet him? Sally refuses to reveal even one detail about him."

Tessa raised her shoulders a smidge. "That's what I used to think about my mother. I didn't see any way to connect with her. When I finally tried, sent off the paperwork to find out about her, God ended up bringing her right to me. God knows how to join the dots, bring people together."

"Sally hates him."

"Yes, I know."

"Do you know why?" Hope filled her at the possibility. And then she realized that Tessa knew a lot about Sally. Yes, Tessa had worked with Sally during her detox from drugs, before they realized they were related. There was probably a bunch Tessa knew about Walter. Sally probably revealed a whole gamut of information during that time, things from the past. Maybe she even communicated her upheaval with Walter and what led up to it.

"Maybe."

Now she felt confused. "You know but you won't tell me?"

"I can't. It's part of our work agreement. We can't divulge client information with anyone on the outside. It's called client/staff confidentiality."

Isabella reached across the table and gripped Tessa's hands. "Please tell me. I have to know."

Tessa shook her head emphatically. "I absolutely can't, Isabella. I'm sorry."

She released her sister's hands and slumped back to her side in defeat. "I need to know something."

The compassion in Tessa's eyes was real but so was her resolve.

Isabella leaned forward again. "Do you know his name?" She wasn't about to admit that she'd found out too.

After a deep breath and heavy sigh, Tessa said, "Yes."

"I thought so."

"Look, Isabella, I can't give you the information you long for. Only Sally can do that for you."

"She refuses."

"Then ask God."

"Ask him what?"

"To reveal it to you."

"You think he'd do that?"

"His ways are so much higher than our ways. He's not limited to our puny efforts. I should know."

"What do you mean?"

"He's redirected my life in some amazing ways."

Isabella wasn't sure what that meant. The confusion must have shown because Tessa smiled. Isabella said, "You'll need to explain."

"I was a bit older than you when God took me back in time and showed me things, things that changed my mindset, my direction in life."

Shock hit Isabella like a punch in the gut and she broke out in an immediate sweat. Her heart pounded frantically in her rib cage and it felt ready to explode. Why had she never heard this before? The revelation was astounding. Her sister had also gone back in time? What were the chances of that?

"Are you okay?" asked Tessa.

"I'm not sure."

"I know it sounds far-fetched and unbelievable, but it truly did happen to me."

The safest thing was to keep Tessa talking. Maybe that would hide her anxious thoughts. "Could you tell me about it?"

"Sure," Tessa said with a slight shrug. "It happened at the Mansion of Hope, before it was called that. Back then it was an old abandoned mansion, decrepit and falling apart. I was with two of my good friends, Luke and Richelle. Luke dared us girls to go in and he finally talked us into it. The moment we crossed a certain line on the yard, past that old oak tree in the front, we traveled back in time and the mansion was restored to its original magnificence, fully occupied."

Isabella listened in rapt attention as her sister unveiled her experiences in the mansion. Tessa went on for some time, elaborating on what she'd experienced there. Hearing of the inhabitants' struggles and pain, things that transpired so many years ago, touched her even now. To realize that the elaborate mansion had eventually been abandoned and left to rot was hard to comprehend.

And then to know that God had used that place to soften Tessa's heart for those in heart-rending situations amazed her. If God hadn't changed Tessa's heart, there was no way she'd have ended up serving those addicted and in bondage to substances. There was no way God could have connected her with Sally. Well, maybe he still could have brought them together but it wouldn't have been God's best.

Tessa shared about a trench-coated, top-hat-wearing angel that was involved in orchestrating every time travel at the mansion. As soon as she spoke of it, goose bumps formed all over Isabella's arms. She'd seen that very man today at the mansion. Or was it an angel? Could it be? Isabella tried to hide her shock and listened until Tessa was done.

When Tessa ended her story, she sighed heavily and stared at Isabella in expectation. "So, what do you think?"

"I know what I should say."

"And what's that?"

"That you're completely off your rocker."

"I don't particularly like rockers."

Isabella couldn't stop the crooked grin. "The story's amazing. A little unbelievable but it is amazing." She knew it didn't feel unbelievable at all. It touched her deeply and resonated strongly with her own experiences.

"I understand." Tessa gave a slight nod. "I don't share my story with very many people. I get funny responses."

"But I believe you."

"Thanks."

"So you think God could do that for me?"

"It's only one way. God's creative. He can get you the information that he needs you to have."

"What if he decides I can live without my dad?"

"Would you be okay with that?"

"No."

"Then ask him and see what he does."

"I already have." As soon as the words left her lips she regretted it. It was saying too much.

"And... has he shown you anything?"

That was the expected question. How would she answer it? "Not enough." That sounded safe without lying.

"Well, he will. He'll show you exactly what you need to know. He knows you better than you know yourself. He also knows your father inside out. Divine connections are a specialty of his."

"You really think God could get us together somehow?"

"Yes, I do."

"Even with Sally's determination to keep us apart?"

"Sally's afraid of a lot of things. Why don't we both pray that God will help Sally overcome her fears?"

Isabella nodded. It sounded like a great idea. She thought Tessa meant to pray later but she reached forward and grabbed her hands, nodded her head and prayed. Isabella joined her with bowed head and waited until the prayer was over. Tessa looked at her, gave her hands a squeeze and let go.

Talk turned to other things, safer subjects. Tessa shared about the kids, their school adventures, extra-curricular activities and Hope's amusing stories. She also shared about her work at the Mansion of Hope. It was fascinating. Tessa's world delved into the darkness of substance abuse, setting women free. It felt like an alternate world hidden away in this life, which so few people were privileged to view.

After an hour of interesting conversation, Tessa stood and grabbed her coat. "I have to go. Faith will be done her soccer practice soon. Cody was going to drop her off but I promised to pick her up on my way home."

"Sure." Isabella stood and slipped into her jacket.

Tessa said, "I really enjoyed this. We should do it more often, sis."

"Thanks for suggesting this. I enjoyed it too."

Tessa smiled and said, "I'll take care of the bill."

"Thanks." She reached for Tessa and gave her a warm hug.

They chatted as they walked back to the Mansion of Hope. Tessa was easy to talk to and Isabella felt so loved and cared for by her older sister.

"Do you want a ride home?" Tessa asked as they got back to the mansion.

"No. I like walking."

"Okay."

Tessa headed toward the back of the huge house where her car was parked. Isabella turned and headed for home. It was only a few blocks from there. Agreeing to go for milkshakes with Tessa had turned out to be a providential meeting. She'd learned so much and felt a special kinship with her sister, more than ever before. The fact that they shared time travel was uncanny. She never knew that before. It brought a warmth and comfort to her insides and made her picture travel feel less ominous and frightening. What if it truly was God's doing and he was exposing exactly what she needed to know, in answer to her prayers? She felt more confident of that than ever before.

CHAPTER 26

Isabella was fuming. Grayson Kendal had talked Sally into taking them both for lunch after church.

Isabella had noticed them chatting again in the lobby after the service and was relieved when Sally finally motioned that it was time to go. As soon as they exited the church building, Sally dumped the news on her, as if she'd be thrilled for the opportunity to have lunch with him. What was her mother thinking?

That Sally gave in so quickly, giving up their one day together to include Grayson was infuriating. Isabella knew she was sulking but couldn't stop it. Fury simmered just below her controlled exterior, as she sat in the passenger seat while her mother drove out of the church yard.

Sally glanced at her several times. Isabella avoided eye contact and chose to study the buildings rushing by instead.

"You don't mind, do you?" Sally finally asked.

"Whatever."

"Oh, so you do mind."

Isabella raised a hand and let it drop. "Let's just get this over with so I can hang out with Abby and Shana." She could feel Sally's eyes boring into the back of her head but she refused to turn around.

"But Sunday afternoons are for us; we have no other time together. You never make plans with Abby and Shana on Sundays."

The pleading in her mother's tone further irritated her. It was entirely hypocritical in her mind. "I always thought Sundays were for us too, until now."

That silenced Sally. After a few minutes, she said, "I'm sorry."

Isabella refused to answer.

"I didn't know how to say no to him. He's been very patient with me and he really is a very nice man."

Nice? My foot. He's old and I don't want him around.

"Isabella, please give him a chance. I think you'll grow to like him. He really wants to get to know you."

Isabella turned and stared at her mother. "You're not serious?"

"Why wouldn't I be?"

"You're thinking of providing a *daddy* at this point in my life."

"I thought that's what you've always wanted."

She released a frustrated breath. "You don't know anything."

Sally puzzled quietly for a few minutes.

Isabella could see the restaurant sign up ahead. It was some kind of cheap family restaurant that served an abundance of chicken. This was quite the way to impress a potential future daughter. The thought made her cringe.

With an edge to her voice, Sally said, "What do you want then?"

Isabella glared at her. "I want you to tell me about my *real* father."

Sally was already shaking her head. It was the usual response and only made Isabella angrier.

"I can't do that," said Sally.

"It has nothing to do with can't. You simply won't."

"You'd hate me if I did."

"I hate you because you don't."

Sally looked at her and then focused on turning into the restaurant parking lot. After parking the car, Sally turned to her and said, "You don't know him like I do. It's best for everyone if he stays away."

A frustrated rush of air escaped Isabella's lips. "Since you won't tell me about my father, let's go inside and get to know this wonderful chap called Grayson." Her voice dripped with sarcasm but she didn't care.

"Why are you so angry?"

"You should know how it feels to be angry. You spent years hating your mother." Isabella said, grabbing the door handle and swinging it wide. She'd said too much again, revealing she knew about Sally's past, but at the moment she didn't care.

Sally got out of the car and stared at Isabella over the car roof. "And how would you know about that?"

Isabella shook her head and shrugged her shoulders dispassionately. "You must have mentioned it."

"I don't recall mentioning it." Sally slammed the door shut and walked around to the back of the car.

They met up as they walked to the restaurant. Sally reached out to touch Isabella's arm and they both stopped. "Please be kind. This means a lot to me. I meant to spend the rest of the day with you, honestly I did. And I'm sorry if I've angered you. That was not my intent. Please let's not spoil the day by fighting."

Guilt assailed her heart. How could she stay at odds with the only family she had? Her mother was her life. If only Grayson Kendal would crawl back into the hole he came from, then everything would be all right. Not wanting to share her mother was definitely revealing her selfish side. Maybe that's what it was. Selfishness was rearing its ugly head and she didn't know how to curb its advance.

With a nod of her head, she said, "I'll try to be civil."

"Thank you."

The relief in Sally's eyes was enough to make Isabella kick herself. Why couldn't she be sweeter, kinder, less self-absorbed? She supposed being a teenager allowed for some grace in developing character but it also revealed the lack of it as well. She promised herself she'd try harder. But she was still dreading lunch.

~~~~~

At home at last. Isabella left her mother in the entrance and headed upstairs immediately. She could feel Sally's eyes on her back as she took the steps two at a time. She just wanted to get away by herself. If she talked, she'd only say things she'd regret later.

On the drive home, Sally had grilled her. What do you think of him? Do you feel comfortable around him? Isn't he easy to talk to? The questions were annoying and difficult. She'd been in no mood to talk about Grayson. Walter - that's whom she wanted to discuss.

Sprawled on her bed and staring up at her ceiling, she didn't know what to think. It was clear that Sally was falling for Grayson. The pain around Isabella's heart told her how scared she was. How could this be happening just when she was beginning to learn about her real father? It seemed so unfair, cruel even. She wanted nothing to do with Grayson Kendal. Oh sure, he was nice enough.

His smile told her he was kind and he really didn't look too old. He dressed nicely, if not as stylishly as her mother. That he treated Sally well was obvious. He opened doors for her, waited until she was seated before sitting himself, gave preference to her in everything and lavished her with eyes full of interest and concern. What woman her mother's age wouldn't fall for such treatment? And Sally had been lonely for a long time.

That thought made her angry again. Wasn't she enough for her mother? But then that was being selfish again. Her head hurt from thinking things through. She felt so confused and didn't know how to make it stop.

A light knock on the door made her turn that way. "What?" It was impossible to keep the irritation out of her curt reply.

The door opened a bit and her mother's face appeared. "Are you all right?"

"I don't know."

"You want to talk about it?"

"No, not really."

Sally walked in anyway. "I'd like to talk."

"As long as you don't ask any more questions."

"Okay." Sally sat down at the edge of Isabella's bed and looked at her. "I love you."

It was her customary statement. "I love you too," responded Isabella.

"I hate it when you're mad at me."

The lost look in Sally's eyes made Isabella's insides twist. She just nodded in response.

"It's true, you know. I spent most of my teenage years hating my mother."

Isabella didn't respond, didn't look at her mother. It was still too difficult. She grabbed one of her throw pillows from her bed and played with the ruffled edge.

Sally sighed and said, "Now I know a bit of what I put her through. I actually hated her for many, many years. I made life very difficult for her."

"Why were you so hard on her?"

Sally shrugged. "We never saw things eye to eye. We were always at odds with each other. I felt she didn't like me very much and I certainly didn't like her for a very long time."

"What does that have to do with us?" asked Isabella without looking at her.

"I don't want us to be that way."

"Then stop seeing Grayson." She felt like a heel for saying it. Her selfishness needed some serious reining in. Why did it feel so impossible?

"That's what you truly want?"

"You know what I want."

"You're angry because I won't tell you about your father." It was more of a statement than anything else.

She looked at Sally then, wondering if she'd had a change of mind.

"When I think about him, whenever you ask me about him, I start feeling light-headed, like I'm about to choke and faint." Sally put a hand to her heart and turned pale.

"But why?"

She shook her head in a sad sort of way. "I just can't talk about him. I'm too terribly afraid to."

"Is it because he hurt you so much?"

With a small, uncertain shrug, she said, "I'm not sure if that's what it is."

"You think he'll hurt me too?"

"Maybe." The concern in Sally's eyes made Isabella take pause and wonder.

"But we won't know for sure unless we try."

"Try what?" Sally asked with misgiving in her eyes.

"Contact him, speak with him, find out where he is and maybe suggest meeting somewhere."

A look of sheer terror slid over Sally's face and her breathing suddenly sounded labored. "No, absolutely not."

Isabella marveled at her mother's state. The woman was scared spitless. "Why are you so afraid?"

Sally shrugged.

"Did you even listen to a word Pastor Chad said this morning?"

Sally stared at her with confusion.

"He talked about faith in God, how faith and fear don't mix. With one we believe God and with the other we believe the lies of the enemy. He called fear 'contaminated faith.' Fear will stop God's power from operating. Our faith in the enemy renders God unable to act on our behalf." Isabella felt like a little preacher, but her mother needed some talking to.

Sally remained quiet, clearly battling to gain control over her emotions.

"Mom, do you really believe God would let anything bad happen to me?"

"I don't know," she said in a small voice. "I don't trust your father."

"That's quite obvious. But do you trust your Heavenly Father? I'm really questioning that at the moment."

Sally looked unsure. "I'm trying to."

"It's not a very believable effort."

"I know." Sally gazed at her hands in her lap, clearly undone by the conversation.

Isabella felt bad for reprimanding her mother's panicked state but she couldn't sit idly by letting Sally be overwhelmed by fear. It had to be stopped.

"I suppose I should put into practice what I hear, huh?"

Isabella nodded in response. Her mother was her rock, her one stable influence. To see her so shaken was disconcerting.

"I'll try to trust God more."

"What about my father?"

"I'll work on that, getting over my fear, that is. You'll have to give me some time."

"Will you let me meet him?"

"Not now."

Isabella knew it was time to back off. Sally's eyes were glazing over again with a film of horror. "Okay."

After a few minutes, Sally gained control again. "I'll give you some space." She stood and went to the door. Turning, she asked, "So, your friends are coming over later?"

"Yeah, they'll be here soon."

"Could you spare the evening for your mother?"

Isabella smiled at her. "Yes, I'll let them know they need to leave for the evening."

"Thanks." She left and closed the door.

CHAPTER 27

Abby and Shana stopped by the house at three and Isabella let them in. They stepped inside in the throes of a discussion, an argument in full bloom.

"What's going on?" asked Isabella. "What's the issue?"

Shana rolled her eyes in frustration. "It's Abby. She's so full of herself that it stinks."

"I am not, Shana. Take that back." Abby's eyes were large and defensive. "Just because I have a boyfriend and you don't doesn't mean I'm full of myself."

"See," stated Shana, pointing at Abby. "She won't stop rubbing it in."

"I can't help it if you're jealous. That's not my problem. If I could get Mark to take an interest in you, I'd help you out."

"See what I mean," declared Shana, crossing her arms. "She thinks she's the only one who can get a guy interested. She thinks I can't even do that on my own."

"That's not what I said," insisted Abby. "I'm just saying I'm willing to help."

"And what could you do?"

"I could put a buzz in his ear, let him know you like him."

Shana suddenly looked deflated, the fight out of her. "I heard he asked Blair out yesterday. They went to see a movie together."

They made their way into the living room and sat down. Isabella and Shana sat on the couch together and Abby was across from them on the love seat.

Abby's face fell at the news. "I'm sorry, Shana."

Isabella reached out and placed her arm around her friend. "I'm sorry too."

"Whatever. Mark wouldn't know a gem even if it's shining directly in his face."

"That's right. That's what you are," agreed Isabella.

"A tall, gangly gem, that's what I am."

"Hey, that rhymes," said Abby. "We should make it into a song."

Shana grinned. Her eyes locked on Abby and waited.

"Let me think. We have to include Mark's name somehow."

Isabella thought for a moment and then held up a finger. "How about, 'Mark's a handsome hunk, my heart is surely sunk...'" That's all she could muster. She'd already run out of ideas.

Shana laughed and then said, "And next would be, 'He never sees the gold in me, another woman holds the key...'"

Abby slapped her thigh and said, "I know, I know what should come next. 'His heart is being led astray, by a luster-less piece of clay.'"

"That's sounds somewhat corny," said Shana. "And mean."

"What does it matter? It's not like anyone's actually going to hear this song."

"Okay. Then we need the other part," said Shana. "I'm a tall, gangly gem, but a gem is what I am." She grinned real big and said, "And then we could add, If Mark could only see, he'd be mesmerized by me."

Isabella continued with the theme, "Then..., 'And though I'm tall as a tree, he's taller and perfect, you see.'"

"Hey, you," protested Shana.

"It's true," said Abby.

"And it rhymes," added Isabella.

Abby and Shana both stared at her and shook their heads.

Shana said, "It doesn't fit with the song."

"Let's try saying it all together," suggested Isabella.

They did but struggled to get the words right. Abby finally wrote it down on a piece of paper and the three huddled together on the couch so they could all see. They decided they actually had two verses and they also came up with a simple chorus. They practiced finding the right melody and getting the words down pat. Finally, after half an hour, they actually sounded pretty good, at least to their ears.

Although their musical ability could be debated, at least their words matched now and the tune was quite catchy.

'Mark's a handsome hunk, my heart is surely sunk.

He never sees the gold in me; another woman holds the key.
His heart is being led astray by a lusterless piece of clay.

I'm a tall and gangly gem, but a gem is what I am.
If Mark could only see, he'd be mesmerized by me.
And though I'm tall as a tree, he's taller and perfect, you see.

I am a gem. Yes that is what I am.
I am a gem. Yes, that is what I am.
Oh I am a gem. Yes, that is what I am.'

Abby suggested, "Hey, you two. We should suggest doing a special number for Youth next Friday. We could get Connor to play the guitar for us. It would be epic."

Shana giggled. "Wouldn't Mark be shocked?"

"He'd know then," said Isabella. "He'd have a fit."

Shana said, "He's so clueless, he wouldn't even know the song was about him."

Abby's nose scrunched up. "Isn't there an old song like that?"

"Yes," said Isabella, "but it's actually about someone thinking the song is about them.

"Oh," Abby said. She giggled then. "I love the song we made up."

"I love it too," Sally's voice came from the entrance to the kitchen.

All three girls turned in unison. "Mom," shouted Isabella, "did you hear the whole thing?"

"It's quite entertaining."

"Oh no," exclaimed Shana. "You can't say a word to his mother."

Sally chuckled. "I promise I won't."

"You weren't supposed to eavesdrop."

"It's hard not to when your voices are projecting through the whole house."

Well, that was true. They weren't exactly trying to hide it

"Would you girls like some ice cream? I just went out to buy some Haagen Dazs and it's sitting on the counter. I bought caramel cone, chocolate almond and blackberry cabernet."

"Yes!" all three shouted in agreement. They followed Sally into the kitchen, eager for an afternoon snack. Having stretched their creative juices to come up with a perfect musical parody, they were ready for some energy food.

Later, in Isabella's room, the three girls lounged on the floor and decided on a game of cards.

Shana was the first to bring up the subject. "What's been happening with the picture travel? Anything interesting?"

After taking a deep breath of air and exhaling slowly, Isabella said, "It's been difficult."

"How and why?" asked Abby. "Because we were really hoping we could join you today."

Isabella's heart sank. There was no way she was taking them with her. The pictures were revealing far too much for her liking. She wasn't ready to expose her father in that way. And her mother was home. It was way too risky. She said, "I've learned things about my father that bothers me a lot. It's explained a bunch of stuff already, stuff I've always questioned. But it's been hard to go back and watch."

"Like what?" asked Shana, her face full of curiosity.

Isabella shrugged. "How he was raised and manipulated by a terrible father to be a certain person."

"So it's all bad?" asked Abby, concern in her eyes.

"It sure isn't good."

"How did his father raise him?" asked Abby.

Isabella felt uncertain. How much did she dare reveal? Would they end up hating him before she even found him? She didn't want that. He deserved a fair trial, at least in her mind. Sally would differ on that point, she was sure of it.

"Isabella?" Shana brought her back to the present.

"His father was a pastor of a church and he dominated everyone and everything. He was also very overbearing in his own home. He made sure he trained my dad to follow in his footsteps."

"So he was cruel and ordered people around?" Shana asked.

"It was more how he treated my grandmother. That bothered me the most."

"What is she like?" asked Abby.

"She is unimpressive, sad, unhappy, submissive and always obedient."

"She sounds incredibly dull," admitted Abby.

"I feel sorry for her," said Isabella.

"Why didn't she ever fight back?"

Isabella shrugged. "She learned not to."

"So, he was mean and cruel," stated Shana.

"He knew how to get people to do what he wanted. His character was very strong and controlling."

"Is he still alive?" asked Abby.

That made Isabella stop and think. "I have no idea."

"What has your mom said about him?"

"Nothing."

"Not a single thing?"

"No."

The room grew silent. The consistent secrecy concerning her father's side of the family was showing itself to be unbearable. There were so many things Isabella didn't know that it still angered her.

"And you know nothing about your grandmother either?" asked Abby. "You know, whether she's still living?"

Isabella shrugged.

"Humph," Abby grunted. "Sure makes me wonder what his family got into. It must be a huge embarrassment for your mom."

"All I know is that I have to find out, no matter what."

"But you won't take us with you?" complained Shana, disappointment in her eyes.

"I can't. It's difficult enough finding things out without having to try to explain it to the two of you. I don't understand it myself."

"We won't make you explain it. We understand that you're just finding out about him."

"Yeah, Isabella. Let us come, please?" begged Abby.

"Not today, not with Sally at home."

"Then when?"

Isabella gazed at Shana. "I don't know."

"Promise us you'll let us go with you sometime," demanded Abby.

"I can't promise that." Isabella felt bad but she couldn't give them anything definitive. She wasn't so sure she'd go back again herself. The picture travel was complex enough without involving others.

Both of them looked at her as if she'd abandoned them.

"You're not much of a friend," grumped Shana.

"That's not fair, Shana. It took a lot of courage for me to show you anything at all."

Shana turned to Abby and said, "We shouldn't pressure her too much. She's under enough stress as it is."

"You always take her side."

"Well, look at her. She's completely torn." Shana looked at Isabella for confirmation.

"I'll let you know, okay. I just can't make a promise today. Yesterday was way too tough."

"All right. It's something I suppose." Abby picked up her hand of cards and made a play.

The afternoon flew by and soon it was time for the girls to leave. Isabella breathed a sigh of relief as she closed the door behind them. She'd enjoyed their company but lately their presence brought unneeded pressure, pressure she could do without.

CHAPTER 28

The week scurried by and Isabella found her school schedule all-consuming with tests, assignments and group projects. By the time Friday rolled around, she was too exhausted to think of going to Youth group. Instead, Abby and Shana were coming over to work on a project the three of them were doing together.

Sally was going out with Grayson again. When she found out Isabella was skipping Youth, she wasn't happy about the decision.

As Sally stood in the kitchen with crossed arms, Isabella felt defensive. "Why is it so important that I attend every Friday?"

"It's what we do," Sally said emphatically.

"No, it's what I do. You go out on a date every Friday."

Frustration played in Sally's eyes.

Isabella said, "I know why you're upset. You want me to go to Youth so you won't feel guilty about going out with Grayson."

"Don't, Isabella."

"Don't what?"

"Don't analyze me. It's infuriating."

"Is that what I'm doing?"

Sally didn't answer. The anger in her eyes was enough of an answer.

"Look, Mom. I've had a hectic week, I'm tired and I still have this stupid project to do. Abby and Shana's mothers let them come over; they let them miss Youth. What's the big deal?"

"It's just not right. You could have worked on this thing tomorrow afternoon or evening. Why did you have to choose Friday night?"

She shrugged. "I don't know. It just seemed smart to get it out of the way."

The doorbell rang and, with a weary sigh, Sally turned and walked to the entrance.

Before Sally got to the door, Isabella asked, "Where are you going?"

"Out for dinner," she said without turning back.

"Have fun." Isabella was in no mood to greet Grayson or attempt to be civil. She stayed seated at the kitchen table sipping her tea. Her friends would arrive soon and then she'd get up and moving.

Shana and Abby showed up half an hour after Sally left. Later, at 8:30, they were nearly done their social project and decided to stop. What they had left, they could complete individually and compile on Monday morning at school before it was due.

After gathering up all the information, papers and graphs, Abby turned to Isabella and asked, "Have you given the picture travel any more thought? Will you take us with you?"

Isabella stared at her friend. "What, like tonight?"

"Yeah."

Shana glanced at the two as she stuffed her things into her back pack.

"I'm not sure."

Abby asked, "What picture were you planning to visit next?"

"I haven't decided."

"We could help you decide," suggested Shana, standing to her feet.

"There's not a lot of time." Sally'd be back soon and there was no way Isabella would take the risk of being discovered up in the attic surrounded by pictures she was forbidden to see.

"Just one picture is all we're asking for. It won't take that long," said Abby, her eyes pleading.

"Please," begged Shana. "It's been weeks since we've gone on an adventure."

"It's not just an adventure to me."

"We know that," insisted Abby.

"I don't consider the picture anomaly playtime. It's all wrapped around my past."

Shana released a sigh of frustration. "We know, Isabella. We're you're friends. Don't you trust us?"

Yes, she did trust them. They hadn't let any information slip since the last time travel. Perhaps she was being too cautious, too afraid of the 'what ifs'. "Okay," she finally said with a sigh, uncertainty still playing at the back of her mind.

"Awesome," shouted Abby.

"Great," agreed Shana.

With some trepidation, Isabella led them to the hall and to where the attic access stood above them.

Isabella took the pole, looped the hook through the metal ring on the ceiling and pulled the opening down, unfolded it, set the base on the floor and straightened the ladder. It looked more like an extremely steep set of steps

She led the way up and her friends followed. Walking over to the far corner, she uncovered the insulation and pulled out the shoe boxes. Shana stooped down to take two of them and Isabella carried the other two over to the light.

They sat cross-legged in a circle with the boxes in the middle. Isabella reached for the safest one, the one with pictures predominantly of her mother. She wasn't ready to reveal her father to them. Lifting off the lid, she scanned the pictures, moving them around to check for ones that looked safe.

One picture caught her attention. She was sitting in a highchair, a cupcake in front of her with two lit candles sticking out from it. Her big, blue eyes were rounder than usual, focused on the flickering flames. She looked so small and adorable. Holding the picture up for her friends to see, she asked, "How about this one?"

Shana shrugged broadly and said, "Sure."

"Just one?" asked Abby.

"It's all the time we have. I really don't know when Sally will be home."

The two girls scooted in close to Isabella and held onto her arms on either side. Isabella looked down at the picture and studied it carefully. The room began to shift and move in violent patterns. The mirage and blending of colors caused dizziness and disorientation. Abby and Shana also came undone beside her, their frames shooting through the room in various directions until they were indistinguishable.

The experience of seeing her friends merge with the kaleidoscopic panorama was frightening. It was a good thing she knew she'd see them on the other side of this or else she'd be tempted to turn the picture face down right now. With terrific speed, everything blended to obscurity, slowed and stopped. The colorful display then twisted backward at an accelerated rate until it too diminished and came to rest.

Two-year-old Isabella appeared out of the confusion and the highchair came into focus. The light converged to the flames on the candles over the cupcake and flickered there. The room gave a small shudder and then everything stilled.

This room wasn't in Sally and Walter's apartment. Isabella knew that immediately. The furniture was recognizable and the familiar dining room brought back a surge of memories. She was standing in her grandparents' home, Vern and Melody Windsor. The wall art was the initial giveaway. A large oil painting of Grandma's favorite artist hung on the wall. Isabella had always loved the garden scene painting. Thomas Kinkade was the artist and his creations all exuded the same quality of serenity.

It was obviously close to Christmas. Having a December birthday insured a Christmas tree close by. Over in the other room the bright lights of the tree twinkled off and on.

Isabella looked first to her right and then to her left. Yes, Abby and Shana had made it here with her. She breathed a sigh of relief and then looked to see who took the picture. Grandma Windsor held the camera in her hands.

Grandma turned to Sally, sitting by the table and said, "Go and stand beside the highchair. I'll take a picture of the two of you."

It was then that Isabella saw her grandfather sitting at the table with Sally, a small smile on his lips and his arms crossed. He looked better, not as red-cheeked as the last time she'd seen him. His eyes weren't bloodshot and he appeared to be sober. This was a good sign. She was grateful for that.

Sally walked over to the high chair. Bending down close to Isabella's cheek, she looked at Grandma and waited for the picture to be taken. The absence of joy on her face seemed out of place at a birthday party. Sally's eyes looked sad and vacant. After the camera snapped, she headed back to her chair without a word and twirled her cup, causing the ice to clink against the glass. Grandma sat down close to the high chair and helped Isabella with her cupcake.

"Now doesn't this look good, Isabella?"

"Ummy. Isy wan it."

"Yes, it's yummy."

"Aw. Isn't that cute?" said Abby to her right.

"Just adorable," agreed Shana

Isabella elbowed both of them. "Stop it and just listen." It was embarrassing enough having them see her as a toddler without them making comments.

Sally sipped at her cold drink. Her father served her a plate with a cupcake but she didn't touch it. The concern in his eyes for her was obvious.

The conversation at the table focused around Isabella eating her cupcake. Sally didn't bother participating.

"She's so beautiful," said Vern. "I'm so proud of my granddaughter."

"And she's a mess," exclaimed Melody. "Look at your dirty face, baby girl."

"Dity." Isabella held up her chocolate covered hands and grinned.

"Very dirty," agreed Grandma.

"Ummy."

"Was it yummy?"

"Uh-huh." Isabella nodded vigorously.

That made Grandma chuckle.

"She's a smart one," said Grandpa with a grin.

"I smart," agreed Isabella, staring at Grandpa.

"And it's your birthday. How old are you?"

Grandma was busy wiping down Isabella's face and hands with a damp cloth at the moment. As soon as she finished, Isabella held up a hand with two fingers raised.

"I two," she shouted.

"How old are you?" asked Grandpa again.

"I two," she yelled even louder.

This produced a small, fleeting smile on Sally's face. Her morose gaze returned promptly.

"Did you want to play with your new toys now?"

"Uh-huh." Isabella squirmed in her high chair restraints, struggling to get up.

"Now, just a minute. Let me help you," said Grandma, standing and unclasping the buckle around Isabella's waist. "There. Now stand up, baby girl."

Isabella stood and then stared at her grandmother. "I not a baby. I two." She held up her two fingers again to prove her point.

Grandma smiled at her and nodded. "Yes, you are two and getting to be so big."

A pleased grin spread across Isabella's face and she nodded emphatically. "I big."

Grandma Windsor lifted her out of the seat and set her feet firmly on the floor. Isabella raced off to the corner to a new, bright pink push car with purple trim. She swung one leg over, sat down, turned it around and pushed herself around the room, making car noises the best she could.

"That is so adorable," said Abby. "You were so cute when you were two."

Isabella looked at her friend in disgust. "Can you please control yourself?"

"How can we when you look so sweet?" agreed Shana.

Grandpa's comment turned their attention back to the table. With a shake of his head, he said, "Walter sure messed things up for himself. I bet he'd give anything to be here with his daughter right now on her second birthday." His crossed arms rested on the table.

That brought a low, disgusted grunt from Sally. "He couldn't care less about Isabella. All he's ever cared for is himself, his reputation, job, career, position. He never did love her."

Grandpa's eyes showed his shock. "That can't be. How could he not love her?"

"He never did," Sally said with dead eyes.

"He must have loved her in his own, strange way," debated Grandma.

"By not spending a lick of time with her? By not holding her? Yes, it was strange all right. He hardly ever saw her and when he did, he wouldn't even look at her."

"But she needs her daddy," insisted Grandpa.

With a snicker of disdain, Sally said, "She's better off without him."

"She has no choice now," said Grandma.

"I hope he rots in jail." The vehemence in Sally's voice was appalling. There was dark revenge in her eyes.

"I wonder what his sentence will be." Grandpa rubbed his chin.

Grandma sighed and then said, "They usually don't give sex offenders much time in the slammer."

"It makes me sick," Sally said in disgust. "They need to lock him up and throw away the key."

Isabella could hardly breathe. The room felt tight and suffocating. Her father was a sex offender? He served a prison sentence? The shock was more than she could take. The gasps coming from her friends beside her told her they were learning far more than what she'd planned on revealing.

Grandpa reached over and rubbed Sally's back in comfort. She allowed it for a time. Grandpa said, "I wish I could take away all the pain you've been through."

"I did it to myself. I married another louse. If only we hadn't had a daughter. How will I ever protect her from this garbage?"

Vern and Melody didn't respond. Sally's question had rendered them speechless.

Sally said, "Moving away is one answer. If he ever does get out of prison, he'll never know where we are. I'll make sure family never lets the information out of the bag. If he ever writes, don't you dare tell him anything. I'll warn Robert too and anyone else Walter might ask."

"If he doesn't love Isabella, why would he try to reconnect?" asked Grandfather.

The words made Isabella's heart hurt intensely. Was it really true? Her father hated her?

"He'll try to get back to me. In his demented state, he thinks he still loves me. According to him, we belong together for life. It's what Sheffield's church always taught: marriage is for life." With a look of complete repugnance, Sally said, "If I never see him again, it'll be too soon. And I'll never let him near Isabella ever again. I swear that on my life."

The intensity of Sally's eyes and the force of her vow spooked Isabella. Seeing her mother so angry and bitter, so full of vengeful hate, astounded her.

"Wow, she really hates him," said Abby beside her.

Isabella ignored her.

"You'll need to forgive him, Sally," said Grandma. "You'll only destroy yourself with all your hate."

"He doesn't deserve to be forgiven," Sally shouted.

"I know. He deserves jail."

"He deserves death."

"Don't we all?"

"Stop it, Mother," demanded Sally. "Don't turn it spiritual. I've had enough spiritual for a lifetime, enough religion to last for eternity. I'm done with it all."

That silenced Grandma.

Grandpa was still rubbing Sally's back but she shrugged him off and stood.

"You're not leaving, are you?" asked Vern.

"I need some strong coffee." Sally headed for the kitchen and returned shortly, carrying a steaming cup.

"I believe that God still loves him, Sally."

Sally stared daggers at her mother.

"I know, I know. I'm supposed to shut up but I just can't. If Walter repents, God would forgive him. How can we do any less?" argued Melody.

"Do you have any idea how hurtful your words are? Do you realize how Walter has crushed my heart and my trust? Do you even care how I feel?" Sally's eyes misted over.

"I do care. My heart has been broken for you. I've cried many times over the whole situation and begged God for mercy for both of you."

"For both of us? Walter's the one who needs mercy. The lying, cheating idiot is the one in need of mercy. I'm sure he'll be crying for mercy sitting in jail."

"And you need God's mercy so you can heal."

"I don't need to heal. All I need is to get away from him and never see him again."

The room fell silent once more.

Isabella didn't know what to think. To see her mother this way was heartbreaking. She'd never known that Walter put her through so much. No wonder Sally refused to talk about him. She'd vowed to keep him away from her and she'd done just that.

Grandpa said, "Sally, I wish you didn't have to move away. We'll miss both of you like crazy."

Sally didn't answer for a while. After a heavy sigh, she said, "It's for the best. I need a new start. To get away from here, from all the memories will be best for me right now."

"What about Isabella?" asked Grandma. "She'll miss us very much."

"And we'll miss her," added Grandpa.

"It can't be helped. I have to do this. If I'm to stay sane, I have to leave Toronto behind."

Grandpa nodded in understanding. Grandma wiped away some tears. Little Isabella had done the loop through the kitchen around to the living room and back to the dining room a handful of times. She stopped, bumped into Grandma's chair and looked up at her with her big, round eyes.

"Why you cry, Gamma?"

Grandma smiled sadly and gazed at Isabella. "Because I want you to stay here always."

"Okay," she said brightly. "I stay."

"Come here, precious girl." Grandma patted her lap and Isabella left her ride-on car and flew into her arms. Grandma held her tightly and Isabella hugged back, resting her head on her shoulder. "I wish you could stay."

"You're just making it harder on yourself," said Sally. "We can't stay."

Grandma looked at Sally. "I know."

"We come back," Isabella said, lifting herself away from Grandma's shoulder and looking at everyone.

"Of course you'll come back," said Grandpa.

"I'll come when I can," stated Sally. "It won't be easy at first. I'll need to establish myself in the fashion industry somewhere else. The details of getting settled will be very consuming."

"Then we'll come visit you," Grandpa said decisively.

"I'd like that."

"Me too," Isabella said with a grin.

Grandma hugged her tightly again.

"So, I take it, you're not staying for the court proceedings?" asked Grandpa.

"Definitely not."

"What if they need you to testify?"

"I already spoke with my lawyer. They have plenty of evidence and many people from the church to testify against him. With all the young girls he molested, they have a stack of evidence to work with. They don't need me. And if they decide they absolutely do need me, then I'll come back. But I'll fight it. I don't want to see his face again."

Grandpa nodded in understanding and Grandma focused on little Isabella who was squirming to get down and back to her toy car. She got on quickly, turned the pink racer around and sped off, her feet whipping it into motion.

Beneath her baggy sweater, Isabella's heart pounded wildly against her rib cage. This single picture travel had invaded her peace like no other. "I want to go," said Isabella quietly. "I've heard enough."

Abby and Shana both looked disappointed to leave so soon but knew Isabella couldn't take any more. She looked faint and sickly. Hopefully she'd make it back without passing out. Her friends held onto her on either side and she quickly flipped the picture face down.

CHAPTER 29

The next day, as soon as Isabella heard the front door close and lock, she swung her feet out of bed and headed to the bathroom. Sleep still pulled at her but Sally would be at work all morning and the attic was free for a few hours. Isabella knew she had no time to waste. She had a lot to accomplish today. She looked forward to Saturday mornings. It was the one day of the week when the house was all hers. There was no risk of Abby or Shana dropping by. Saturday mornings were their sacred, beauty sleep time.

After a quick shower, she towel-dried her hair, brushed through it and put on a pair of sweats and a big sweatshirt. She hurried downstairs for a bowl of cereal and glass of milk. The coffee maker hadn't timed out yet. The red button still shone red, showing the carafe was hot. As she placed her bowl and cup in the dishwasher, she decided to take a cup of coffee up to the attic with her. The caffeine would help wake her up.

She searched in the cupboard for one of those thermal coffee mugs her mother kept on hand. One year Sally had some made for the office, all with the words, "House of Windsor Fashion" on the front, the name of her shops. Her staff all used them faithfully; at least that's what Sally claimed. As Isabella pulled one bright red cup from the cupboard, she smiled at it. One Christmas, everyone on Sally's wish list had received either a red or green cup. In the spring, Sally had ordered a new batch of pastel colored thermal mugs. She even sold them in her shops. Apparently they were quite the hit.

Upstairs in the hall, Isabella set her cup down and retrieved the long pole from the closet. After pulling down the ladder and setting it firmly on the floor, she picked up her coffee and carried it carefully as she ascended to the attic.

She pulled the shoe boxes from their hiding spots and placed them close to the light. There she situated herself and reached for the box she knew she needed to search. Lifting the lid, she saw one of the large brown envelopes on top. She took it out and saw the second one tucked underneath. Glancing inside the first envelope, she noticed it contained Walter's childhood pictures, the few that there were.

Before, she'd only glanced at the pictures in this envelope. She discarded it, reached for the second brown envelope and placed it in her lap. She slipped the meager contents out onto the floor before her and gazed at the newspaper clippings. Looking at them more carefully, she could see they were all about Walter. A mug shot and article had been snipped out of a newspaper. That must have been when he was first arrested. His eyes looked wild and confused and his hair was tussled, unlike his usual, sophisticated look. His white shirt was creased and dirty with a tear and blood stain on one shoulder. He must have had quite the struggle during his arrest.

There were numerous articles concerning the court proceedings, the jury's deliberations and his final conviction. Time magazine had done an interview with him shortly after his incarceration. The article had been carefully cut out and placed with the other clippings. The title read, "Inside the Mind of a Sex Offender."

Another article, on faded newsprint, caught her eye. Walter was shown sitting in a sealed room, behind a table, his arms resting on it with his hands clasped. He looked years older, lines creasing his forehead and his eyes emitting a sad and defeated appearance. The caption beneath the picture read, "Convicted Sex Offender Rehabilitated?" The question mark made her curious. She glanced at the article and read the first few sentences.

"Sex Offender, Walter Tassey, incarcerated in Kingston Penitentiary, in Kingston, Ontario, has been serving a twelve-year sentence for sexually abusing underage girls. These victims were all part of the same church organization, Tassey Sanctuary. It appears they were brainwashed into believing their salvation was conditional on performing the act of sex with a church leader. The church, run by Walter's father, Sheffield Tassey, shut down after the arrest of both father and son. Now in his sixth year in prison, Walter claims he's overcome his baser instincts, found a true relationship with God and has seen the light. His claims are fairly grand. He agreed to an interview to share his newfound *faith*."

With the article in her hand, Isabella reached over for her mug of coffee and took a sip. The liquid was beginning to cool, the temperature was perfect. She took a few big gulps and turned back to the clipping she held in her hand.

She had to think of him as Walter now. To say "father" gave her too much uncomfortable attachment to a criminal. It was still difficult to accept the truth. Last night, after her friends left and Sally retired for the night, Isabella had cried herself to sleep. The knowledge of what her father had done was shameful and horrifying. She'd cried until her eyes were bloodshot red and her head ached in pain. Not only did he not love her, but he'd done some awful things, things deserving prison. The man was a sicko.

The fact that she'd never known, never been told the truth, aggravated her. She understood Sally's reasons but that didn't make it any easier now. And to have had her friends in on the revelation was even more upsetting. She made them promise to keep it quiet. Hopefully they'd zip their mouths and hold the secret.

It was more than Walter's poor choices that had made her cry last night. Watching Sally in the picture travel had also greatly upset her. Anger and bitterness had poured out of her. The hurt and pain in Sally's eyes had been too much to witness. Walter's unfaithfulness, and the awfulness of it, had done her in. The vows she made after his arrest and incarceration produced huge repercussions, effects that Isabella was feeling now in full force.

Why had he done it? That was her main query in all of this. If he claimed to love Sally, why would he do it? If it was true that he meant to stay with her for a lifetime, why would he risk their marriage with such stupidity? Being involved in the church the way he was, should have helped him avoid such pitfalls. But it was obvious from the article that the church was the reason he did it at all. Further down in the article, the writer declared Tassey Sanctuary a cult.

There was only one way to find the answers. She had to visit some of these newspaper clippings, hear the conversations. She didn't know if it was possible yet but figured that if they were here, in the same box as the pictures, she'd be able to time travel into them too.

Setting her mug down, she sent up a quick prayer and focused on Walter's distressed face in the picture. In her peripheral vision, she noticed the attic disintegrating, detaching and distorting wildly. Swirls of insulation, wood grain, her bright red mug and streaks of light from the bulb meshed together and swooshed around her tempestuously. She placed a hand over her heart to still the frantic beating. This initial detachment from reality caused her the greatest anxiety. Coming back was always easier.

The frenetic churning of the room slowed, stopped and then began its backward spiral. Colors and forms rushed to and fro in a barbaric sort of dance, swirling and churning chaotically. Gradually the room stilled and Walter's face appeared and came into focus. Where the newspaper clipping had been devoid of color, the black and white image now gave way to the true color of the day.

Walter's drab prison clothes were unimpressive against his once attractive face and warm-toned skin. His dark hair now showed streaks of grey but his large, sky-blue eyes, although troubled, still held a mesmerizing quality. He sat at a table of plain metal, which was firmly attached to the floor, with a plastic cup of ice water next to his extended arms. He had a gaze of bored acceptance, while the camera's flashes kept lighting up the room.

Isabella looked over to see a young man holding the camera. He set it to rest on his chest, supported by a strap around his neck. There was a video camera set up on a tripod on the far side of the table. The young man went to stand behind it. Another gentleman, sitting across from Walter, cleared his throat. He looked seasoned in his job. His sharp features and graying temples, along with a confident posture, gave him an air of experience.

"I have a few more questions and then we'll wrap up."

Walter waited.

"You say that your recovery started when a pastor visited you here."

Walter remained quiet.

"Is that correct?"

"Yes."

"What's his name?"

"His name is Gareth Theor. He holds services in the chapel here every week."

"How did the two of you meet?"

"After service he's allowed to visit the different recreation and lounge rooms. I never attended his services. After what happened at my father's church, I didn't see much point."

"Why is that?"

A small, cynical smile curled his lips. "Tassey Sanctuary destroyed my life. I didn't want to give any religion another shot at me."

"So you believe that what transpired there was wrong?"

Walter nodded. "My father deceived me."

"How was he able to do that?"

"He told me it was the only way I'd make it to heaven."

"By molesting young girls?" The reporter seemed shocked.

"Oh, that's not the way he put it. My father is very convincing and knows how to craft words in order to manipulate."

"I've seen that first hand. I interviewed him last week. He truly believes God will reinstate him to his church and that it will be bigger than ever."

Walter looked surprised. "He said that?"

The reporter nodded. "He claims he already has quite a following."

Walter didn't look impressed. "He's a confused and deceived old man."

"Why do believe that?"

"He tricked me into believing that by molesting young girls I'd not only save them but save my own soul. To make it possible for them to achieve heaven was the highest call. He said the only way to shine like a star in heaven was to bring many souls into the kingdom."

"So salvation comes through sex abuse?" The straight face with which the reporter asked it showed he'd had experience interviewing the mentally twisted.

"That's what my father believed. He was the one who initially offered this service to the young girls and new potential converts. It was a revelation he'd come up with. He brainwashed me with it shortly after I married."

"You were married?" The reporter scanned his notes.

"My father insisted I share in the responsibility. I initially refused. I knew it would be devastating should my wife ever find out."

"And I suppose it did devastate her?"

Walter nodded sadly.

"So what has changed?"

His eyes brightened slightly. "I've changed."

"Religion has changed you?"

"No, not religion. I met Gareth Theor. Like I said, he was allowed to visit the recreation areas. That's where he found me and started talking with me. He treated me like I was normal, like a friend treats a friend. At first I resisted him. I didn't want anything to do with religion and told him so. No matter what I said or how I treated him, and I said a lot of nasty things, he wouldn't leave me alone. He'd give me tracts, articles to read, even some books. Most of them I never touched. I'd had my fill of my father force-feeding me his garbage. But then, one day, I decided to read what he gave me, just to try it. It was a tract about having a relationship with Jesus."

"Sounds like you found religion to me."

"No, it wasn't religion. Religion was what my father had. This spoke about something completely different — a relationship with the God who loves me. That's when I realized I didn't know God at all. I'd never heard him speak to me in a still, small voice, like that tract talked about. When I thought about God, all I could see was my father's angry, controlling face. That tract gave a completely different picture of God. One that looked inviting."

"So what happened then?"

"I asked him, Jesus, to be my friend, just like Gareth was trying to be a friend to me."

"And...?" the reporter encouraged when Walter went silent.

"I began to change, little by little. Gareth agreed to counsel me, help me work through all the deception and the lies. He showed me from the Bible about what God is really like. My mind began to heal and the twisted thinking began to straighten out."

"So you're fully recovered then?"

Walter gave a weak smile. "No. I've only started. I still have a long way to go. With Gareth's help and God on my side, I know I'll make it out of this place a changed man."

"What does your wife think? Does she ever come to visit?"

Sorrow filled his face at the questions. He shook his head slowly. "No. She's divorced me and gone on with her life."

"Does she live around here?"

"I don't know. I've written her repeatedly but she never responds."

Isabella never knew that. He'd written Sally? Why had she never mentioned it? Of course she wouldn't have. But the knowledge that he'd tried, hoping for some communication, was encouraging.

"If you've written her you must know where she lives. Right?" asked the reporter.

"I send the letters to her parents in the hope that they'll forward them. I don't know whether that happens, if the letters ever get to my ex-wife."

"Do you have any children?"

Isabella stared at him, wondering if he'd even admit it. If he truly hated her, like Sally insisted, this was a perfect opportunity to announce it to the world. Her heart thudded in fear of what he'd say.

"Yes," he whispered.

"How many children do have?"

"One. I have a daughter."

Isabella was shocked that he revealed that and couldn't take her eyes off of him. What else would he say?

"Were you close to her?"

After a deep sigh, Walter said, "Sadly, no. I was too wrapped up in my father's world to give her any attention. His brainwashing was too complete. I couldn't get close to her back then even if I'd tried."

"How old was she when you last saw her?"

Walter thought it over for a while. "I think she was around two."

"So she wouldn't remember you. Have you seen her since? Has she come to visit?"

"No," he answered sorrowfully.

Isabella wondered. Did it really make him sad or was this all an act?

"How old would she be now?"

"Eight, I think. She was born in December."

At least he knew that much about her. She'd checked the date on the article before reading it. At the time of the interview, she would have been eight. It was encouraging that he cared enough to remember when she was born.

"Do you think you deserve visitation rights to her?"

Walter leveled weary eyes at the reporter. "I don't know. Her mother would say no, but…I long to see her. I think about her every day."

"What's her name?"

"Isabella."

"It's pretty."

Isabella's head was spinning. Could it be true? Did he actually long for her? The revelation brought a warmth that spread through her chest and spanned outward until her whole body quivered with the knowledge.

"She was a very pretty baby."

"You haven't even seen a picture since then?"

With wary eyes, Walter refused to answer. He stood, signaling he was done. Walking to the door, he waited for the guard to open it for him so he could leave.

The reporter gathered up his papers and said, "Thank you for your time, Walter Tassey."

Walter turned back just as the guard unlocked the door. "You're welcome." Then he was gone.

Isabella looked down at the newspaper clipping and turned it upside down. The room bucked horrifically and the lights from the ceiling crashed down at her. The reporter and cameraman distorted violently and swirled into the color mirage. The thriving, pulsing mass of twisted color grew more distorted and gyrated through the room in spastic pulses until slowly the convulsions grew quieter, stopped and hurled themselves backwards.

All light converged on a single point and the bulb came into view. The attic access straightened and developed, until it rested in its rightful spot. A red, dancing blob took shape and came to rest on the floor. Her coffee cup finally stilled and took on its proper contour.

Isabella's heart raced in trepidation. She was back and glad of it. After her heart stilled and her breathing slowed, she looked at the turned-over clipping in her hand. She set it down and looked at the other articles laid out around her. Did she have the courage to visit another? She wasn't so sure. The positive experience of the last one pushed her to scan some others.

One bright spot stood out from the drab newspapers articles. She pulled at the colorful corner sticking out, revealing a snap shot. Staring at it, she knew someone had taken a picture of Walter in prison, during visitation. He sat behind a protective glass barrier so his face wasn't quite clear.

Who could have taken this? Did he have visitors? But who?

Isabella studied the picture and she didn't initially notice the room coming unglued.

CHAPTER 30

By the time Isabella looked up, the room was in full motion, swaying and gyrating with intensity. It sent her head spinning and her equilibrium floundering. She found herself swaying to one side. She noticed and righted herself

The room slowed, stopped and reversed its dramatic seething. Gradually the room took shape, revealing a metal divider, counter and glass partition. Walter's face appeared on the other side, gradually growing clearer until his features grew solid. Finally the woozy feeling stilled and Isabella felt the floor stop, her body finally planted on solid surface.

With a hand to her head, Isabella turned to see Lynne Tassey to her immediate left, seated and with a camera in her hand. Isabella stood just as the flash lit up the area as Lynne snapped the picture.

"I wish you wouldn't," Walter said dispassionately.

"It's been years since I've taken your picture." Lynne slipped the thin camera into her purse on the floor and looked up.

"I don't want to remember this."

"I do."

Walter only stared at her.

"I went to see your father last week."

A sound of disgust escaped Walter's mouth.

"I won't go again."

"Why? You've been so faithful in your visitations."

"He's more delusional than ever. There's no hope for him. According to him, he's gathering a multitude of followers in prison. Apparently they'll join him when they get out of the slammer. Can you imagine a church like that?"

Walter shook his head.

"I'm surprised and happy they keep the two of you in separate divisions."

"Maybe they're afraid we'll brainstorm and get reestablished," he stated with a cynical edge.

"I've talked to a lawyer."

With a hint of interest, Walter looked at her.

"I want a divorce."

Walter's eyebrows rose in disbelief. "Why now? He'll be out in a few years. The two of you can carry on business like usual."

With a heavy sigh, Lynne placed a hand on her forehead and rubbed the spot as though it hurt. "No." After a deep breath and long exhale, she said, "At the beginning of his prison term, I was hopeful that he'd change. I was willing to give him another chance, for the family." She shook her head. "But I don't think he'll ever change."

"You'll actually do it? You'll divorce him?"

She nodded but there was fear in her eyes.

"You'll have to move, change your name, something to keep him away," Walter said with some urgency.

"I already thought of that. I talked to my lawyer and he suggested both, changing my name and moving."

"Where would you go?"

She shrugged. "It doesn't really matter. The only thing that matters is that I don't lose you."

"You won't. I'll need a place to live when I get out." He smiled crookedly.

"You'll be welcome, my son," she said as she smiled gently.

He looked at her with what resembled compassion. "We've put you through so much. How do you bear it?"

"I keep my eyes fixed on Jesus. That's the only way I've stayed sane. I also focus on the future, when you'll finally be free again."

"It's been eight years," Walter said incredulously, "and the only thing keeping you going is waiting for me to come home?"

She nodded. "And Jesus."

"You have a pathetic life, Mother."

Her eyes gave off a wounded glow.

Walter leaned forward. "I didn't mean it that way. I meant that I'm not worth waiting for. For you to put your hopes on a pathetic individual like me is, hypothetically, pathetic."

Lynne shook her head decisively. "You've changed. I can see that God has done a work in you. I can genuinely see it. You're not the same Walter that went into prison. That man that's counseling you, he's really helped you. It's obvious you have a relationship with Jesus."

He stared at her. "You can see that?"

"Oh, yes I can. You treat me better and your views have changed."

"Humph."

Silence stretched between them for a minute.

Lynne gazed at her son and asked, "Has Sally written?"

Walter shook his head.

"Phoned?"

"No. Mother, please don't ask. It just reminds me of all I've lost."

"Do you still write to her?"

"Once in a while but I've almost given up hope."

"What about Sally's mother? I thought you wrote her, asking for information?"

"Yes. She wrote back but she refuses to tell me much of anything. Sally insists on privacy and has sworn her mother to secrecy."

Isabella stared at the man she knew as father. He'd written Sally? And he'd written Grandmother? Why had no one mentioned this? The secrecy vow was running strong. Irritation caused her heart to pick up speed.

"I miss Isabella," said Lynne.

Isabella stared at her. She'd never imagined Lynne missing her. She knew this woman only from the picture travel. That Lynne had known her, held her or cared one whit for her had never crossed her mind.

"I miss Sally too, but Isabella is my only grandchild and I feel I've lost her forever." A tear trickled down Lynne's cheek. She swiped at it in anger.

Isabella took note. The woman had more guts now than she'd ever seen in any of the previous pictures. Perhaps all the adversity and heartache had finally brought out some fight in her. More likely, being away from Sheffield's high-handed, domineering ways had also changed her. It wasn't much, but the vigor with which she'd wiped at her face said something. And now to realize that she was considering divorce, which would definitely incur Sheffield's wrath, said a lot for her bravery.

The sorrow on Walter's face overshadowed the courage on Lynne's. "I wish so many things."

Lynne gazed at her son and touched the glass. "Like what? Tell me."

Sighing heavily, Walter said, "I wish I hadn't been so gullible. I wish I'd been raised by a different father. I wish Sally would have stuck by me. I wish she hadn't denied me my daughter and I wish Isabella, once she's grown, would come and see me."

A quiet understanding flowed between the two, each sharing in each other's sorrow. Lynne nodded sadly.

Finally, she said, "I've wished for many things in my life. Very few have actually materialized. One thing definitely has."

Walter stared at her, question in his eyes.

"You've come back to me."

"I'm in prison," he said blandly.

"That doesn't matter. The real you has returned to me. You no longer reject me. I know that you love me now. I've known for a few years."

Walter nodded in understanding. "Mother, I'm so sorry."

"I don't blame you."

They both stared at each other and knew they didn't have to say a word.

Walter turned away, coughed, looked back at his mother and asked, "How's your job going?"

She shrugged. "It's going well. The Little Coffee Shop chain loves my baking. The owner is thrilled that I've lasted this long. The previous baker only stayed for three years. I've been their chief baker now for seven years. Can you imagine that?"

He replied with a grin.

"The hours work for me. I can do a lot of baking right in my own kitchen and they pick it up right at the house."

"Do you still work the early morning shift at the main store?"

With a nod, she said, "Yup. They need their biscuits, bagels and English muffins fresh for the breakfast crowd."

"You're amazing, Mother. I always knew you were fantastic in the kitchen but that you're actually working, supporting yourself, is awesome."

A smile of pleasure broke across her face. "Thank you."

"It's not too much for you?"

Lynne waved his question away with a flick of her wrist. "No, I absolutely love being independent and self-sufficient."

"You'll need that if you divorce Sheffield."

"Yes, I will." She said it with a great deal of confidence and meaning.

Isabella stared at her in wonder. Here was an entirely different person than what she remembered. The changes in her were astounding. She even worked and supported herself.

"When will you let him know?"

"I'll have the lawyer mail him something."

"You won't give it to him yourself?"

"I already told you that I'm not going to see him again."

"You're serious?"

"Absolutely serious."

A slow smile spread across Walter's face. "I'd love to see his face when he reads the divorce papers."

Lynne shook her head. "I don't want to be around when that happens for sure."

"He won't sign them. You know that, right?"

"My lawyer says I can divorce him on grounds of unfaithfulness. Then there's the fact that he's in prison. Having a husband that's a convicted sex offender doesn't stand well in his stead either. He can't contest it."

Walter's smile faded and a look of regret replaced it.

"I'm sorry I brought that up," Lynne said, compassion filling her eyes.

"It's okay. The truth is the truth."

"I pray every day."

"I know."

"God still answers prayers."

"That's what you keep telling me."

"Just look at you."

Walter nodded.

"He can bring Sally and Isabella back to you."

After a heavy sigh, he nodded and said, "I pray for that too, a lot."

"I do too. If the two of us are praying for the same thing, who knows what will happen?"

He nodded.

Lynne gazed at him affectionately for a while.

He looked away and studied his hands.

"How are you doing?" she asked in her quiet way.

With a grunt, he said, "Prison life isn't easy, but I'm managing. Gareth Theor, the pastor that comes in, is one bright spot in here. He's a true friend." He sat erect in his chair and with a turn of his neck, said, "I've made friends, guys who've found a relationship with Jesus, brothers in Christ. That's made things easier to handle."

Lynne nodded.

"I miss your cooking and baking. I've grown a lot thinner in here."

That made her smile. "In a few years you'll be out and I'll fatten you up."

Isabella started at that. He'd be out soon? When was this picture taken? It must have been years ago. Was he out already? Why had she not considered the possibility?

He tilted his head to one side and said, "My goal isn't to get fat, Mom."

"With all the weights you lift and the exercises you do, you'd never gain weight."

It was true. Looking at him more closely now, Isabella could tell he was ripped. Through his t-shirt she saw that his upper body was bulging with muscles. Although his face looked strained and visibly older, the years of prison having taken their toll, his body looked fit and trim.

"I do what I can to survive."

The joy drained from Lynne's eyes, worry replacing it. "Is it that bad?"

"I've learned to cope. Don't worry about me."

Lynne reached down for her purse. "I hate to leave but I have to get back to work."

"I'll be thinking of you."

Lynne stared at him fondly.

"The kitchen full of delicious baking; I can imagine what your whole house would smell like."

Her eyes watered. "Soon, Walter. It'll be sooner than you think and you won't have to imagine it anymore."

He crossed his arms and nodded.

"It might seem like a long time to you, but it's not." With that she stood and pushed the chair in beneath the metal table. She placed a hand on the glass partition affectionately.

Walter stood, lifted his hand and placed it to hers on his side of the partition. They stood that way for a moment, each looking into the other's eyes.

"I love you, Walter."

"I love you too, Mother." With that he let his hand drop, turned and walked to the back door where a guard waited to let him out of the visitation room.

Lynne watched him leave then turned to the exit. Although her eyes were filled with tears, there was a resolute strength to her posture as she walked out.

Others were in the room, visiting friends and family in prison. The room buzzed with the many conversations. The partition between them kept the words muffled and indiscernible.

Isabella looked down at the picture. She was thankful for the great deal it had revealed. Her heart felt lighter knowing that her father thought about her and wished to see her. She flipped the photo face down.

CHAPTER 31

Isabella thought it was irresponsible that she'd never thought of going online and checking on her father, a complete oversight on her part. Anyone, who had any sense at all, would do an immediate search online. Why hadn't she thought of it?

Actually, no, the idea had been there all the time, nagging at her. She hadn't had all the information necessary but the idea of finding out everything from a computer terrified her. Learning about her father in such an impersonal, clinical way seemed unfair to him, to both of them. The computer offered information without emotion and with no possible solution. It offered basic facts and that was all.

Picture travel had brought a bounty of information. With it came understanding and empathy toward Walter and others that an online search never would have produced. That's why she'd never Googled him before.

But now, sitting in front of her computer, she was ready. Typing in his name, "Walter Tassey," numerous sites popped up. Many of them were articles written about him in different papers and magazines. Wikipedia was one of the first sites on the list and she clicked on it. It documented his date of birth, childhood, his indoctrination by Sheffield Tassey's church, his crimes, arrest and incarceration. It told her nothing she didn't already know. Scrolling further down, a heading caught her attention: "Release Date." She read through it quickly.

Pulling away from her desk, she clasped her hands and allowed her breathing to still. He'd been released from prison over a year ago. His father, Sheffield, was scheduled for release in two years.

Sitting forward, she opened a new window and typed a name. Even if Lynne had moved, finding her place of employment shouldn't be too hard. The information popped up and Isabella transferred it to a Word document. A phone call would tell her all she needed.

~~~~

Impatience gnawed at Isabella while she waited for her mother. Saturdays were her short days of work, so why wasn't Sally home yet? She glanced at the clock on the wall. It was already after 5:00 and supper would be late again. Releasing a huff of air, she looked down at her cell phone. She'd texted Sally numerous times but still there was no reply.

Frustrated, Isabella headed to the kitchen. Her belly signaled that it was time to fill the hole. She made herself a bowl of instant noodle soup, toasted some bread and slathered it with butter. Sitting by the table, devouring her toast first, waiting for the hot soup to cool, she heard the front door open and close.

She rolled her eyes. At times it felt like she was the mother and Sally the child.

Noise from the entrance told her that Mother was tired. Shoes went flying, landing with a thud in the closet and her purse landed with some noise on the tiled entrance.

"Isabella!" yelled Sally.

She clinked her spoon against the side of the bowl to signal where she was.

A moment later, Sally's head popped in and the irritation in her eyes made Isabella stop the onward advance of the spoonful of noodle soup to her mouth. She lowered the spoon and said, "What?"

"You're eating."

"I was hungry and it was getting late." Isabella stared back, mirroring her mother's irritation. "I texted you a bunch of times. You never replied."

Sally released a pent up breath of air and held up her phone. "It went dead." Walking over to the kitchen junk drawer, she pulled out her charger, inserted it into the wall outlet and plugged the cell phone in. She turned and leaned against the counter, her arms crossed. "So, now that you're full, what's the plan?"

Stuffing the full spoonful of noodles into her mouth, Isabella shrugged. She swallowed and said, "I could make you some gourmet, instant noodle soup, along with vintage toast drizzled with butter." She raised and lowered her eyebrows a few times and allowed a small smile.

"It sounds better than nothing."

Isabella wasn't offended that Sally didn't look impressed. It hadn't seemed that appetizing when she'd first decided on her dinner menu either, but now, eating it, it was going down incredibly well.

"What were you planning on?"

"I was going to order in, pizza or something."

"That would have been good but hey, this stuff isn't too bad."

"Promise it won't kill me?"

Slurping the last spoonful of noodles, Isabella swiped her mouth with her sleeve and said, "I promise." She went to the counter and placed her dishes in the sink. "Sit down, Sally. I'll make your delicious dinner."

Her mother looked more exhausted than usual.

While she allowed the water in the small pot to come to a boil, Isabella said, "You know that business trip you're going on next weekend?"

"Yes," Sally said dispassionately. "That's why I was so busy today, organizing everything so I can get away. There are endless things to put in place whenever I leave."

Sally did this business trip every three months, to oversee her various stores. Her first franchise was just getting off the ground. The manager of another one of the stores was considering buying a franchise as well. Right now, Sally was busier than ever but she kept making assurances that once things settled, her pace would slow down. Isabella was looking forward to it. Work was holding Sally captive. She hated her being so wrapped up in it.

Isabella had been brainstorming all day and prayed the idea she had would pass inspection. After a nervous swallow, she turned to Sally and said, "I've been thinking."

"Sounds dangerous," Sally said with a slight turning of her lips.

"This weekend will be a long weekend so I'll have two extra days off and you'll be gone that whole time. I don't really want to stay with Tessa and Cody…not that I don't like being there." But she had a plan. "While you're away, why don't I fly to Toronto and spend time with Grandma and Grandpa? I haven't seen them in months. I could fly out Friday morning when you're heading to New York. We could go to the airport together. Grandpa could pick me up in Toronto. I'm sure he wouldn't mind."

Sally's intense gaze was unnerving but Isabella wasn't going to back down.

"Where did you come up with that wild idea?"

Isabella shrugged. "I thought it would be nice to see them again. I miss them."

Guilt paraded across Sally's eyes. "I'm sorry. I should take you to see them more often."

"I don't mind going on my own."

Sally studied her. "Are you sure?"

"Yes, I'm sure."

"A last minute ticket will cost me a bundle."

With a sheepish look, Isabella said, "I know."

"You could have given me some warning."

"I suppose I should have. It didn't cross my mind until today."

"What made you think of them?"

She couldn't say the real reason although the one she'd formulated wasn't a lie. "I was just thinking of them and realized how much I miss them. The last time Grandma was here was August. It's been months."

Sally nodded. "Two months."

They often traveled to Toronto at Christmastime but that was still over a month away. She couldn't wait that long and this time she didn't want Sally there with her to waylay her plans. "Please, Mother." Begging wasn't her style but she just had to get to Toronto somehow.

"You're calling me 'Mother' now? You must be desperate." Sally stared around her and asked, "Are you timing my soup or is it mush by now?"

"Oh. I forgot to add the noodles." Isabella took the lid from the bubbling pot of water and felt dismayed that a good portion of the liquid had evaporated. She added more water and then watched for it to boil. It didn't take long. Adding the noodles to the pot, she stirred them, turned the temperature down and set the timer.

"I'll make the arrangements tonight."

Isabella beamed at Sally. "You will?"

"Yes. I'll eat and then get on the computer and book your flight."

"Thank you so much," said Isabella with studied calmness.

"My, my, you sure are excited about visiting some old folks."

"Mom, they're your parents."

"I'm still surprised you want to head out there by yourself. Wouldn't staying with Tessa, Cody and the kids be more interesting?"

Isabella shrugged. "I see them all the time."

Sally nodded. The point had been taken.

Tingles of excitement rode up Isabella's spine. She couldn't let Sally see the extent of her enthusiasm. Sally's suspicion could be aroused and that wouldn't help her cause.

"All right. I'll book your flight."

"Thanks, Sally."

She nodded and smiled. "So, now that you've gotten your way, it's back to Sally?"

Isabella shrugged, went to her and wrapped her arms around her mother's neck. She squeezed and gave her a kiss on the cheek. "Thank you, Mom."

Sally patted her arm. "You're welcome, my dear."

Pulling back from her mother, she said, "You don't have to book the flight tonight. Why don't you just relax? Maybe we could watch a movie together. You'll have lots of time tomorrow to book it."

With a deep sigh, Sally said, "You're right. I need time to chill."

The beeper sounded and Isabella turned to the oven to switch it off.

CHAPTER 32

The flight to Toronto was smooth and the ride to Markham from the airport was enjoyable. Grandpa was thrilled to have her to himself. He chatted warmly and asked questions. When she asked why Grandma hadn't come along, he said, "She's busy baking up a storm and cooking supper for us. She's fully expecting you to eat like a horse."

It was Grandmother's way. To her, hospitality meant lots of food. Isabella already knew that the bedding would be washed and clean on the guest room bed, fresh towels would be placed in a pretty basket and set on the nightstand and fresh cut flowers would be resting in a glass vase on the guest bathroom vanity. Her room would smell like lavender and vanilla from an air freshener placed there the day before.

To say that she always felt welcome in their home was an understatement. Grandmother's thoughtfulness and desire to serve created an aura of warmth and generosity. There was always something to eat with Grandma's delicacies filling the kitchen.

Grandpa's specialty was making sure there was an abundance of activity and recreation. His supply of games was limitless and as soon as one was done, he speedily suggested another. The Nintendo system he'd bought years ago was still in working condition and he loved to compete with Isabella. She quite enjoyed it too. When it came time to play Nintendo, Grandma was content to watch and cheer, but she was a wicked card player.

Isabella stared out the window at the light dusting of snow everywhere. Everything appeared clean and pure. The sight of it made her heart race. Snowflakes were still falling from the gray skies above. Just maybe she'd have the chance to make a snowman, her first of the season. Back home they still didn't have a speck of snow.

"How's your mother?"

She turned to her grandfather. "Sally's fine. She's always busy working."

"That's why you're here, right? She's off on a business trip again."

"Yeah." She caught herself. "I mean yes. Sally's always reminding me to speak properly."

He turned to her and grinned. Looking back to the road, he said, "I'm so glad you suggested coming here. It's been too long and I missed you like crazy."

"I missed you too."

"I've planned out our games for this afternoon."

"I bet you have," Isabella said with a nod.

"It's going to be epic."

"Epic?"

"You taught me that."

"I guess I did." Isabella gazed at his profile and smiled. She loved him dearly. He was very special to her, her only grandfather, the only stable male influence in her life. If only she could spend more time with him. They lived too far apart.

Grandpa said, "I think this time we'll keep track who wins which games. We'll have our own winter games."

"Will Grandma join us?"

His lips tightened as he thought it over. "Well, she won't play Nintendo with us."

"No, but we could include her in the other games."

"Yes, of course. We'll do that."

"It sounds like fun."

"Robert, Emily and the kids are coming over tomorrow night for dinner."

Isabella clapped her hands in delight. "Wonderful. I haven't seen them in ages."

"Not since last Christmas."

With a sigh, Isabella said sadly, "I wish we didn't live so far away."

"I wish that often. I should suggest they come earlier and we could include them in our winter games."

That would completely shred her plans for tomorrow. "Oh dear. I was hoping to go shopping in Toronto tomorrow afternoon.

Mother insists I need some better clothes and since I refuse to wear most of what she buys me, she suggested I shop on my own."

Grandpa glanced her way. "You want me to drive you there?"

"No. You'll be bored following me around. I'll take the GO train downtown."

"Are you sure?"

"Yes. I'll do my shopping and I'll be back before dinner."

"Grandma won't like it."

"I know, but we'll have the rest of the weekend together."

~~~~~

The next morning Grandma stood with her back against the kitchen counter and scowled. Even with her forehead creased in worry, she still looked lovely and stylish. Melody knew how to dress well and with her regular regimen of exercise, she was in great shape. Her jeans fit her to a 'T' and her Marc Jacobs striped sweater flattered her. Years ago she'd had a heart attack and since then had changed her eating habits and started a work-out routine. She admitted to feeling as healthy as a twenty-year-old.

"I wish you'd stay with us. Does Sally know you were planning a trip to Toronto by yourself?"

Isabella nodded. "Yes, she even gave me my own credit card to use."

"You have to pay for your own clothes?" Her consternation was amusing.

With a wide smile, Isabella said, "No, of course not. She'll pay the bill."

"Well, that's a good thing." With a hand to her heart, she said, "I still don't like you going off on your own."

"I'll be fine, Grandma. I'm on my own all the time. I don't mind it. I actually prefer it most times. It's what I'm used to."

"It doesn't seem right. Why won't you let me go with you? I love to shop and I won't be any bother."

Isabella went to her and gave her a hug. "Maybe next time. I hate shopping as it is and I'll make your day miserable if you come." She pulled away and looked at her grandmother. "Don't worry about me, Grams. I'll be just fine." She dug into her jean pocket and pulled out her cell phone. "You can always call me."

"You wouldn't mind if I called you every hour on the hour?"

Isabella stared at her, her head cocked to one side. "Are you really that worried about me?" It felt odd to have someone so concerned over her whereabouts. Sally trusted her unconditionally and gave her a wide berth of free range. To have Grandma fuss over her well being felt somewhat stifling.

Grandma nodded.

"You worry too much, Grams. I go off on my own all the time. Sally never concerns herself with my coming and going."

Biting her lip in anxiety, Grandma took a deep breath, released it nervously and said, "Okay, I'll let you go, but only because Sally instructed you to. I wish she'd said as much to me."

"You can trust me, Grandma."

"Oh, I know I can. It's everyone else out there that I'm not so sure about."

Isabella reached for her again and squeezed tightly. "I'll be back before you know it." She headed for the door but turned back and said, "Thanks for the pancakes. They were awesome."

With a hint of a smile, Melody said, "You're welcome."

At the door, Grandpa met her. "Are you ready?"

"Yes." Isabella pulled on her Army Surplus boots and slipped into her coat. Although she'd suggested taking the bus to the Markham GO train terminal, Grandpa had insisted he give her a ride there. She'd conceded that much.

From the kitchen, noise alerted them and they both watched Grandma walk toward them. "Let me know when you get to Toronto, okay?"

"I will," answered Isabella.

"And call if you need us. We'll come get you immediately if anything happens."

Isabella stared at her. "Like I buy too much stuff and I can't carry it back? That kind of thing?"

Grandma looked taken back. "Well…yes…I suppose so."

"Look, if I get abducted or some other strange thing, it'll be too late to call."

"Don't say that, Isabella."

"It's true."

Grandpa placed an arm around Isabella's shoulders and squeezed. "Our girl here will be fine. She's street smart and knows her way around a city."

"Not Toronto," stated Grandma indignantly.

Grandpa stared at her. "Where's your faith in God?"

"Hmph," she said but the point had been taken. "I'll be praying for you."

"Thanks, Grams." With that Isabella turned and followed her grandfather into the garage to the car.

She buckled herself in and watched as Vern backed the car out of the garage, engaged the gear shift into drive and headed down the street. Maybe she should feel guilty for the things she left unsaid but her grandmother's anxious ways didn't leave any room for doubt. This is the way things had to be. They could not know the full extent of her afternoon's agenda. It would turn Melody's worries into full-blown fear. If Grandpa knew, he'd turn the car straight around and march her back into their home, no questions asked.

CHAPTER 33

Isabella disembarked at Union station and headed north toward the Eaton Centre, located right in the heart of downtown Toronto. It was a mere fifteen minute walk and with the moderate temperature, it was pleasant. She still needed her jacket; the wind was strong, but at least it wasn't biting cold, as she expected with the dusting of snow they had yesterday.

There were people everywhere, the sidewalks crowded with shoppers and business people.

She walked into the massive mall, cited to be the third largest in Canada. She'd Googled it before she came. She'd shopped here with her mother before. It was bright and airy with vaulted glass ceilings and open, multi-levels of shopping. More than two hundred and fifty stores graced the halls and levels of this enormous mall. It even had underground pathways, linking businesses and shopping stores.

Isabella stopped on the third level and looked up at the feature in the open, arched area. She'd read the plaque detailing the featured artist's work. Canadian artist, Michael Snow, had created quite the whimsical illusion of a flock of geese sailing high above them, suspended from the ceiling. The name he'd given his collection of sculptures was Flightstop. She loved the visual artistry and beauty it gave the huge, open space. It gave the illusion of standing outdoors in spring or fall, on a raised outcropping, within easy view of the marvelous creatures.

Tearing her eyes away from the scene, she checked her cell phone. Then she remembered that she'd promised to call Grandmother. After a quick call, assuring her that she was fine and safely at the mall, she said goodbye; Melody thanked her and Isabella placed her phone back into her purse. She had a couple of hours of shopping before their meeting. She didn't know how she'd be able to concentrate on clothes with the planned rendezvous. But she dared not head back to her grandparents without any bags on her arms.

Being warned to stay away from low-class clothes, Isabella headed to the top floor where all the expensive shops were located. After browsing through a few, she sighed in frustration. None of these clothes suited her. They were too sophisticated, too severe and old. If only there were an Army Surplus store here, she'd head straight for it, much to her mother's chagrin. That made her smile as she headed down the escalator.

No. She'd promised Sally she'd behave and buy some proper clothes. She noticed some stores more to her liking, with window displays that caught her eye. Walking into Dynamite, she tried on a few tops and bought three. The Guess store's window display was interesting. Trying on a few pair of jeans there, she decided on two of them. They fit tighter than her usual preference but Sally would approve and besides, Sally was the one paying. She also tried on a few cute tops and purchased another four. An off-white sweater went amazingly with one of the scooped tops she purchased so she decided to get that as well.

All this shopping was making her hungry. She stopped at Jugo Juice for something refreshing and she couldn't resist getting some caramel popcorn at Kernels. Sitting down in the food court, she watched as people walked past. The mall was getting busy now that it was past noon. There was still more time to waste so after eating half the bag of popcorn and finishing her fruity slushy, Isabella got up and kept going.

Another stop at Garage and The Gap added another two bags to her load. Heading back up to the third level, she found an adorable, red, leather jacket at Coach that she just had to buy. They also had a red, leather purse that matched spectacularly. Sally would love it. It wasn't one of Sally's favored designer labels but it would garner an approving nod for sure.

For someone who hated shopping, Isabella thought she had done pretty well. She glanced at the time and realized she had thirty minutes left. They'd agreed to meet at Starbucks on the second level. She was too nervous to keep shopping and wanted to give herself enough time to get there. It was only a level down and right behind Jacob. It wouldn't take her long at all. She'd checked the mall directory when she first arrived and had memorized where the Starbucks was located.

Heading down the escalator, her heart thudded loudly in her ears. She was surprised others didn't hear it and stare. It sounded otherworldly to her. To say she was anxious about their meeting would be putting it mildly. She was excited, scared and uncertain. There was no way to predict how things would go or what he'd be like. She'd fantasized about meeting him for so long it was ridiculous. To place some sort of expectation on their first meeting was stupid, she knew that. It could very likely turn out to be a huge disappointment. But, oh, she hoped for so much more.

One part of her told her it was crazy. The man had spent time in prison, molested under-age girls. The girls had consented of course, but he was a felon. From the outside it had appeared he'd changed, but was he really different? What if she was placing herself in terrible danger? Once a criminal, always a criminal?

No. She couldn't look at Walter as a criminal. He was her father and she was about to meet him. It sent tingles of excitement up her spine.

Sally would be beside herself with fear and fury if she knew she hadn't been able to dissuade Isabella in the least. Sally's secretive ways and tight-lipped withholding of truth had backfired. Her mother wasn't the only one capable of keeping secrets.

By the time she reached Starbucks, she was a few minutes late. It was better than getting there too early, looking too desperate. Inhaling a deep, cleansing breath of air, she released it slowly and walked inside.

She saw him immediately, on the far end, sitting in the corner by a small round table. He locked eyes with her as she entered. She stopped and stared at him.

CHAPTER 34

That he was her father was completely obvious. She recognized him from all the picture travel. He looked better now than he had in prison. There was a genuine hope shining from his eyes and a brightness to his gaze.

He stood and took a few steps toward her, his expression full of anticipation, which encouraged her. Isabella matched his step and walked toward him. With uncertainty, he held out a hand in a formal handshake.

"Hi," he said. "I'm Walter."

"Hi, I'm Isabella."

"I can see that." He smiled then, relief filling his face. "You're beautiful." He stared at her as though mesmerized.

Isabella looked down. "Thank you."

Slowly he came out of his stupor. "Uh, do you want anything? I'm buying."

Isabella shrugged. "Sure."

"Their Frappuccinos are fantastic," he said enthusiastically.

"What kind do you suggest?"

"I particularly like the strawberries and cream version."

"Sure. It sounds good."

"I'll be right back." Walter turned past her and headed to the front desk. The eagerness with which he did everything was amusing.

Isabella sat down at the table and watched him with a mixture of trepidation and wonder. Sally's voice was shouting in her mind that she was irresponsible, crazy even, to meet him unescorted. "How could you ever do this?" She'd be so horrified. But when she looked at him, all she thought of was how amazing this moment was. He was taller than she remembered from the pictures and his smile was brighter, filling her with warmth. With all the positive vibes she felt as soon as she saw him, she knew this moment couldn't be wrong.

Her returned to the table, handed her the frosty drink, which was lathered with whipping cream, and sat down opposite her.

She took a sip and nodded. "It's good."

He pointed to his cup. "I got one too but it's almost gone. I came early."

So he was as eager to meet her as she'd been to meet him. Looking at him, she asked, "Do you live close to here?"

"No. I live on the outskirts of the city, in Scarborough."

"Do you live with anyone?"

He gave her a funny look. "I live with my mother."

Isabella nodded. That's what she wanted to know. She'd suspected as much because when she'd called Lynne's house, Walter had answered immediately.

"She's here, you know?"

"Who?"

"My mother."

"Why?"

"She really wants to meet you. She's missed you a lot."

With furrowed brow and anxiety threatening, Isabella said, "I don't know her."

"I know." He nodded, with a concerned look. "She's shopping right now and if you don't want to meet her it's okay. I'll call her and tell her to stay away."

All of this was overwhelming. Just to meet Walter on her own took great courage, especially after a lifetime of fear imparted by her mother. "I don't know."

"Let's not worry about it. Let's just enjoy our time together, okay?"

Isabella nodded. The thought of his mother brought other questions to the forefront. Sally had told her virtually nothing about Walter or his family. "Do you have any siblings? I was just wondering if I have any more aunts and uncles."

"Sally never told you?"

Isabella shook her head, feeling badly for him.

"I'm an only child. You don't have any aunts or uncles on my side."

"Thank you. I've wondered about so many things."

"Why wouldn't Sally have told you about things like that?"

"She's stubborn."

Walter nodded and changed the subject. "What grade are you in?"

She was grateful for the switch in topic. "Ten."

"What are your marks like?" He smiled.

"I do well enough."

"Do you like school?"

With a shrug, she said, "It's okay. I have some good friends so that makes it bearable."

"I'm glad." He swallowed hard. "I want to ask you something but you don't have to answer if you don't want to."

"Okay."

He looked nervous, as though his future depended on what she'd say. "Has Sally told you anything about me?"

"Not much at all. All I've ever heard is that you're not worth the trouble and that I'd be better off without you."

Pain clouded his eyes and Isabella regretted being so honest. "I'm sorry."

"No, no, I asked."

"I've drilled Sally about you often but she's adamantly remained tight-lipped."

"I wrote her a lot, asking for information. I sent the letters to your grandmother, Melody Windsor, in hopes that she'd send them on to Sally. In every letter, I asked about you. Any information would have been encouraging."

"I didn't know that." (Isabella hadn't known that until one of the last picture travels. It wasn't really a lie.)

"How did you find me?"

"I had to do my own research. It took me a while." The thought of telling him about the pictures made her uncomfortable. He might not believe her and it sounded bizarre even to her. Tessa had seemed almost eager to share her time travel experience from long ago but Isabella couldn't be that open, not yet.

He nodded. "I don't blame her for hating me. I did the unpardonable in our marriage. I'm sure you know from your research."

"Yes, I know it all."

Looking down at his hands, he fell silent for a moment.

Isabella had so many questions. She didn't know where to start. "What do you do now? Do you have a job? Do you work?"

He looked up at her, regret still in his eyes. "Yes. I deliver equipment to various construction sites. I'm a delivery boy. It took me a while to find work. No one wants to hire an ex-convict. My mother supported me while I searched for a job. She's been very kind to me after all I put her through."

Isabella nodded.

"Now, I help to support her."

"Does she work?" Although she already knew this, she had to appear eager for information.

"Yes, she does all the baking for a string of restaurants. It keeps her very busy but she's exceptionally good at what she does."

Isabella nodded. "It's surprising you're not fat, you know, living with her and all. If she's that good of a baker, I would gain weight in no time."

He chuckled, low and deep and it warmed her to her toes. He said, "I've learned to resist and I work out so that helps."

There was a question nagging her that she had to ask. "What about your spirituality? Do you still believe in God? I wouldn't be surprised if you didn't. Do you go to church?"

"I attend a small church run by a man that helped me in prison. His name's Gareth Theor. His congregation is made up of a lot of ex-convicts. It's not your typical church. He counsels me and helps me understand the Bible. I'm still trying to sort out the lies from the truth."

"Did it scare you to be back in church?"

"Oh, yeah," he said soundly but then grew pensive. "I don't ever want to be deceived like that again."

"I can't imagine being involved in a cult. How does that happen?"

His eyes grew dark and piercing. "I grew up with it. My father indoctrinated me well. It was truth to me."

"Did you ever read the Bible?"

"My father didn't allow it. He insisted that I would be led astray reading it. He believed that God spoke and imparted the correct interpretation directly to him. Reading the scripture was his job and then he'd teach us."

"Do you read the Bible now?"

"Yes. Gareth encourages me to study on my own and always ask Holy Spirit to help me understand it. He says Holy Spirit is the one who moved men to write the very words of God. If anyone can interpret it, it would be Holy Spirit."

To hear it from his lips was encouraging.

"I've found out that the Bible is the Truth. Learning the truth is gradually setting me free from the mental bondage I was in." He gazed at her quizzically. "Are you a Christian, Isabella?"

She nodded. "Yes, I am."

"Sally takes you to church?" He looked surprised.

"Yes, since I was young."

He looked skeptical. "Why would she do that after all she'd been through with Tassey Sanctuary?"

"God healed her heart years ago."

"How?" he asked with keen interest.

"She told me about it once. She was hooked on drugs and had to go to drug rehab. It was there, at a Christian-based rehabilitation home, that God ministered to her and healed her. She met her oldest daughter there. Did you know that she has another daughter?"

"Really?" Walter sounded shocked. "No, I didn't know."

Isabella nodded. "Yes, she gave her up for adoption when she was in her teens. I should rephrase that. Her mother forced Sally to give up the baby. But her daughter, Tessa, worked at the rehab home and the truth came out eventually. Meeting her older daughter did wonders for her. God reunited them at a time when Sally needed a huge amount of emotional healing. After that, she started taking me to church."

"I see." He remained silent for a time. "It's a lot to absorb."

She felt sorry for him. He'd missed so much of their lives and he seemed so desperate to soak up as much as he could.

Moisture filled Walter's eyes. "I'm glad. I'm grateful Sally didn't turn her back on God. I was afraid of that. Afraid you'd be brought up without any sort of faith. My prayers were always for your protection and salvation, at least after I turned my heart to God and truly got to know him."

Isabella didn't know what to say so she waited.

His eyes looked wounded. "Sally never forgave me. I wonder why?"

Thinking it over, Isabella decided to attempt shedding some light. "She was afraid of you, afraid for me. Fear is her constant companion. I know it shouldn't be. She's a Christian but she's vowed to keep me safe."

"Safe from me," Walter said gloomily.

"I'm sorry."

"No. I brought it on myself. I should have known she'd respond that way. I don't really blame her. I was just hoping…"

"I do more than hope. I pray for her. She needs to let go of her fear."

"Will you tell her?"

"What?"

"Will you tell her about meeting me?"

Isabella looked away. She wasn't sure. What if she wanted to meet Walter again sometime? If Sally knew, she'd probably forbid it. She'd watch her like a hawk every time they visited grandparents. It was a huge risk. "I'm not sure."

"You should tell her."

It made her angry. She glared at him. "Why?"

"Because she's your mother and she loves you."

"Even if she forbids me to see you again?"

Hesitancy returned to his eyes. His chest rose and fell visibly. "Let's hope she won't do that."

"We live in Chelsey, Minnesota. You need to know."

"Why are you telling me this? Sally wouldn't like it."

Releasing a groan of frustration, Isabella said, "I'm tired of what Sally wants and what Sally likes or doesn't like. What about what I want? I wanted to meet my father. I want a relationship with you. I want you part of my life. And I'm tired of Sally forbidding me everything I want."

He stared at her, his mouth slightly ajar.

"It's true. Why do you think I'm here, sitting across from you in Toronto, Canada?"

He didn't answer.

"Sally's on a business trip. I was supposed to stay with my sister, Tessa, her husband and kids this weekend but I asked to fly to Toronto instead and stay with my grandparents. I wanted to see them, but my plans held an ulterior motive."

"You planned all this just to see me?"

"Yes."

His eyes watered again while he gazed at her in surprise.

"I've been curious about you for a very, very long time," she explained.

"I've never forgotten about you, Isabella," he said with a quiver in his voice. "You've been in my heart and mind for years."

The honest confession touched her deeply.

"I wanted so desperately to make things right, to be the father you deserved. Everything I tried, all the letters I wrote, proved pointless. Sally refused to let me back into her life and I thought you were lost to me forever." He reached back into his jean pocket and pulled out his wallet. Flipping it open, he pulled out a picture and handed it to her.

Isabella took it and stared. It was of her when she was around ten. It looked well worn, frayed at the edges. She looked up at him.

"Your Grandmother Windsor sent it to me years ago. That's the only picture I have of you."

"Melody wrote to you?"

He nodded. "I only received two letters from her." Pointing to the picture in her hand, he said, "She sent that with her last letter."

"I didn't know."

"Melody told me that Sally didn't want anything to do with me, that she'd moved away and made her promise to keep her whereabouts secret."

Isabella nodded. "That's Sally's way alright."

Remorse returned to his eyes for a moment.

Isabella raised her head and said, "But even she couldn't stop God's plan."

Walter stared at her with what looked like pride. "Yes, that's exactly it. God's answered all my prayers."

She grinned. "Mine too."

He tilted his head sideways, grimaced and said, "Well, not quite. There's still Sally. I've prayed for years that her heart would soften towards me."

"It just might."

With intensity of focus, his big blue eyes mesmerizing her, he asked, "Is she seeing anyone? Has she remarried?"

The question shocked her. Was he thinking of attempting to woo Sally back? The thought was exciting but hardly possible. Sally was too hard and cold toward Walter even to consider such a prospect. The odds were squarely stacked against the two. "She hasn't remarried but she is seeing someone."

"Do you like him?"

Again, his question startled her. No one had ever asked her opinion like this before. The opportunity felt divine. "No."

With a crooked grin, he asked, "Why?"

She shrugged and said, "He's not you."

Slowly he nodded and smiled again. "Good answer."

She smiled back, feeling a sudden bond with him she'd only dreamed about. "And, what about you? Are you seeing anyone?" she asked.

"I've dated a few women." He played with his empty cup for a few seconds and then looked up to lock eyes with Isabella. "None of them measured up to Sally."

It warmed her right down to her toes. He still cared for Sally and appraised other women based on her. This was better than Isabella had expected, much better. But caution won out. She'd had too many years listening to Sally's warnings, hearing her negative slant against him and too many years of his absentee presence.

"So, what's your plan?" asked Isabella.

"Regarding Sally?"

"Yes."

"I don't know that I have a plan. I just learned you were coming out to Toronto a few days ago and that you wanted to meet. The last few days I've been biting my nails in anxiety about where to meet and what to say. I haven't had time to process Sally yet. And it'll all depend on what you tell her. If you end up hating me and go back with a horrible report against me, that'll end the chapter there. If you herald my praises," he shrugged, "who knows what'll happen."

Isabella narrowed her eyes and asked, "Are you trying to bribe me?"

"If it works." He grinned at her.

She gazed at him for a while and then said, "I like you more than I thought I would."

He leaned forward and held out his open hands on the table.

Isabella wasn't sure if she was ready to touch him. She wasn't certain she could trust him yet. The moment seemed to hang in the air, waiting for her willingness to risk. Pushing aside her misgivings, she reached for his hands and placed hers in his. His grip was warm, tight and firm.

"I love you, my daughter. I love you, Isabella."

Something inside her broke at his words. She felt her guarded reserve crumbling and moisture filling her eyes. A tear slipped down her cheek and her throat constricted. Everything grew blurry and she couldn't tell what his response was. She heard his chair squeak and his hands slipped from beneath hers.

Strong arms lifted her to her feet and then wrapped around her in a firm hug. Her hands rested on his back, his frame dwarfing her.

Walter whispered close to her ear. "I've dreamed of holding you in my arms. When I had the chance, when you were little, I never took it. I've regretted that."

Tears flowed freely now and she tried not to sob. They were causing enough of a scene as it was. It felt like her heart was being mended on the spot. To have her father admit his love, his regret, and hold her this way did more to heal her pain than anything else could. To know she was loved reconstructed her broken image so that she actually felt a shift inside.

He released her slowly and moved away. Lifting a napkin from the table, he handed it to her.

She took it willingly and wiped her face. Sitting down, with a shaky voice, she said, "I'm sorry I made such a scene."

"I'm only sorry I couldn't hold you sooner." His face held a mixture of gratitude and regret.

Isabella nodded.

CHAPTER 35

Walter's phone rang and he answered it. After he was done, he looked at her.

Isabella knew who had called.

"What do you think? Do you want to meet your grandmother?"

She did now. Although it was getting on in the afternoon and she'd arrive late for dinner at her grandparents', she wanted to meet Lynne Tassey. She nodded.

"She's just down the hall. I'll call her and tell her to come."

"No, why don't we go and meet her." Isabella stood. "I really need to get going. My grandparents are expecting me back in half an hour. There's no way I'll make it in time. Can we make this visit short?"

"Sure," he agreed, but he looked disappointed.

They'd spent two hours together and yet he seemed in no rush to leave. He called his mother back and told her the plan.

Isabella grabbed her numerous shopping bags and Walter reached over to help. He carried three, while Isabella took the rest.

Walking beside her father down the main corridor of the mall felt wonderful. She wanted to remember this moment. There was no guarantee it would happen again. After all, she was still fifteen, underage and not really permitted contact with her father, at least according to Sally.

"I wish this walk would last forever," Walter said, glancing sideways at her.

She gazed up at him. "I was thinking the same thing."

After nearly bumping into a young mother and her stroller, they kept their gaze focused ahead and concentrated on where they were going.

Isabella spotted Lynne, sitting in a center lounging area with two shopping bags at her feet. She was still plump and, with her short frame, her feet barely reached the floor. Her hair had a lot more white but it was styled neatly in a short cut. Her face held great anticipation as her eyes found them.

Walter waved and Isabella looked down at the floor. She couldn't show that she recognized his mother. He'd wonder about that.

As they drew closer, Walter reached for her arm and guided her to the sitting area. "There she is." Releasing her arm, he pointed to Lynne.

Lynne stood and waited for her to approach.

Isabella shifted her bags and held out a hand. "Hi, I'm Isabella."

"I'm Lynne Tassey, your grandmother." There was so much emotion in her eyes — regret, joy, sorrow, relief — it was hard to tell which dominated.

"And I suppose I'm your granddaughter."

"Yes." Lynne looked uncertain but she stepped forward and opened her arms.

Isabella let her bags drop and stepped into her arms. They held each other for a moment. The top of Lynne's head came just below her mouth. Pulling away, Isabella looked into Lynne's eyes. The woman had been through so much and yet she looked strong and resilient.

"It's good to meet you."

"I can't even begin to tell you what this means to me." Lynne's chest rose and fell rapidly with all the emotions raging inside her. Her eyes misted as she said, "I've dreamed of this moment for so long, being reunited with you."

Isabella nodded. There wasn't much she could say. All she'd ever dreamed of was meeting Walter. She'd never considered her significance to her other grandparents.

Lynne pointed to the seat next to her. "Please sit."

"Oh, I'm sorry, I can't stay."

Disappointment clouded Lynne's eyes.

"I'm very late. I promised my grandparents I'd be back for dinner. My uncle and his family are coming. I haven't seen them in almost a year."

"I haven't seen you in nearly fourteen years."

Guilt rushed in and Isabella didn't know what to say. She'd never considered Lynne's desperation to be with her.

"Okay." Isabella sat and turned toward Lynne. Walter took the third seat and Isabella could feel his eyes on her.

Lynne looked unsure and nervous and yet her face emanated with anticipation. "How's your mother, Sally?"

"She's doing well. She works a lot and is very successful. Her stores are beginning to franchise and she's so excited about it."

"Stores?" asked Lynne.

"Yes. She has women's fashion design shops and she calls them House of Windsor Fashion."

"Innovative," said Walter with respect in his voice. "Sally always had that intensity about her, eager to succeed."

"You must be very proud of her," said Lynne.

"Oh, I am. I just wish I had more time with her. So much of her life is wrapped up with work. But that's what franchising her stores will do, free up some of her time."

Lynne looked nominally interested. "And, how about you, Isabella? How are you doing?"

"Well." She glanced at Walter. "Better now."

He grinned in delight.

"What grade are you in?"

Was she really supposed to answer all these questions again? She didn't have time for this. After a deep breath and exhaling slowly, she said, "I'm in grade ten."

"Do you like school?"

"I do. I have good friends and I do pretty well in my subjects."

Lynne nodded. "That's great."

She asked other questions, about church attendance, friends, family, possible step-father, where she lived and the list went on. There was such a hunger in her eyes for information; Isabella felt badly for her. The desire in her eyes to know Isabella was distinct. And to think she never even gave Lynne a thought over the last — how many years? It shamed her. But then again, she never knew Lynne even existed until recently.

She'd come to Toronto to spend time with her mother's parents and not once considered that Lynne Tassey would be yearning for a sliver of time with her. She was the only grandchild Lynne had. Now, sitting here, answering her assorted questions, seemed like the right thing to do and the perfect place to be. Her other grandparents would be waiting but they had the rest of the weekend to spend with her.

Time slipped away as she gave her grandmother the coveted insight into her life. Lynne smiled and soaked up the information like drought-parched ground in a sudden downpour. Lynne talked of her life, her work, struggles and joys.

After an hour of conversation, the hub of people passing by them in the halls forgotten in the midst of the reunion, Lynne gazed at her with wonder in her eyes and said, "I so appreciate you taking this time for me."

"It was wonderful for me too. I'm sorry if I seemed hesitant to stay and talk. I needed to do this and I'm so glad I did."

A slow smile spread across her pudgy face. "Thank you." She stood then. "I know you have to get back."

Isabella also stood and reached out to embrace the older woman. Lynne held tightly and squeezed.

"I'll miss you, Isabella."

They pulled apart and Isabella looked at her grandmother. "I'll miss you too."

"I truly wish your mother would allow visits. Then this parting wouldn't be so painful." Tears welled up in her eyes and a single tear trickled down her cheek.

Isabella shrugged. She couldn't make any false promises. "I don't know what she'll do. She doesn't even know about this visit."

Lynne nodded. "I know."

If only this were easier. If only this weren't the only time, the only visit. They were part of her already, woven into the fabric of who she was. Meeting them only cemented that fact more firmly in her heart and soul.

"I can talk to Sally and see what she'll say." The very idea of doing such a thing was terrifying but how else would she ever get back here to them?

Lynne reached for Isabella's hands and held them tenderly. "Oh, please do."

Isabella nodded but she wasn't sure she'd have the courage.

"And I'll be praying for you. God will help you and give you the words to say."

"Thank you."

That Lynne still held onto her faith after all she'd been through was astounding. But here she was, encouraging and promising prayer support.

They hugged one last time and then Walter had her in his arms, holding her so tightly that it was hard to breathe. It was then that the tears came and wet her cheeks. If only this wasn't a final goodbye but that's exactly how it felt. The heart-wrenching finality of this visit hit Isabella like a blow. She wasn't ready to let him go. They'd only barely met.

"My baby girl. It's so hard to let you go." Walter's voice sounded husky and full of emotion.

"I don't want to go," Isabella said shakily.

Walter finally pulled away and held her at arm's length. Gazing deeply into her eyes, a hint of a smile spread across his face. "This visit was an answer to prayer. Even if we never meet again, I'll always remember and thank God for this time together."

"We will meet again. I'll be eighteen in a few years. I'm turning sixteen next month."

A shadow of pain flitted across Walter's irises. "It feels like forever to me."

She nodded, her heart mirroring the agony in his eyes. Oh, if only.... but no. This is how things were. The only way things would change is if Sally would change.

Walter took one hand and touched her cheek. "I'll be praying for you. I'll be praying for Sally too."

Isabella nodded, the tears starting anew. She felt like a fool and she didn't want him to remember her this way, a blubbering idiot.

"Oh." Walter pulled away and reached into his jacket pocket. "I almost forgot something." He handed her a small, silver jewelry box.

She took it and stared at it.

"Go ahead, open it."

Lynne stood to the side, watching their exchange.

Isabella lifted the hinged lid and gasped. In the purple velvet lining sat a dazzling ring.

"It's real, sterling silver and ruby, surrounded by diamonds." Walter looked beside himself with anticipation. "Try it on."

She stared at him. "Why? Why did you buy me something so expensive?"

He matched her gaze. "Because I've missed so much of your life, birthdays, Christmases, and I had a lot to make up for."

Tears were threatening again.

"Here, I'll help you." Walter reached for the box and took out the ring. After handing the box to his mother, he took Isabella's right hand and slipped the ring onto her ring finger. "It fits. I went on memory. That was Sally's ring size."

Isabella stared at it, mesmerized by its beauty and size. "I love it."

"Good," Walter stated emphatically.

Looking up at him, her heart felt full of gratitude and wonder. "Thank you so much."

"Now go. You'll be late."

Isabella nodded but she had no desire to be the first to walk away.

"Oh wait. I almost forgot something else."

She stared as Walter dug in his pocket again. He'd bought her something else?

He pulled out his phone and said, "I need a picture."

"Oh." That made sense. She should get a picture of him too.

He took a picture of her and then handed the phone to his mother. "Take one of us together." Scooting close to Isabella, he placed an arm around her waist and waited until Lynne took the picture.

Isabella pulled out her phone and gave it to Lynne. "I need one too. Take a couple of pictures."

The two posed as Lynne snapped the pictures.

Isabella took her phone back and handed it to Walter. "I want one of Lynne and me too."

Lynne smiled in unexpected pleasure. After the picture was taken, Lynne turned to Isabella and said, "There's something I should tell you before you go. I changed my name to Lois Throne. It was necessary in beginning a new life without my former husband."

"Ok," Isabella said, surprised with the information. The name felt strange and would be hard to adjust to. She'd always know her grandmother as Lynne Tassey.

With pictures all taken and nothing else to discuss, the three stood and looked at each other for a moment.

"I should go." Why was this so hard?

Walter nodded. "Yes you should."

After a few more moments with not a movement, Walter said, "Okay, Lynne and I will go first. Your grandparents will start to worry if you don't get back. We'll head to the elevator and you need to take the escalator."

Isabella nodded, tears filling her eyes again.

"Now don't cry, Isabella. You have to be strong." Walter didn't look that tough either. His eyes were beginning to mist. "Just remember, you have my number and you can call anytime."

Isabella made a derogatory sound. "Not if Sally has anything to do with it. She'll confiscate my phone if she finds out."

"We'll trust God to work things out." He grabbed his mother's hand then and turned away. Turning back once more, he said, "Good bye, Isabella."

"Good bye." She turned in the opposite direction toward the escalator. When she glanced back, she noticed the two disappear around a corner. That was that. He was gone out of her life again and her heart twisted in pain.

CHAPTER 36

As soon as she entered the GO Train and sat down, her phone began to ring. The call display indicated her grandparents were calling. She answered and assured Melody she was on her way but that she'd be late. Grandmother was upset. Isabella knew by the questions she asked.

It was hard to explain why shopping took half a day to complete and why it couldn't have been done in Chelsey before she came. The comment that they only had a brief weekend together was sign enough that Grandmother was already regretting agreeing to this shopping trip. She questioned whether she should keep supper warm until Isabella arrived. Robert, Emily and their three children were already there, waiting.

Isabella assured her that she didn't want to keep anyone waiting. She gave permission for them to go ahead and eat. Warming up the leftovers would be fine. She did enough of that at home. Eating alone didn't bother her.

By the time she exited the train, Grandfather was there waiting for her. He smiled when he saw her, gave her a hug and then took some of her bags and carried them to his car. The ride home was quiet, too quiet.

Isabella looked at him. "Are you angry?"

"No. Why would I be angry? You come to visit us all the way from the United States of America. Why would that possibly bother me?"

That made her smile. "Chelsey, Minnesota isn't that far away."

"It's far enough that it requires getting in a jet and flying through the clouds. Not exactly a hop, skip and jump."

"That's true." She was silent for a moment. "I'm sorry I'm so late. Time just got away on me."

"By all those bags you were carrying, I'd say you've been busy." He glanced at her and grinned.

"I was." And yet she felt guilty, guilty for not revealing everything.

At the house, Grandpa took her bags and carried them to her room while Grandma fussed over her. "Now come into the kitchen. I have a hot plate of food ready for you."

"Give me a second, Grams. I need to say hi to Uncle Robert and Auntie Emily."

"Oh, all right, but come soon." Melody turned and headed to the kitchen.

Isabella could hear them in the living room. Katie came racing through to the entrance and grabbed Isabella around the waist.

"Hi, Isabella." Eight-year-old Katie was a bundle of energy and her bright eyes were always full of mischief.

"Hello there."

"Gramps set up the card tables and we're all waiting for you. It'll be an epic and colossal Windsor battle."

Shy, ten-year-old Reginald appeared from the living room. He leaned up against the wall and crossed his arms. "Hey."

"Hey, Regi. How are you?"

"Okay."

"Are you excited about our Windsor winter games?"

"I'll show everyone up."

Katie's eyebrows nearly met in the middle with her confident look. "You will not. You don't even like games that much. I'll be the winner for sure. Or Grandpa. He's really good too."

"We'll see," said Reginald. He didn't appear fazed by his sister's enthusiastic belief in herself. He pushed himself off the wall, gave Isabella a weak wave and headed back to the living room.

Isabella followed him into the room. She noticed Robert and Emily sitting together on the couch and Trent sitting across from them on the loveseat. Trent was her oldest cousin. He was thirteen and as outgoing as Reginald was introverted.

He jumped up when he saw her.

Uncle Robert said, "Hi there, Isabella. Long time no see."

"It's good to see you," said Auntie Emily.

"Thanks, everyone."

Trent reached her then, stood inches from her face, smiling and nodding. "Good to see you, Cous."

"Good to see you too."

He pointed to the room and the three card tables set up. "Gramps has got the entertainment covered."

"I see that."

"So, why'd you get back so late? What could be more enthralling and exciting than being with us?"

"It was tough staying away."

"So you admit it? You tried to stay away, and on purpose too?" Trent's face twisted in disbelief.

"No, of course not. I'm a girl and I was shopping. That's all the explanation you need."

"Amen to that," agreed Auntie Emily.

Isabella gave her an appreciative look. It felt great to have support.

Grandpa entered the room then, walked past her and patted her on the back.

She glanced at him as he scooted past and took his regular seat on the big, lounge chair.

"I hate shopping," admitted Katie. "It's boring."

"You might grow to like it," said Isabella.

Katie's face scrunched comically as she stared up at her. "I doubt it."

"I hope you do," said Auntie Emily.

Isabella said, "I'll be back. Grandma has my dinner ready."

In the kitchen, Melody was sitting at the table waiting for her. When Melody saw her, she pulled off the foil wrapping over the hot plate of food and placed it in the spot where Isabella usually sat.

Isabella sat down and looked at Melody. "I'm sorry, Grams. I wasn't planning to be out so late. Time just got away from me."

"Don't worry about that now. Eat before it gets cold again."

The roast beef and gravy smelled divine. The mashed potatoes were a bit hard and clumped but they still tasted wonderful. Mixed vegetables finished off the hot items and in a bowl on the table was Grams' amazing Caesar salad. She made the dressing from scratch and it was the best Isabella had ever tasted. No restaurant could compete with her.

While she ate, Melody stayed at the table but didn't stare. Her eyes stayed glued to the book in her hands. When Isabella finished her meal, Melody lifted her eyes from her book, closed it and set it down. "Do you want dessert too?"

Placing a hand over her full middle, Isabella said, "I'm stuffed. Maybe I'll have some later."

The look in her grandmother's eyes made her stop and stare. "Are you okay?"

With a shake of her head, Melody said, "No."

She felt like a heel. "Is it because I got back so late? I said I was sorry."

Melody shook her head. "No, it's not that."

Isabella waited.

"I had a nap this afternoon."

"You're not feeling well?"

"I feel fine."

"Oh." Maybe she should just hush and let her grandmother speak.

"While I was napping, I had a dream."

"Okay," Isabella said after some silence.

"You were in my dream."

"Really?"

"Yes."

Why did her grandmother look so accusing and why did her eyes emit such hurt, like Isabella had done something wrong intentionally. She couldn't be held responsible for what others dreamed about her.

"I saw you sitting in a coffee shop."

When Melody fell silent, Isabella felt her skin begin to crawl. "And?" she asked cautiously.

"Your father was sitting there with you."

How in the world would she know that? This is completely freaky.

Melody continued, "You were both smiling, enjoying yourselves. So much talk, so much joy on both your faces." She looked agitated. "It shook me up."

She'd been found out? God ratted on her? Her head felt light and her heart raced wildly in her ribcage. "I don't know what to say."

"Just tell me if it's true. Were you with him today?"

She stared at her grandmother. "Do you really want to know?"

"I have to know."

"Can we discuss this later, after Robert and his family go home?"

"No, it can't wait."

Drawing in a ragged breath, Isabella released it slowly as she stared at Melody. She still didn't know how it was possible.

"It's true, isn't it?" Melody was trying to make this easy for her.

Isabella nodded. "Yes, it is. I met him and we talked."

Grams nodded. "I thought so." She stood then. "We'll discuss this later."

Isabella sat transfixed as she watched Melody take her plate and place it in the dishwasher. Not another word was uttered, not another question asked. She felt like a criminal. Had she done the wrong thing? Did Melody feel taken advantage of? She hadn't come all this way just for Walter. Grandmother had to know that as a fact. She'd come to see them too. The last thing she wanted was to alienate herself from her grandparents. They meant the world to her.

Melody finished at the sink and waved to her. "Come on, let's go join the others."

Isabella nodded and followed, guilt hounding her thoughts.

CHAPTER 37

Home is where the heart is. That statement rang true as Isabella stepped inside the door. It was good to be back. Setting her suitcase by the wall, she stopped and took a deep breath. The smell of home was sweet to her soul.

Sally stepped in behind her, carrying one of Isabella's bags for her. She set it down and went back to the car for another suitcase. Isabella followed her out and helped with the rest of the luggage.

Their flights had coordinated well. Sally's flight came in earlier and she waited until Isabella's jet arrived shortly afterwards. Connecting at the airport and driving home together had worked out for them.

On the drive home, Sally had filled her in on her business dealings and meetings. She'd had a productive weekend. She grilled Isabella on her weekend and Isabella divulged as much as she was willing to at that point.

Isabella still hadn't decided how much she'd say, if anything.

Setting the last suitcase to the side, Sally turned to her and said, "Why don't we unpack? I'll start laundry and then we'll order something in. We have the whole evening together and we can tell each other more about our weekends."

Isabella shrugged. "Sure. Sounds good to me." As she headed up the stairs with her bags, she couldn't help feeling a twinge of guilt. Grandmother had made her promise she'd tell Sally everything. Now, trudging up the stairs, she felt paralyzed by fear. She wasn't ready to face Sally's fury. And she was sure that's what her news would elicit from her.

During her flight, all she could think about was Walter and how amazing it was to meet him. Other thoughts invaded as well, thoughts about Sally and how she'd take the news. Visions of Sally erupting in anger made her push those thoughts firmly away. Now that she was home, she couldn't evade the nervousness she felt.

Perhaps, while she unpacked, she'd find some courage and get rid of this unreasonable dread that was hounding her.

~~~~~

Sally didn't know what it was, but there was something different about Isabella. She appeared agitated and she couldn't place her finger on it. Everything Isabella told her about her weekend seemed acceptable. She'd spent some time shopping and had shown her all the items while on their trip home from the airport. The wardrobe she'd purchased was quite impressive. That girl's style was improving and Sally was glad.

As Sally cleaned out her suitcase, she thought over the other things Isabella had mentioned. The Windsor winter games, all the card games they'd played. Even Robert, Emily and their kids had joined in. That sounded safe enough. Melody and Vern had taken Sally to a nice steak restaurant one night. They'd gone to see a movie another night. Robert and Emily had Isabella over for a meal and treated her to ice cream at Dairy Queen.

It all sounded so circumspect, maybe too sterile and safe. But what else did she expect from Isabella's visit with her parents? It wasn't like they'd take her sky diving or bungee jumping! She trusted her parents emphatically with her daughter.

No, it was more than that. The look in Isabella's eyes had flagged a warning. But why? What could possibly have happened in Toronto that would cause Isabella to act guilty and nervous around her?

Sally placed all her dirty clothes in the hamper she'd pulled from her closet and refolded the clean items from her suitcase and put them back where they belonged. As she zipped up the empty suitcase and hauled it to her walk in closet, she decided to do more digging tonight. She hated having something between them. Isabella was everything to her and there was no way she'd allow suspicion and secrets spoil their close relationship.

The phone rang on her night stand just as she was about to leave the room, hamper in hand. She stopped and stared at it. Dropping the hamper, she hurried to it. She lifted the handset and checked the caller ID. It was Grayson. With a smile, she hit the talk button and raised the headset to her ear.

"Hi Grayson."

"Hi there, beautiful. How was your weekend?"

"Lonely, but productive."

"Mine was miserable. My two favorite girls were gone and I was scrambling to keep from crawling the walls."

"Wow, we did that to you?"

He chuckled and it made Sally smile. He had this uncanny way of making her feel wanted, light and happy again.

"So you're glad we're back?" Sally asked.

"I'm ecstatic. I can't wait to see you. Can I drop by tonight?"

"Oh..."

"That doesn't sound too positive."

"I was hoping to have a deep, heart-to-heart talk with Isabella. I haven't been with her all weekend and I really missed her."

"I see." By the sound of his voice, he was disappointed.

Sally was sorry for doing that to him. She should have told him how much she missed him, couldn't wait to be with him. Why didn't she? "I'm planning on a half day of work tomorrow. Why don't we meet for a late lunch, let's say around 2:00?"

"I think I could swing that."

"I'm sorry it can't be sooner."

"I understand."

"I'm looking forward to seeing you, Grayson."

"You have no idea how much I look forward to seeing you."

"I have to run. We'll talk tomorrow. Bye, Grayson."

"Bye, love."

Sally clicked the phone off and returned it to its base. Releasing a heavy sigh, she turned back to where she'd dropped the hamper, picked it up and left her room. All she could think about at the moment was clearing the air with Isabella.

CHAPTER 38

Isabella didn't know why the atmosphere was so fraught with tension. Could Sally feel her anxiety? They'd eaten in near silence, Sally's questioning gaze assessing her oddly. It made Isabella uncomfortable.

Now, sitting in the living room, Sally scanning through television channels, Isabella still felt an unfamiliar strain between them. She was sure Sally could feel it too.

Without looking at her, Sally said, "I have a feeling more happened in Markham than what you're willing to say."

Isabella stared at her. What did she mean? And what was she implying? Only one possibility came to her. "Did Grandma call you?"

Slowly, Sally turned to lock eyes with her. "No. Should she have?"

"I don't know." Isabella shook her head. "I don't know why she would."

After a few more moments of strained silence, Sally said, "Did something happen that you'd like to share?"

"No," she said, without blinking an eye. There was nothing she particularly wanted to share.

"Then, is there something you probably should share?"

This was her opportunity but it felt more like a long, dreadful walk to the guillotine. She was afraid of her mother. Sally could be scary if she chose to be. Not knowing the exact outcome of her confession was the biggest deterrent at the moment. Would Sally see to it that she'd be cut off from her father forever? The risk felt so great and the benefit too small.

But then they'd always been open with each other — in every area except the topic of her father. They were extremely close and yet there was this huge elephant between them, this issue of Walter, which kept them at polar opposites.

If only they were both adults and could discuss it without hysterics. The only adult between them, Sally, was the one who was most likely to take a dive off the deep end.

In Isabella's mind, she was the more stable one and able to process it all with some reasonable thought. Sally was sure to differ on that.

So, how was she to go about this? Should she just blurt it all out? Go slowly? Give Sally a bit of information at a time? Should she leave parts out? What she did know was that she gave her word to Melody that she'd confess to Sally. Why exactly had she agreed to that again? It eluded her at the moment.

Off in the distance she heard someone call her name and she distractedly turned toward her mother.

"Isabella. Isabella."

"What?"

The look on Sally's face bordered on alarm. "I called your name at least five times. What's wrong with you?"

Isabella shook her head to clear away the fog. "My mind was on something else. I'm sorry."

"Out with it," Sally ordered. "What happened in Markham or Toronto or wherever?"

Words lodged solidly in her throat. This was it. She had no way out. "You won't like it," she squeaked.

"I won't know until you tell me what it is." Sally grabbed the remote and clicked the TV off. Crossing her arms, she gave Isabella her full attention.

"I didn't really mean to go behind your back but I had to know."

"Know what?" asked Sally, fear entering her eyes, replacing the stern look.

"If only you'd given me some information, told me something about him, maybe I wouldn't have been so determined to find out."

"Him who?" Alarm began to register in her eyes.

"Walter Tassey."

Sally uncrossed her arms and her eyes grew large and frightened. "How did you find out? Did Grandma tell you his name? I warned her."

"No, no. Grandma didn't tell me a single thing about him."

"Then how could you possibly know his name?"

"From the pictures."

"What pictures?" Sally's eyes, surprisingly, grew even larger.

If the conversation weren't so serious Isabella would have chuckled at the sight. She swallowed hard and said, "The pictures in the attic, the ones Grandma brought here that I'm not supposed to see."

"How did you know?"

"I overheard more than you could possibly realize."

Sally groaned as though in pain. "But how would you know his name from those?"

This is where the conversation would get sticky. How much should she say? Would it help to explain the picture travel? Would Sally believe her? She'd gone this far. She may as well delve into it all. "The pictures have a special power. Whenever I looked at one, it sent me back to that time, into the picture and I saw what happened and what was said."

Sally sneered in derision. "That's the best you can come up with? Why don't you tell me the Easter Bunny visited you and told you about your daddy? It would be as believable."

Isabella gazed at her. It was the expected response and yet it hurt to have Sally doubt her, mock her.

"Who really told you about Walter?"

"I already told you. I found out about him through the picture travel."

"Isabella, stop lying to me. It's not like you and I don't appreciate it."

"I'm not lying," she yelled right back. "I can prove it."

"How?"

"I know things about your past, about all your relationships. I know things about Walter's upbringing, things you probably don't even know. I know about the cult he was in and how controlling his father was."

"Stop, stop! That's impossible."

"If you'll let me talk, I'll tell you some things I know."

Fear leapt into Sally's eyes, but she visibly controlled it, nodded and said, "All right, talk."

So she did. She told her mother everything she could remember, things Sally knew about and those she couldn't possibly know, items from Walter's childhood, damaging, scarring things.

When she finished retelling the things she'd seen and heard, Sally looked shocked and deflated.

"I want you to show me," she said with shaky voice. "I want to know this is true."

Isabella wasn't sure she'd heard correctly. "You want me to show you the pictures? You want to go back to the past?" She hadn't expected this kind of response.

Sally gave a slight nod. "I have to know for sure."

"Okay." Isabella stood and headed to the stairs, Sally following close behind.

CHAPTER 39

Sally wasn't sure about this at all. Going back in time sounded terrifying, especially visiting her own past. But she followed and her curiosity won out over the terror she felt.

While Isabella pulled the attic access ladder down, Sally watched, wondering if there was any truth to it at all. Maybe Isabella was only prolonging telling her the truth by this cleverly-spun tale. The direct gaze of her eyes as she told her things she could never have known attested that maybe she was being truthful. But that was crazy. Going back into a picture was impossible and ridiculous.

Isabella headed up the steep steps and Sally begrudgingly followed. With a flick of the switch, Isabella flooded the small attic space with meager light. As Sally's feet settled on the plywood floor, she noticed Isabella at the far end, pulling shoe boxes out from the insulation.

Confusion rattled her. That's not where she'd put the pictures at all. Who'd moved them? Then it all became clear. Isabella had, of course. She'd even gone to the bother of safeguarding them, hiding them from her own mother. It flooded her with guilt and anger concurrently. Sally reined in her frazzled emotions and asked, "You've been up here a fair bit then?"

Isabella nodded. "You could say that." She set the boxes on the floor, close to the light. "Why don't we sit down here and decide which picture to visit."

Sally smiled nervously. "You make it sound like such an everyday occurrence."

"It can be if I choose it."

Sally's smile vanished. How could her daughter be so sure about something that sounded so bizarre? She joined Isabella on the floor and watched her daughter remove the lids from the boxes and scan through pictures Sally had long forgotten about. The way

Isabella sped through them gave the clear impression of familiarity. She quickly discarded some to the side, keeping only a few directly before her.

Sally pointed to the small pile. "Are those the ones you're considering looking at?"

Isabella lifted her head and met her gaze. She placed a hand on the miniscule stack and said, "I haven't visited these ones yet and I thought they might interest you."

"Really?"

Her daughter lowered her eyes and sorted again. Watching her was therapeutic in a way. That Isabella potentially knew so much about her past and her life was certainly traumatizing, yet somehow comforting. She'd worked so hard to keep all these secrets hidden. Now that Isabella knew, or at least seemed to know certain aspects, it took a weight off her shoulders she didn't even realize she'd been carrying. It surprised her that she wasn't angrier. She should be furious and yet there was this uncanny relief filling her heart and soul.

Isabella looked up and said, "I've decided. We'll look at this one." She held up a picture that Sally had never seen before.

Reaching for it, her mouth ajar, she stared at the photo in shock. "It's in prison."

"I thought so, but I wasn't quite sure. Did Grandma take the picture?"

"I didn't even know she brought her camera."

"I thought you never went to see him in jail."

"I went to see him once," She lifted her eyes to lock her gaze with Isabella, "after his arrest, before his sentencing." Isabella didn't need to know more than that.

"Can we visit it?"

Sally couldn't stop the skepticism from filling her chest. Let her try. "Sure."

"Okay. You have to hold onto me so that we end up there together. You can't let go. When the room moves and comes undone, don't freak out and let go. Everything will settle in a bit and we'll be there."

"Whatever you say." She'd humor the girl and soon it would be Isabella who felt the fool. Perhaps then she'd break down and tell her the truth. That's what she hoped for out of all this nonsense. Sally moved closer to Isabella and placed her hand on her arm. "Like this?"

"Yes, and don't let go."

"Okay." She watched as Isabella lifted the photo and gazed intently at it. The quicker this charade finished the better. The floor was too hard and sitting cross-legged was painful. She should have thought of bringing a throw cushion up here to sit on.

"Do you see it?" asked Isabella.

"What?" Sally said, feeling some confusion. But then, when she shifted her eyes, she saw.

The room was buckling and heaving out of shape, the floor rising and throbbing until it released and let go, meshing with the sagging ceiling joists up above. The light, from the single bulb, shot through the mirage like an arrow heading for a target, but then slowed and curved into a long, snake-like apparition. The light separated and scurried throughout the space, creating sparkling stars that encircled her. The pictures that were scattered on the floor were now strewn throughout the room, images of a younger Sally distorting before her eyes, some moving in close, others speeding away into the distance.

Sally closed her eyes tightly. She was sure she was only hallucinating. It reminded her of her drug days. That it was happening here, in her home, up in the attic, was alarming. Maybe it was occurring because of Isabella's assertions that it would, mind over matter. Her mind was probably just playing tricks on her. Opening her eyes slowly, she realized that nothing had changed. The room was still in full swing.

Isabella's bright pink top had come undone and had sprinkled the air with bubbles of color. It was quite a pretty sight, if not for the fact that it was her daughter's body that had unglued and was drifting through the room. Terror filled her throat and she screamed.

"Mom, just hold on a bit longer. Everything will stop soon."

Hearing Isabella's voice brought back some calm. She was still alive and well. Gradually the frenetic display slowed, stopped and reversed, rushing backward in a flurry of activity. The kaleidoscopic spectacle began to separate, colors severing from the mass of disjointed shapes. Distinct forms began to appear, colors converging on singular points, uniting to make a whole.

Walter's face came into view and then his body took shape and stilled. His tortured eyes caught her attention first. She couldn't remember him being so upset that day or that his eyes showed such remorse. All she could recall was how angry and hurt she'd been and how fully she'd let him know.

When everything stilled and settled, Sally noticed how white and sterile the room was. The single table in the room was unoccupied and Walter stood beside it, a pleading look in his eyes. A younger version of herself stood at a safe distance, behind a chair, her whole stance one of defense. Her mother stood behind her, a camera in her hand and the picture just taken. Her mother slipped the camera into her purse and the deed was done, just like that, without her knowledge at all.

That's why she was here, staring at herself and the louse that ruined her life. Sally allowed her gaze to lock on Walter and she felt the familiar hatred and bitterness.

"You can let go now," said Isabella beside her.

Sally looked over, surprised to see her here. "Of course." She released her grip on Isabella's arm and turned her attention back to Walter.

"Please, Sally," begged Walter, "give me another chance. I'll make it up to you. When I get out of here, I'll be a different man, I promise."

The younger Sally sneered. "You'll never change, Walter. I warned you, over and over again."

"But I know I can change," he said with desperation.

"I don't want to wait for you. You haven't given me any reason to want to. The only reason I came to see you, is to say good bye. Forever."

"No, Sally!" He took a step toward her.

She held up a hand and yelled, "No! If you take one more step I'll leave."

He stopped and looked at her with a completely broken, defeated look. "Please don't leave me. I'll die without you."

"You should have thought of that a little sooner, Walter."

A tear slipped from his eye and trailed down his cheek.

Sally stared at him. She couldn't remember him crying that day, not that she felt sorry for him. The younger version of herself was speaking so she turned and listened.

"I also wanted to come and tell you that you'll *never* see your daughter again. I will move away and *no one* will *ever* tell you my address. I'll make sure of that. You didn't want anything to do with her while you lived with us so I'll just make things easy for you. Isabella is, from this moment, cut off from your life *forever*."

The vehemence with which the younger Sally spoke shook her. To have Isabella hear this disturbed her. She glanced at her daughter and saw tears trailing down her face, her eyes glued on her father. The sight of Isabella in such a state made her heart twist.

"No, please don't do it. I want to be a father to Isabella, to teach her and train her."

A sound of utter disdain passed the younger Sally's lips. "Just like your father taught you? Is that your idea of proper parenting?"

Walter looked helpless to respond.

"I think not. The best thing for Isabella is to stay as far from you as possible."

Walter's sobs came then. "I didn't…want this. This is…not…what I…wanted."

"That's too bad, Walter," the younger Sally said coldly. She crossed her arms and stared daggers at him. "If you think your crying will soften me, you're dead wrong." Her chest rose and fell, anger flowing out of her in waves. "It's too bad you couldn't think for yourself. You let your daddy do all the thinking for you. He thought you right into adultery, into having sex with underage girls and you didn't have the guts to refute him."

"I tried. I told him…no…often."

"But daddy always gets his way," Sally said matter-of-factly. "So, where is daddy now?"

"His name is Sheffield," Walter said, his tears drying up and his back straightening.

"He's in prison, Walter, just like you."

Walter didn't respond but deep shame exuded from his eyes.

"Where's all his power now?"

Walter stayed silent.

Sally shook her head in utter disdain, scorn for Walter worn like a mask.

"Please, Sally. I'll do anything to change, to get my family back."

"It's much too late for that." Her voice sounded tired now, her pain showing through. "I'm leaving and never coming back. You'll never see me or Isabella again. Good bye, Walter."

"No!" he cried out. "Please."

But she turned and walked to the door, signaling to the guard that she was through.

Melody stayed where she was and gazed at Walter with sorrow, regret in her eyes. Then she turned to follow Sally.

The lock turned and the door swung open. The two left with Walter crying out after them, begging for Sally to change her mind. As the door clanged shut, Walter crumbled to the floor, his wails of distress loud and disturbing.

Sally turned to Isabella and said, "Can we get out of here, please?"

Isabella's cheeks were wet with tears, her eyes red and her face scrunched in turbulent emotion. She nodded through her misery, looked at the picture in her hand and was about to flip it over when she turned back and said, "Hold on to me."

Sally grabbed for her daughter's arm and nodded. "Okay."

Isabella flipped the picture over and the room came unglued, colors rushing to and fro, objects distorting and flying apart, whipping about the space in segregated particles.

CHAPTER 40

It had been four days since the bizarre episode in the attic and Sally was still an emotional wreck. Every time her mind veered that direction, her hands started to shake and her heart began to palpitate frantically. The experience had completely unglued her. Her calm, capable exterior was, for now, in a shattered state. Work was nearly impossible and she took more time off than she should.

Isabella was different now, though. The picture travel had done something to her too but she was calmer about the whole thing. She'd been pretty upset initially. Seeing the two of them that way, Sally so angry and hurtful towards Walter, had wounded her. Isabella had admitted that she loved her father, had seen him for what he is now and that he had indeed changed for the good. Developing a relationship with him was more important to her than anything else. Isabella admitting that had hurt Sally. Badly.

Sitting at her desk, looking at the long list of things needing attention, Sally's mind wandered away again. Having protected Isabella from Walter for so long and now to have all the carefully constructed walls come crumbling down around her, was devastating. The idea that Isabella went behind her back, contacted him and even met him shook her to the core. She'd taken all these safeguards for nothing? Moving to another city, even another country hadn't been enough. Why hadn't it been?

She rubbed her forehead with the tips of her fingers. She could feel another headache coming on. It was becoming the norm this week.

Then there was the picture travel, an anomaly that was impossible to explain. How did it happen and who was responsible? Was it her mother's doing? Had it happened to her? Was she trying to get rid of the pictures for a reason? Perhaps she'd been hurled back in time every time she looked at the pictures. Bringing the box here, to Sally, she finally got rid of the Pandora's box and then scurried back to her home in Markham.

She'd talked to her mother, called her long distance. Melody knew very little except that Isabella had met with Walter. She'd gone behind her grandparents' backs too. Melody had made Isabella promise to tell Sally about the whole thing. At least she'd done that much.

Pointing the finger seemed futile at this juncture. Isabella insisted it was God's doing because she'd prayed and begged for years for her father to enter her life. Then Grandma brought the pictures, the picture travel began and information flowed. Sally should be angry at God then. If this was his doing, he was intentionally messing up her well-laid plans. Having Walter hurled back into her life certainly wasn't anything she'd ever planned.

Isabella admitted to meeting her Tassey grandmother and the things Isabella said about her surprised Sally. The woman had spunk to divorce Sheffield and go out on her own, work full time and support herself. She'd never known Lynne that way. Although Lynne Tassey no longer went by that name, she'd changed her name to Lois Throne to bring finality to her separation from Sheffield Tassey and had no contact with the man. She'd moved to a suburb of Toronto and left no forwarding address. Sheffield was scheduled to be released from prison in two years. That thought caused a host of anxious emotions. The right thing to do would be to lock him up for life and throw away the key.

Then there was Isabella to consider. When she talked of Walter, her eyes lit up and her lips turned upwards in a smile. She was obviously completely taken with him. She had nothing but praise for him. Isabella was insistent that she have regular visits with Walter. She wanted to know her father and in her mind it was time for it.

Just the thought made Sally's stomach queasy. There was no guarantee that he could be trusted. Her initial gut reaction was a definite and resounding "No!" and she'd told Isabella as much. Isabella's angry reaction made her take pause. She'd made a good point. If this was God's doing, bringing Walter back into Isabella's life in direct answer to her prayers, then perhaps it was time to let him in. Sally finally agreed to pray about it, seek God's wisdom and get back to her.

Isabella waited patiently for Sally to decide, which was commendable. But she wasn't any closer to a decision now than four days ago. If only she could make this all go away. She didn't want Walter back in her life and she certainly didn't want him in her daughter's life.

The phone rang beside her and she jumped. She released a pent-up breath and shook her head. She had to get a grip on her emotions. As frazzled as she was, she couldn't even answer the phone without composing herself first.

Lifting the receiver to her ear, she said, "Hello, House of Windsor Fashion."

"Hi, Sally. How are you holding up?" Grayson's voice was a godsend.

She could feel the tightness around her chest ease some. "Not good."

"Have you made a decision?"

"No."

"How's Isabella doing?"

"She's patient with me but I can see it in her eyes. She wants to know."

"I can't imagine how stressful this must be for you."

"It's absolutely horrible. It's like my worst nightmare coming true."

"Why don't I take you out tonight and we can talk? It'll help release some of the tension."

"I'm not so sure it'll accomplish that. I'm wound up as tight as a jack-in-the-box."

"Let me help to unwind you."

"Grayson, I appreciate it, but I just can't. I have to figure this out on my own."

"Okay." He sounded disappointed. She'd been ignoring him for days.

"I've been praying for the two of you, especially you, Sally. You have a lot of soul-searching to do."

His comment irritated her. He had no clue what she was dealing with. He wasn't the one Walter had cheated on. "What do you mean?"

"You're full of fear. If this is God, why are you so afraid?"

"I'm not afraid." It was a lie of course, but she felt defensive at the moment.

"Okay, whatever," Grayson said in concession. "I'll still be praying."

"I have to go."

"Give me a call when you want to see me."

"I will." She hung up and stared at the phone. He was upset. That he didn't say good bye, using a sweet name for her, was the sign.

She was so confused she didn't know what to do or say anymore. Isabella was unhappy with her, Grayson was upset and her mother had highly encouraged her to listen to Isabella.

A thought invaded the cloud of bewilderment hovering over her: *"Peace I leave with you, my peace I give you."* It was a portion of a scripture and it made her wonder. Peace was a scarcity this week. Another scripture permeated her thoughts. *"Do not be anxious about anything, but in every situation, by prayer and petition, with thanksgiving, present your requests to God."* Sally released a disgruntled breath. She was purposely rebelling against that command. Anxiety and worry could be added to her name. They'd become like faithful dogs tight on her heels.

Thinking it over, she realized she hadn't once prayed about the situation. Four days had passed in frantic worry and not once had she thought to pray. It shamed her now. Others had been praying for her. But her? Worry and fear had her completely wrapped up and tied with a bow.

She looked up at the ceiling. It was a silly habit. Jesus had promised never to leave her or forsake her. She knew that well. She also knew the scripture that said, *"Christ in you, the hope of glory."* Pastor Chad recited that nearly every Sunday before his message. It was his signature saying. If Christ was in her, how could he be up by the ceiling?

She lowered her gaze, folded her hands in her lap and said, "God, I'm sorry I forgot about you. I feel like such a fool. Please help me here. I've been trying so hard to figure this all out on my own. I'm scared and don't know what to do. Please show me, give me some wisdom. That's it. Amen."

Not much felt different. If she allowed her mind to roam to her dilemma, fear would invade again like an old friend. She pushed the feelings aside and said, "You have to help me overcome this fear, God. I can't do it alone."

With great control, she set her mind on her to do list and began to tackle one item at a time. She'd think this all through again when she was done work. Now she had to focus.

CHAPTER 41

Impatience nagged at Isabella but she kept reminding herself to give Sally time. Her meeting with Walter had so shocked her mother, sending her compass into a tailspin. Isabella could see it in her eyes. Sally was beside herself.

In the last four days they'd hardly spoken. Sally would come home, they'd eat in silence, and then Sally would often leave shortly afterwards. Her excuse was that she had to think things through. She'd go for a drive or a walk in the park or sit at a coffee shop alone. It was completely out of character for her.

Isabella found herself praying more frantically lately than ever before. She knew her mother needed to let go of all the misgivings, fear and unforgiveness she'd held against Walter for years. Could that be done in a matter of days? Isabella wasn't sure but she prayed that God would work a miracle.

All Sally's anxiety had accomplished was to bind her up with all the hypothetical negative possibilities that could happen. She was in a prison of her own making and yet she didn't see it. Trying to be Isabella's protector, defender and savior must be exhausting work. Now, with the realization that all her hard labor had amounted to nothing, her very life's agenda was spinning out of control and threatening to crash on the rocks.

The confusion in Sally's eyes was foreign. Her usual strength of character and firm control of every situation had taken flight. Isabella didn't like this new Sally and yet it couldn't be avoided. Sally had to work through this and this was the only way. Isabella believed it was God's way of bringing things to a place of change.

Isabella shook her head at the thought. She felt sorry for Sally. So much fear dominated her and so little faith in God. Her heart cried out to God for her mother and she prayed the best she knew how.

Sally's car was waiting for her by the curb after Youth group. Isabella got in and looked at her mother.

Sally gave a small, uncertain smile. "How was Youth?"

"Good."

Sally turned and veered into traffic.

"How was your evening with Grayson?"

"Tense and difficult."

"Really?" Isabella said, feeling hopeful.

"Not in the way you think. We talked about you and Walter. I always get tense discussing him."

"Oh." Isabella's heart dropped.

They were silent for a few minutes. Sally cleared her throat and said, "I want to apologize for being so distant this week. My mind's been full of everything you've told me and the time travel experience. I couldn't concentrate on anything this week. It's been a nightmare."

"I've noticed."

Sally nodded without looking at her. "I'm sorry."

"I understand."

"How about we stop at a coffee shop, visit for a while?"

Isabella shrugged. "Sure."

Sally pulled the car into the next coffee shop they could find and parked. They walked into the place in silence, ordered their drinks and sat at a corner table. The place was nearly empty, probably due to the fact that it was after 10:00 at night.

After a few sips of her decaf coffee, Sally looked at Isabella, sighed deeply and said, "Tell me what it means to you to have contact with Walter. I need to hear it again."

After a long swig on her straw from a frosted fruit drink, Isabella said, "Seeing him meant the world to me. I've wondered about him all my life, wanted to see him, know his name, get to know him personally yet it all seemed so out of reach. You refused to tell me anything about him and it made me angry."

Sally nodded.

"Then when the picture travel started, it opened up a whole new world to me. I not only learned about Walter, but I also learned about you and your life."

"Not a pretty picture," Sally said sadly.

"But it explained a lot to me. It helped me understand why you're so afraid of everything."

"I'm not afraid of everything," Sally said defensively.

Isabella shook her head and rolled her eyes. "Get over it, Mom. Yes, you are. It's obvious to everyone around you."

Sally stared daggers at her but Isabella refused to divert her gaze.

After a moment of reining in her emotions, Sally said, "So, why is it so important to have contact with him? You've seen him, talked with him. Isn't that enough?"

Isabella couldn't believe the absurdity of the comment. "What if you'd been separated from me for a lifetime? Would spending one day with me be enough for you? Would it have been enough to meet Tessa once and then never see her again?"

A look of shocked understanding filled Sally's eyes. "You're turning my question all around."

"But it's true. It wouldn't be enough for you. And spending one day with a father I've wondered about for a lifetime isn't enough for me either."

When Sally said nothing, Isabella continued. "He loves me and wants to be a father to me. He said so. And he apologized for all the mistakes he's made."

A look of disdain paraded across Sally's face. "I just wonder about his motives."

Isabella felt suddenly disgusted. "And what were your motives in keeping me from him? You hurt him too, you know. Was it revenge? Are you still trying to pay him back for all he did to you?"

Surprise lit her eyes. "I *never* hurt him as much as he hurt me."

"How do you know? You've never given him a chance to tell you how he feels. And besides all that, what you did, all your secrecy and your anger toward him, hurt me. Walter is my father."

Sally stared at her, looking somewhat dumbfounded.

"If you won't let me see him, I can always take things into my own hands."

"You wouldn't."

Isabella thought it over and shook her head. "No, I wouldn't. Walter wouldn't let me."

Confused, Sally asked, "What do you mean?"

"He told me I should tell you everything and that I shouldn't have gone behind your back. I asked him what he'd do if you cut off a relationship between me and him. He said he'd have to accept it for now."

"For now?"

"I will be eighteen in just over two years." Again Isabella felt like the parent, instructing her mother on the facts of life.

With fear reappearing in her eyes, Sally nodded. She lifted her coffee cup and silently took a few sips.

Isabella felt sorry for her. If only she'd give Walter a chance, get to know him again, she'd see that he was completely harmless. Then she could finally let go of all the terror locked up inside.

Sally looked up with a look of false bravado and said, "What if we try supervised visitations?"

Isabella's forehead creased in bewilderment. "What do you mean?"

"Well, I was thinking. At Christmas, it's only about a month away, we'll be heading to Toronto and we could set up a meeting with Walter." Her voice quavered as she said it.

Isabella's heart swelled. "Yes, I'd love that."

"I discussed it with Grayson tonight."

It made Isabella immediately angry that Grayson was involved in any way with this decision.

"He doesn't like it at all."

"I don't care," Isabella said in defiance.

"He's concerned for you."

"Again, I don't care," Isabella said, crossing her arms.

That made Sally smile. "But he's far more concerned about me."

"Why?"

"He doesn't want me falling for Walter again."

That's exactly what Isabella had been hoping and praying for. With Sally thinking of meeting him at Christmas, her whole wish seemed much more feasible.

"I will *not* fall for Walter again, Isabella." Sally stared right through her. "I am in love with Grayson. We've been discussing a future together."

Isabella could feel her heart tighten in a knot of mixed emotions. The words sounded like a death knoll in her soul. All her dreams of getting her parents back together had been spoiled by Grayson Kendal. It made her hate him even more.

Sally's voice brought her back. "You need to be very clear about where I stand. I want to be happy for you but I still plan to protect you from Walter. I will not allow you to see him on your own." She waved a hand in the air. "Once you're eighteen, I suppose you can decide what you want. I'd still like to supervise you at that age, but I can't force you."

"How could you possibly fall for Grayson?" asked Isabella angrily.

Sally's face softened. "Isabella, you said it yourself. You'll be eighteen in two years and I'll soon be alone. I don't want to be alone for the rest of my life."

"I don't want you to marry him."

"We haven't made any firm decision yet."

She looked at her mother. "Can you please wait with a decision until after you've met Walter?"

Sally took a deep breath and exhaled slowly. "Yes, I'll wait."

Driving home, Isabella's mind was full of future possibilities. She berated herself for being so idealistic. After all, her sixteenth birthday was in a few weeks. She was old enough to know better than to paint fairytale endings to their lives. Sally despised Walter. How could Sally change her opinion so quickly and fall in love with him again? It was unrealistic to think that way.

But in her heart of hearts, she still hoped and prayed.

CHAPTER 42

Six months had passed since Sally's brave decision. Isabella was proud of her. She knew it took great courage to do what her mother did. Isabella sat in her bedroom, at her desk, and allowed her mind to wander, revisiting the whirlwind of the past few months. The memories brought a smile to her lips.

On her birthday, early December, Walter sent her a card stuffed with gift certificates. Each one was worth one hundred dollars and there were five of them. He'd taken note of the bags she'd carried that first day they met at the mall and specifically bought gift certificates from those stores.

Isabella and Sally met Walter in Toronto at Christmastime, at a restaurant close to downtown, and he treated them to a wonderful meal. He'd been charming and wonderful, just as she remembered. His humble, quiet approach had caught Sally off guard and she ended up warming to him, at least toward the end of the visit. Isabella had insisted on having him come for the Windsor Christmas celebration at her grandparents' and Sally had reluctantly agreed.

That was her first Christmas with her father and the memories of that day could potentially last her a lifetime. The gifts he brought, just for her, were extravagant and outrageous. He also brought gifts for her grandparents for hosting Christmas, and he brought a gift for Sally too. She'd been embarrassed, demanding that he take it back, but he never did.

He gave Sally a diamond necklace, a large stone hanging on a wide silver chain. Isabella noticed that sometimes when Sally wasn't with Grayson, she'd wear it.

It was at Christmastime that she realized that Uncle Robert knew Walter very well. They'd worked together in real estate for years. Their relationship took off as though nothing had ever happened between them. It was amusing listening to the two talk and joke around.

With Sally's permission, Walter had flown out to Chelsey the middle of February. He stayed at a hotel and had taken them out quite a few times together. It was like a dream come true. They watched stage productions, went to movies and dinners and had long talks. Spending time with both her parents at the same time was hard to believe.

At some point, Sally's opinion of him began to shift. She started to see him with different eyes. His attentiveness and his caution not to offend her slowly began to win her over. He did nothing without her approval.

He'd offered to fly Isabella to Toronto to watch the Blue Jays play baseball. Sally had been completely against it at first. She was busy and couldn't take time off to supervise, but Isabella had worked on her, begging non-stop.

They'd finally worked out the details. Isabella would fly to Toronto and stay with her grandparents in Markham. Vern would chaperone the baseball outing with Walter. Isabella would be accompanied by either her grandmother or grandfather everywhere she went. At no time, would Isabella ever be alone with Walter.

Isabella hadn't been happy with that at first, but if that was the only way to see a baseball game with her father, she was willing to comply with her mother's stipulations. It had disappointed her that her mother was still wary of Walter. She'd thought Sally had made some progress in her feelings. Although the visit with Walter was amazing, the realization of Sally's guardedness and careful precautions was disheartening.

Isabella had never been to a professional sports game before and the energy of the crowd was electric and exciting. Her father promised that once she turned eighteen, he'd fly her to New York to see the New York Yankees play. She couldn't wait. To go anywhere with her father and do things that he enjoyed felt like making up for years of lost time.

Although Walter hated the restrictions on their relationship, he always expressed great gratitude for what he'd been given. Every time they saw each other, he'd tell her how he thanked God for bringing her back into his life. Restoration, that's what he called it. God had brought him restoration.

Isabella pondered that. It's what he'd done for Sally too. She was no longer so afraid anymore. God had begun to restore her by bringing Walter back into her life. She no longer dreaded seeing him, which was a huge answer to prayer. He was coming out again in July to see them both.

Sally's relationship with Grayson had been put on hold. They still saw each other from time to time but there was no more talk of marriage. He wanted it; Sally wasn't sure. Isabella had asked her why she decided not to marry him. Sally said she didn't want to do anything that would drive a wedge between her and Isabella.

It made her feel guilty again. Was she being selfish? She wanted her mother to be happy. If marrying Grayson would make Sally happy, Isabella shouldn't spoil things for her. But Sally did seem content lately. She worked less hours now, took every Saturday and Sunday off, even some Mondays. Overall, she appeared more at peace with her world. Isabella liked the change.

Her heart was full of gratitude. God had done amazing things, brought restoration in such a short time, what for years she thought was completely out of her reach. If He chose to do it in such an unconventional way, like photo travel, who was she to argue?

EPILOGUE

Just Over Three Years later.

Isabella stepped into her mother's house, suitcase in hand, and set it down in the entrance. The familiar smells of home wafted toward her and she breathed deeply. Sally entered behind her and closed the door, shutting out the chill breeze that filled the entrance. Isabella had just arrived for Thanksgiving weekend and Sally had picked her up at the airport.

Isabella was in her second year of university, taking a business degree at the University of Toronto. Grandparents had insisted at first that she come live with them while in school. Isabella had graciously declined the offer, insisting that the reason she chose to move away from Chelsey, Minnesota was to try out her wings and obtain some independence. They'd been disappointed by her decision but had conceded on the stipulation that Isabella come see them often during weekends.

Isabella went to visit her grandparents whenever she could manage, since assignments and studying occupied much of her weekends. Grandpa Windsor usually came to pick her up on the rare visits to see her grandparents. She also was able to spend a lot of time now with her father, one of her main reasons for moving to Toronto.

Sally had rented a basement suite for her close to the university campus. A short bus ride took her a mere fifteen minutes to get to her first class. It was a perfect location.

When Isabella had decided to go straight into post secondary schooling and chose to take a business degree, Sally was full of ideas for the future. She'd suggested that Isabella join her franchise business, perhaps eventually taking over as Operations Manager. Isabella wasn't ready to jump that far ahead immediately. She told her mother that it might be a possibility but she needed to find her own way. Isabella wasn't prepared to make any promises yet.

After Sally hung her coat in the closet, she turned and said, "I'll put on the kettle for some tea or I could make coffee. Which would you prefer?"

"Definitely coffee. I'm a little hooked."

"Will do." Sally walked toward the kitchen and Isabella followed. "I also bought some Danishes at the bakery you love."

"Yum."

With coffee made, they sat at the table and talked.

Sally's frequent smiles were the sign she was thrilled to have her daughter home.

"I like what you're wearing, Isy."

"Mom. My name's Isabella."

Sally's lifted her chin and said, "I'm your mother. I'm allowed to call you Isy."

Isabella shook her head and looked down at her outfit. "It's one of your creations."

"I know. It looks amazing on you."

"Thanks."

"No, thank you for your suggestions on the Windsor Fresh Apparel."

Isabella shrugged.

In her last year at home, Isabella had made numerous suggestions to her mom for some new and innovative clothing designs that targeted younger women. Sally listened and expanded her influence to include young women of fine taste. Her franchise stores had exploded with increased clientele and renewed accolades. Sally had been thrilled for the changes in Isabella's style and was delighted that she suddenly cared how she dressed.

"So, what was Derek doing this weekend?" Sally asked.

Isabella had met Derek at her grandparents' church in Markham, Ontario in her first year of university. Derek was taking engineering at Seneca College in Toronto and was in his fourth year. He was two years older than she and they'd been dating for about six months. "He's working and had a ton of homework. Canada's Thanksgiving was in October so it's just a regular weekend for him."

"That's right. I should have remembered." Sally smiled again. "How are his courses going?"

Isabella smiled. "They're keeping him quite busy but he's enjoying them."

"I'd like to meet this young man sometime."

"Maybe you could meet him when you come up to Markham at Christmas time."

"I'd like that." Sally smiled and asked, "Your grandparents are doing well?"

"Mom, you call them every week. I'm sure you know."

"That's true, but sometimes they evade the tough questions they don't want to answer."

"They're doing great. Grandpa's still working part time. Grandma wishes he'd retire. She wants to travel more and enjoy their years before they get too old. He's actually considering retiring."

"Yeah. Your grandmother told me that. She's quite excited. Maybe they'll come see me more often."

Isabella nodded. "Grandma still loves to cook up a storm, feeding me every chance she gets. I think she's attempting to fatten me up."

"That's her style."

It grew silent for a minute.

Sally asked, "Do you see your other grandmother sometimes?"

"I do. Walter takes me to her house occasionally and she cooks a feast every time. Between my two grandmothers, it's surprising I haven't increased a few sizes."

Sally chuckled. She paused a few moments, then asked, "Any news of Sheffield?"

"Neither Grandma nor Walter have any interest in reconnecting with him. All I've heard is that he's living in Mississauga somewhere. He's called Walter a few times, tried to strong arm him into joining his new church venture. Walter refuses to meet with him. He actually changed his cell number recently to cut off all ties with Sheffield. Walter and Grandma live in Scarborough, which you already know, far enough away that Sheffield should never find them — at least that's what Dad hopes."

"So Walter never speaks to Sheffield anymore?"

"He's called him once since, used one of the rare payphones downtown. Walter wanted to see if his father had changed and give him one more chance. As they spoke, it became clear that Sheffield was actively gaining a following and only getting worse in his delusions. Walter told his dad in no uncertain terms that he wanted nothing to do with the church. Sheffield insisted that Walter and his mother were the deluded ones and needed to repent. The call didn't last long. Walter told him he wouldn't call again and hung up."

Sally looked disgusted. "The man is so sick. Why didn't you tell me about it sooner?"

"It only happened a week ago."

Sally nodded and changed the subject. "So, you're getting together with Shana and Abby tomorrow?"

"Yeah. We're meeting for lunch, catching up."

"How's Abby doing in Chicago?"

"She's loving university."

"How is she handling being away from home?"

"She loves it. She lives in one of the dorms and really enjoys it."

"It sounds like Abby. She was always an extrovert. Is she dating?"

"When is she not dating? Yes, she's dating. I forget the new guy she's with. I think it's Dale or Don or something."

"And Shana? She's still living at home, attending Chelsey College?"

"Yep. She called me a few weeks ago. Remember Mark from Youth?"

"Yes."

"They started dating! They both attend Chelsey College and were friends first for a while. I guess he finally realized the gem she is." Isabella grinned, remembering the corny song she and her friends wrote years ago.

"I'm happy for her."

Isabella decided to change the subject. "What time is Dad flying in tomorrow?"

"His flight arrives at four in the afternoon. It's too bad the two of you couldn't fly together."

"He couldn't get off work any sooner." Isabella tilted her head and asked, "So, how are things going between the two of you?"

"Good."

"That's it? That's all you're going to tell me?"

A stubborn look entered Sally's eyes. "What does Walter tell you about us?"

"He's told me he's madly in love with you."

"He did not."

"Uh-huh."

The two of them had been seeing a lot of each other in the last year. Walter would fly to Chelsey often to spend time with Sally and she made plenty of trips of her own to Toronto. Sally always cloaked the purpose in the excuse of seeing Isabella and her parents but she spent a lot of time with Walter on those visits.

Sally's eyes turned dreamy. "I don't know what to think. My heart has changed so much in the last few years. What I adamantly insisted would never happen has happened. I never knew it was possible to forgive him and for my heart to be healed and restored to this extent."

"So, what exactly are you saying? It's a little vague."

"I think I love him. When my mind wanders to the past I still get this scared feeling but it never lasts long. Our new history is overshadowing the past. When I think of Walter, the thoughts that come to mind are his attentiveness, kindness, humility and eagerness to please me, the things that first made me fall in love with him so many years ago. Plus, he's still awfully good-looking."

"Why has it taken so long? It's been nearly four years since you were reintroduced to him."

Sally shook her head. "I was very wary of him, Isy. I wanted to be sure that the changes in his character were legit."

"And…"

"And what?"

"Do you believe the changes are real?"

Sally slowly nodded. "I do."

"So…when will you guys get engaged?"

"Isabella!"

"I'd say it's way overdue."

Sally shrugged again. "Walter won't do anything without my approval. I think I'll have to be the one to suggest it this time."

"Unless he's coming out here with a ring in his pocket and a proposal on his lips."

"Did he tell you that?"

Isabella chuckled. "No."

She wasn't about to tell Sally that she'd visited jewelry stores in Toronto with her dad the last weekend they spent together or the motive behind it. She couldn't wait for Thanksgiving Day. Thoughts of her parents remarrying made her feel giddy. She felt like pinching herself sometimes to make sure she wasn't dreaming.

Isabella grew pensive and thought back on the picture travel anomaly. She thanked God once more for answering a young girl's prayers to have her father back, and for the dramatically supernatural way he changed the course of their lives.

She would be forever grateful. Her days of limiting God's ability were in the past and she looked forward to what lay ahead for all of them.

###

THANK YOU

Thank you for reading *Time And Restoration*, the final book in the *Time Trilogy Series*. If you enjoyed it, won't you please take a moment to leave me a review at your favorite retailer? And check out my other novels on my blog - www.colleenreimer.ca or www.colleenreimer.com.

OTHER NOVELS BY AUTHOR

HEAVEN ON EARTH SERIES:

Assignment Code 110
Assignment Code 123
Assignment Code 321

TIME TRILOGY:

Time and Destiny – Book 1 of Trilogy
Time and Healing – Book 2 of Trilogy

For more information about these books go to www.colleenreimer.ca or www.colleenreimer.com. On her website, Colleen also has a blog where she posts short stories and quotes. To sign up to receive her short story notifications, go to her web site and enter your email information.

ABOUT THE AUTHOR

Colleen Reimer lives near Calgary, Canada with her husband and four children, although only the youngest two still live at home. She has lived in multiple places over the years, in many different Canadian cities and also spent seven years in North Carolina.

Besides writing, Colleen also enjoys gardening, travelling, chatting with friends, a hot cup of Chai tea and chocolate.

Manufactured by Amazon.ca
Bolton, ON